"Johnson initiates another swoon-worthy historical series with this emotionally charged romance in which passions run high and things are not always what they seem."

—*Library Journal* on *Love's Rescue*

"The first in Johnson's inspirational romance Keys of Promise series sails off to a strong start with a sweet love story that skillfully incorporates fascinating facts about the nineteenth-century salvage and wrecking trade into a quietly moving plot about the importance of family, faith, and forgiveness."

—*Booklist* on *Love's Rescue*

"This action-packed tale is one to keep readers engaged and rooting for the heroine from the first page to the last."

—*RT Book Reviews* on *Love's Rescue*

"Once again author Christine Johnson demonstrates her impressive mastery of the romance genre with *Honor Redeemed*, a deftly crafted and riveting read from beginning to end."

—**The Midwest Book Review** on *Honor Redeemed*

Books by Christine Johnson

FREEDOM'S PRICE

A NOVEL

Christine Johnson

Revell

a division of Baker Publishing Group
Grand Rapids, Michigan

Published by Revell
a division of Baker Publishing Group
P.O. Box 6287, Grand Rapids, MI 49516-6287
www.revellbooks.com

Printed in the United States of America

Library of Congress Cataloging-in-Publication Data
Names: Johnson, Christine (Christine Elizabeth), author.
Title: Freedom's price : a novel / Christine Johnson.
Description: Grand Rapids, MI : Revell, a division of Baker Publishing Group,
    [2017] | Series: Keys of promise ; 3
Identifiers: LCCN 2016056145| ISBN 9780800723521 (softcover) | ISBN
    9780800728854 (print on demand)
Subjects: LCSH: Man-woman relationships—Fiction. | Family secrets—Fiction. |
    GSAFD: Historical fiction. | Christian fiction. | Love stories.
Classification: LCC PS3610.O32395 F74 2017 | DDC 813/.6—dc23
LC record available at https://lccn.loc.gov/2016056145

Scripture quotations are from the King James Version of the Bible.

17 18 19 20 21 22 23   7 6 5 4 3 2 1

For the mothers and fathers who sacrifice
so much for their children.
I love you, Mom and Dad!

Prologue

Staffordshire, England

Catherine Haynes pressed her ear to the study door. A girl of thirteen knew better than to eavesdrop, but how could she not? She had never seen the stranger before. He appeared Arabian or East Indian. Exotic. A tiny scar beneath one of his black eyes. His gaze had swept over her as he passed her in the hallway. In that instant, he'd claimed her imagination.

She must know why he had come to Deerford.

She listened to the conversation as best she could. Alas, Papa's voice did not carry through the thick oak door, and the stranger's was muffled.

"Get away now." Mrs. McCready, the housekeeper, tugged her from the door. "Your father's business is his alone and not for young lady's ears."

Catherine obliged her by going to the library and then returned to the hallway the moment the stranger burst from the study. Again, his gaze raked her. She could not breathe, could not move. He smiled, nodded, and then strode past, carrying a small strongbox.

Papa followed, his smile dimming when he saw her. "Go to the drawing room, child."

She bristled, ready to object that she was not a child, but he and the man hurried past. She raced to the library window and followed their progress from the house. Papa shook the man's hand. Then the stranger stowed the strongbox in a saddlebag, climbed onto his black steed, and raced away without a backward glance.

Early June 1856

"Miss Haynes!"

A rude masculine voice pulled Catherine from that long-ago memory. For months she'd dreamed of the stranger's return and had romanticized him as a conquering knight. Ten years later, all such fantasies had come to a halt. Dreams were for children. She must deal with reality.

She set her jaw and returned her cousin's glare. By very subtly lifting her gaze above his piercing gray eyes and fixing it on the portrait of her mother hanging behind Papa's desk, she could maintain the illusion of control.

"Well?" Ugly red suffused Mr. Roger Haynes's neck. "I am waiting for an answer."

In the months since he and his family first arrived at Deerford, she had learned one important trait about her cousin. He expected compliance. This time she would not bow. Nor could she find words of refusal.

The mantel clock ticked off the seconds.

Cousin Roger braced his hands on the desktop, leaning forward like a snarling lion eager to capture its prey. "Your reply."

Not a question.

Catherine drew an imperceptible breath and imitated Maman's calm. "I cannot."

"You cannot?" The sentence exploded with unspoken threat. He would force her into this marriage.

Again the ticking of the clock filled the silence.

What would Maman do? Faced with similar prospects upon her return from the grand tour all those years ago, Catherine's mother had abandoned her chaperones in the dead of night and eloped. Catherine had no such escape available.

Cousin Roger's smile menaced. "If you continue in this stubborn refusal, you will lose what is left of your family."

Meaning him. She had no one else. Not here. Maman's family was in faraway Louisiana, and the decision to elope had cost her all contact with them. No letters. No word of any kind. How the separation must have hurt, for Maman often regaled her with stories of plantation life, of balls and soirees and golden days running between the tall rows of sugarcane. Catherine had begged her mother to take her there, but Maman said it was not possible. Then she'd died.

Only the portrait remained. Maman's rose-colored gown flowed from her waist like that of an empress. At her throat rested the ruby brooch Catherine had often run her finger across when she was very young. She had not found it with Maman's jewels. Papa must have buried it with her.

Dear Papa. Catherine tugged at her heavy black sleeves to hide the welling of tears.

"I suggest a different answer," cousin Roger said.

Catherine brushed away the past. It could not solve this dilemma. She chose her words with care. "Mr. Kirby does not suit me."

"Does not suit? You act as if you would bring an heiress's

fortune to your marriage. May I remind you that the terms of your father's estate leave you but five hundred pounds?"

"And fifty pounds per year." Eight months had not changed that fact. The passing of time had only increased her cousin's urgency to be rid of her.

"Until you wed."

That was the crux of it. Once she married, the annual payments would cease.

Her cousin settled into Papa's chair.

She clenched her jaw against a wave of revulsion. He might have gained the estate through settlement, but he did not belong in her father's place.

"I do not intend to wed. Allow me to manage the estate—"

He snorted derisively. "Is that what you call your playing around in the accounts?" He filled a pipe from Papa's tobacco jar.

Angry words rose to the tip of her tongue and stopped there. Very few men considered a woman intelligent enough to manage accounts, least of all an estate. Cousin Roger was not one of them.

"If you examine my entries—"

"I have." He slammed shut the ledger before him. "Some might consider them adequate, considering your gender, but I found them entirely insufficient."

"Insufficient! Compare my skills to any man—"

"Use those skills to benefit your husband."

She choked. "I am in mourning and cannot consider marriage."

"You have worn black long enough. It's time to move on. I suggest you change into something more cheerful." His cold gray gaze, fixed above fashionably long sideburns, bored into her. "That would be welcomed by our guests."

Mr. Kirby and Mrs. Durning, whose husband had just left

for Liverpool to provision his ship for the crossing to the West Indies, were expected. Neither cared about her attire, but at least it gave her an excuse to leave this unbearable interview.

"If you will excuse me, then." She reached for the doorknob.

"Not quite yet." He drew a breath on the pipe and exhaled a cloud of rich smoke.

If she closed her eyes, she could imagine Papa sitting there, his spectacles resting on the tip of his nose, where they would slide after his hours of agonizing over the accounts. Papa had been a kind and generous man, often excusing debts and allowing rents to remain in arrears far too long. Of course, she hadn't known that until he fell ill and she had to take on the accounts.

Her cousin cleared his throat. "At three and twenty you will soon slip from a marriageable age."

"Apparently not, if Mr. Kirby is still calling."

His jaw tightened. "His long association with the family places him in a rather fortunate position."

"Fortunate? That is a matter of perspective, is it not? As you just stated, I bring a pittance into any marriage."

"Precisely. Few would consider a wife who brings only five hundred."

She could not resist poking at his unstated desire. "You might continue the fifty pounds per year. We are cousins, after all."

"Let me spell out what you could never have gleaned from your pitiable scribbling in the ledgers. Your father's estate is in ruin."

She opened her mouth to protest, but he lifted a finger to silence her.

"Even if I manage to collect the arrears, which I fully intend to do, it will not offset the losses."

Catherine would not be set down so easily. "Then how do you intend to pay the dowry?"

His lips twitched, signaling triumph. "I will sell the estate."

"Sell Deerford?" The words barely escaped her constricted throat. "You can't!"

"As you well know, I can. In fact, a buyer is at hand."

"A buyer?" She clawed at hope. "Mr. Kirby?" Perhaps she would agree to marry him if it meant saving Deerford.

He laughed. "Certainly not."

"Then who? Will he continue the tenants' leases? Will he keep planting the land as always?"

"This clay soil was never suited to farming, dear cousin. It will fare much better in the hands of the pottery manufacturer that is buying it."

"A factory?" Her head spun. "But . . . the house."

"It would have been too costly to maintain."

"What will happen to the tenants? You must take care of them. They have worked Deerford land for generations."

He leaned back and blew out a plume of smoke. "They can apply for employment at the factory."

"But they're farmers." Each face flashed through her mind, from old widow Evans to the two-year-old Herring twins. "They don't know anything else."

"Then they can move elsewhere."

His cold statement sent shivers down her spine. She must help them, but how? The few guineas in her possession wouldn't feed them long. They needed lands to tend.

"You must find them new homes," she pleaded.

"Sometimes progress demands change. For them and for you." He paused. "Deerford is extinct. You have nowhere to go. Perhaps a husband—especially one as charitably minded as Mr. Kirby—would find a place for your tenants on his father's or future patrons' lands."

Her throat closed. How carefully he had crafted the snare.

If she hoped to help the displaced tenants, she must marry Eustace Kirby.

Cousin Roger seized his advantage. "I suggest you give full consideration to Mr. Kirby's suit."

She sank into the closest chair. "But he's a clergyman."

His brow quirked. "Do you harbor resentment against that noble profession?"

Her cousin would not think so highly of the ministry if he had been forced into it as Mr. Kirby had been.

"I wouldn't make a good minister's wife."

"Let us hope Mr. Kirby doesn't see that fault before the blessed event. I shall give him my blessing."

"But I did not agree to marry him."

"You would destroy your father's hopes for you and leave your beloved tenants without a future rather than commit to a life of serving the Lord?"

Put that way, it did sound rather selfish, but she could not marry Mr. Kirby. The mere thought of kissing him made her stomach turn. Having children? Settling into a country parish? Impossible.

"There must be another answer." Yet she could not see it.

Cousin Roger leaned back with a contented smirk and puffed his pipe. "Make no mistake, dear cousin, fifty pounds will not go far. Once you have no home . . ." He let her imagine the result.

She clawed at the pit that was swallowing her. Above her cousin, Maman's portrait smiled placidly at the terrible scene unfolding below. She would never have agreed to this manipulation. *You have my wits*, Maman had often told her, *and your papa's compassion.* What to do?

She tried to breathe, but the strictures of both garments and circumstance made it difficult to draw in enough air. Papa's halting words on his deathbed echoed in her mind. *Forgive me for losing what was yours.* Now she knew what he meant.

"So you can see," her cousin was saying, "Mr. Kirby has presented a most opportune offer. I suggest you accept."

He had left her no escape. Her head spun, and spots danced before her eyes.

"Are you unwell?" He rose.

She shook her head rather than admit weakness. Several short breaths restored her vision, though her stomach still quaked.

He moved toward her, a glint in his eye, and brought to mind again the shadowy memory of the stranger, dark as tea. He had cast her the same look when he passed her in the hallway outside Papa's study. The dark stranger's victorious smile, like that of a king, had claimed her imagination. She'd peppered her father with questions, but he would tell her nothing, only that it did not concern her.

But perhaps it did. What if this dark stranger had come from Maman's glorious plantation? What if contact had not been cut off forever? His glance toward her had not borne malice. No, it seemed to say that she belonged elsewhere.

The study door opened.

"Excuse me, Miss Haynes, Mr. Haynes." The housekeeper dipped into a slight curtsy. "Mrs. Durning has arrived, and she says that Mr. Kirby will be here shortly."

"Good," cousin Roger said. "Tell Mr. Kirby to join me in the study. We have business to discuss while Miss Haynes entertains Mrs. Durning."

The housekeeper bustled off.

Cousin Roger drew again on the pipe. The set of his jaw meant the decision had been made. With or without her permission, he would give his consent to Eustace Kirby's suit. He believed he had trapped her.

14

Well, he could give all the blessings he wished. He was not her only family, and Mrs. Durning could very well give her the escape she desperately needed.

She stood, reinvigorated. "I request the annual sum due me."

He set down the pipe with a thud. "What?"

"The fifty pounds specified in Papa's will."

"You will waste it on the tenants?" he sneered.

She could no longer help them. Unless . . . "And an additional ten pounds per tenant family."

He guffawed. Then paused, surprised that she didn't waver before him. "You are jesting."

"I am not."

"It's not in the terms of the will."

"I propose new terms. In exchange for the ten pounds per tenant, I will waive all future annual payments."

"You will anyway, once you marry." The smirk was back.

She drew in a deep breath, never more certain. "I do not intend to marry. I am rejoining my mother's family in America."

He stared, struck silent for the moment, but soon she saw the gleam of self-interest as he calculated the benefits of her plan. This would spare him not only the continued fifty pounds per year but also the five hundred upon her marriage, for she would have difficulty claiming it from America.

She assumed all the risk, leaving intolerable security for the unknown. Surely her mother's family would welcome her, if not with open arms, then at least with sympathy for her predicament. Surely they would not hold Maman's sin against the next generation.

1

August 27, 1856
Off the Bahama Banks

Catherine shot to her feet at the loud crack that shivered through the *Justinian*. The sound, earsplitting as cannon fire, overpowered the winds that screamed around the ship. The vessel, heeled hard to larboard, shuddered and righted for a moment. Then the roof of their cabin shook under a sudden barrage of something very hard and weighty.

Mrs. Durning held on to the frame of the bunk so tightly that her knuckles turned white. "Are we under attack?"

"Who would attack us?" Though Catherine had never traveled by sea before, she suspected a source other than cannon fire, one that could prove much more dangerous in this tempest. Since the vessel had begun to pitch and roll wildly, she sat heavily on her bunk.

"The Spaniards might have declared war in the time it's taken to cross the Atlantic," Mrs. Durning suggested.

"Unlikely."

"They might take advantage of our focus on the Crimea."

Though anything was possible, Catherine knew better than to speculate on the unknown. At present her chief problem was a roiling stomach. Judging from Mrs. Durning's pale countenance, she too was suffering a recurrence of the malady that had plagued them the first two weeks of the long voyage. On their fifty-ninth day, she had not expected to revisit it. These were exceptional conditions. Captain Durning had suggested his wife spend the night with Catherine in order to "see her through the rough seas," rather than wait alone in his cabin.

"I will be busy," he had said with great affection. He then kissed his wife of thirty years on the hand as if they were still courting.

Mrs. Durning had warbled her delight at the time. Now she clung to Catherine.

"My George is a fine master." The woman's voice trembled. "He will keep us safe."

As if the crew had heard her words of confidence, the wild motion of the ship ceased, and Catherine could try to settle her stomach with a sip of mint tea.

Then footsteps scurried across the roof of the cabin. Catherine looked up. She had grown accustomed to the occasional footfall, but this sounded like an army of men.

"Cut the lines," one of the crew shouted directly overhead, his voice carrying to them despite the tempest.

Mrs. Durning stared upward, her eyes round. "Lines? Are we at anchor?"

"I don't know." Catherine rose, more sure of her footing now that the pitching had leveled off. "I will check."

"No you won't. It's too dangerous. You heard our captain."

Indeed Catherine had. They were to stay in the cabin until told otherwise. Some hours ago, a steward had brought a light supper of oily sardines and biscuits with tea. She had barely been able to stomach a biscuit and none of the sardines before he whisked them away. After that, no one visited the cabin. To distract herself from the dreadful howling winds and groaning of the ship, Catherine had plied Mrs. Durning for anything her husband might have told her of their destination, Jamaica.

"Mr. Durning fears it will be too hot for me," she had told Catherine. "He would have discouraged my joining him if not for you. He will secure a safe passage for you from Kingston to New Orleans," she'd added with a squeeze of Catherine's hand. "He knows the ships that call there and will know which one has a good Christian master and crew."

Catherine doubted the religious affiliation of the ship's master guaranteed her safety, but it was better than finding herself at the mercy of an unscrupulous man. It had not taken long aboard the *Justinian* to learn that some of the crew viewed her with interest if the captain was not within earshot. From then on, she'd taken great care to have Mrs. Durning at her side whenever she took the air and to lock the cabin door when alone.

Tonight, the shrieking winds and the scraping overhead did nothing to calm the fears that kept creeping to mind. Unwanted attention was not the worst they would have to contend with.

A sharp thump was followed by another and another. Then the ship lurched again, throwing Mrs. Durning backward and Catherine onto the cabin floor.

She tried unsuccessfully to stand and then resorted to crawling onto the bunk.

"Are you all right, dear?"

"Yes. Fine." Catherine tried to calm her spinning head and shaky voice. "Clumsy of me."

Yet they both knew the fall was none of her doing. The ship was foundering in a terrible sea. Now Catherine clung to the frame of the bunk as tightly as her companion did.

In the light cast by the gimbaled lamp, Mrs. Durning's kindly brown eyes brimmed with tears. "I always feared my George would come to such an end but never imagined I would."

"We won't. We saw land yesterday. Remember? We have reached the Caribbean Sea. Your husband will find safe harbor." Speaking the hope made it somewhat more real.

"I wanted to share in this life he's led for so many years. I wanted to see my George captain a fine ship."

"And so he has." Catherine seized the change of topic. Anything to ignore the pounding overhead. "Thirty years, has it been?"

"Thirty-five, since before we met. He loves me true, he does. I've never known a finer man."

"That's how I remember my father." Yet he hadn't been able to prevent the land settling upon her cousin Roger, who had destroyed the work of generations of Haynes men.

"Aye. A good man. Pity he couldn't leave you a decent living."

Papa's dying words came back to mind. *Forgive me for losing what was yours.* But Papa hadn't lost Deerford. He'd been bound by terms of a settlement formed generations before. Perhaps he had tried to change the settlement but failed. Such generational documents could be impossible to derail. Unfortunately, her cousin had found a way.

"What's done is done. My future rests with Maman's family."

"I hope they will welcome you."

"Why wouldn't they?" Catherine spoke with more vigor now that the tromping overhead had ceased. "My letter explains everything. When I show them my baptismal record, all doubts will be erased."

"I hope you are correct, but one can't know how those Americans might react. They are different, you know, especially those . . . not of English blood."

"French." Catherine didn't mind stating it. Though enmity between the countries was currently at an ebb, attitudes didn't change. "You're referring to Maman's family name, Lafreniere."

"It doesn't matter now, I suppose," Mrs. Durning grumbled. "They're all Americans."

Catherine managed a bit of a smile. "I suppose you're right." But Maman had often spoken French to her when she was a child. Alas, Catherine recalled very little. Would Maman's family still speak French? The thought had occurred to her, as well as the trepidation that she would not fully understand them if they did. If they were anything like Maman, filled with gentle grace and a bold spirit, language would not prove a barrier. "I'm looking forward to meeting them."

"Goodness, you're a brave girl, heading across the ocean to throw yourself on the mercy of kin you've never met."

The thought unsettled her almost as much as the rolling seas. "If I'm fortunate, I'll meet someone like your husband."

That turned Mrs. Durning's attention in a positive direction. "I'll pray you do. Your relations will introduce you to many gentlemen. There's bound to be one or two of quality. I suppose they have some sort of entertainment too, though certainly nothing as grand as our Season."

Catherine recalled her mother's descriptions. "They hold balls and soirees. New Orleans is bound to have theaters and operas and symphonies."

"Indeed." Her tone made it clear she didn't approve of some of those entertainments. "Just take care to follow your family's guidance. Perhaps your grandmother is still living. Or another female relation. An aunt or even an older cousin."

"Maman's brother must have had children. He was much older than her. There could be many in the family by now." The idea of having cousins both excited and terrified Catherine. As an only child, she had not known the trials and joys of siblings.

Regardless, it was better that Mrs. Durning focus on matchmaking or even her prejudices against France and Spain than the battering the ship was taking in this storm.

"My mother described the plantation as having endless fields of sugarcane stretching from the river as far as one can see."

"Oh my. Then your relations must be very rich." Mrs. Durning absently touched the yellowed lace collar of her muslin dress.

"Perhaps. Or perhaps that is only the impression of a young woman. She left when she was but seventeen."

"And met your father." Mrs. Durning knew the details of the story by now. Such a long voyage made for familiarity.

"And met my father."

Footsteps raced overhead again. Catherine instinctively looked up. Seeing nothing, she returned her attention to Mrs. Durning and spotted a droplet upon the woman's shoulder. The ceiling was leaking. She supposed that was to be expected, given the savagery of the storm. At least she hoped it was.

"I'm sure it's nothing out of the ordinary," she murmured.

"What is?"

"Nothing of import."

The door to their cabin burst open, and the steward popped his head into the opening. "Stay in your cabin until someone fetches you."

Catherine rose. "What's happening?"

He slammed the door without answering her question. Catherine strode across the room, holding herself steady against the wall. "I'm going to find out what that was all about."

"It's exactly what Mr. Durning told us."

Not exactly. Captain Durning had said nothing about being fetched.

Catherine flung open the door and poked her head into the narrow hallway. The first officer, Mr. Lightwater, stood just inside the door that opened to the deck. The steward, holding a lantern, had joined him. Through the open doorway, she saw the lashing rain, blown sideways, in the light of his lantern.

Neither man noticed her.

"Get the passengers ready," Mr. Lightwater charged. "The captain is launching the ship's boat."

Ice flowed through Catherine's veins. A boat in such weather? She'd seen it lashed to the deck. It might hold everyone but nothing else. No belongings. What would happen to her three trunks, the family Bible, Maman's portrait, and the daguerreotype of her family taken shortly before Maman's death? A small boat allowed nothing but oars and necessities like food and water. She must at least bring the Bible and the daguerreotype. The fancy gowns and childhood mementos could sink to the bottom. Even Maman's portrait must go, but she could not sacrifice everything.

"Aye," the steward said, eyeing the howling winds. "But if you don't mind my saying so, we'll need help from above to pull this off."

Catherine pressed against the wall, overcome. The steward was right. In such winds, how could a tiny boat prevail?

"You have your orders," Mr. Lightwater said brusquely before returning to the maelstrom on deck.

Catherine ducked back into the room and closed the door before the steward spotted her. Her knees threatened to give way at the thought of what faced them. Winds and horizontal rain were just the start. The waves could swallow such a small boat. She collapsed against the closed door and squeezed her eyes shut against a flood of images.

Surely there was some hope if the captain had ordered the

boat launched. Perhaps they were near the land she'd spotted earlier that day.

"What is it?" Mrs. Durning didn't attempt to hide her alarm. "What did you see?"

Catherine had never considered the possibility of shipwreck or becoming marooned, least of all drowning. Even if they somehow managed to reach land, many of these islands were savage. Some fell under unfriendly control. An Englishwoman might befall precisely the sort of indignities that Mrs. Durning had hinted at during her cautions.

Her heart pounded. Pirates still lurked in the dark corners of this part of the world. What would such men do to Mrs. Durning and her? Romantic tales would not measure well against cruel reality.

The ship lurched, and she bounced against the cabin wall.

"Are you hurt?" Mrs. Durning had somehow managed to reach her in spite of the heaving decks.

Catherine rubbed her shoulder. "I'm fine." But the ship wasn't. "I believe it is time to pray in earnest."

Tom Worthington crushed the letter in his right hand. How could she? This was not the sort of information he needed to receive the morning after a big storm.

"Is everything all right?" asked Jules Ledbetter, the bringer of the bad news.

Tom weighed his words as the jeweler on the other side of the shop counter slipped back to the worktable and resumed tinkering on a watch. Tinker! He let out a cynical snort. How could his mother remarry so soon?

"Barely in the grave," he muttered.

"Someone died?"

Tom shook away the cobwebs of regret. "My pa."

"Sorry. I didn't know." Jules cast him an appropriately sorrowful expression though he'd never known any of Tom's family. "I wouldn't have brought the letter 'cept Captain said it might be important. Tough luck."

"What?" Tom stared at the lad until the bits and pieces fit together. Oh. Jules thought the letter announced Pa's death. "He died seven years ago."

"Oh." Jules squinted at him. "Then why're ye upset now?"

"Because she's remarrying."

"She?"

"My mother. Doesn't she have any respect for Pa? Marrying his sworn enemy, no less. That man didn't have one kind word to say about Pa when he was living. Now she says he's all sympathetic about their situation and wants to take care of them." That put a bitter taste in Tom's mouth.

"Sorry." Jules shuffled his feet again, appearing chagrined but certainly not sympathetic.

"It gets worse. My brothers and sisters are taking that man's name. Tinker." He smacked his fist into his other hand. "How could they?"

Jules shrugged. "He's gonna be their new pa."

"He'll never be their father. Not really." He stared down the lad. "Don't you have something better to do?"

Jules backed away, eyes wide. "I'm s'posed to give you a message. Captain said we're ta set sail within the hour. Ship's aground inside Washerwoman Shoal, and everyone's headin' out ta help in the salvage. Didn't you hear the bell?" He scooted toward the door.

Whenever a wreck was spotted, the bells would ring from the lookout towers. Tom hadn't heard. He'd been too intent on questioning the jeweler. Jules's news sent a thrill through his veins. A wreck would take his mind off trouble at home. A wreck could bring him enough wealth to avenge his father and prove that a Worthington was better than a Tinker any day. The pitying sneers would be replaced by respect.

"Tell Captain O'Malley that I'll board the *Windsprite* as soon as I finish here," Tom called out.

Jules paused in the doorway. "Captain says you're ta take the *James Patrick* out with Rander and pilot in a barque that lost her mainmast."

"Do what?" Piloting brought in a pittance compared to a wreck, where salvage could make a man's fortune. Rourke O'Malley knew how desperately Tom wanted to salvage a big wreck. He would never deny him the opportunity. "You must have misunderstood."

Jules shook his head. "That's what he said."

"I see. Rander is going to follow me back to port in the *James Patrick*, and then we'll head out to the wreck."

Jules hopped from foot to foot. "Nope. He's ta head straight ta the wreck after droppin' ye off."

"What?" Tom couldn't believe his ears. If he didn't participate in the salvage, he earned none of the reward. "He can't leave me grounded."

"That's what the captain said. You can ask him yerself." Jules took off at a run.

Tom raced to the door, but the youngster was already halfway down the street.

"Change your mind?" the jeweler asked behind him.

Tom stuffed the crumpled letter into his jacket pocket and returned to the counter, where the jeweler had laid out a golden brooch.

"Your special lady will treasure it," the jeweler said.

Tom wasn't going to admit he had no special lady. No one

lived up to his criteria. She must be beautiful, compassionate, and elegant like the captain's wife. And honest. Tom couldn't abide the slightest hint of dishonesty. The woman he loved would be exquisite, a jewel.

"All I'm asking is who sold it to you," he prodded. "Was it a Spaniard or Cuban named Mornez?"

"Can't say. It was a long time ago."

Tom laid on the countertop a gold doubloon that he'd found while diving the reef. "Try to remember."

The jeweler reached for the coin, but Tom covered it with his right hand. "Information first."

"Don't know any names, but the gentleman who brought it here claimed it's from nobility and has a great secret behind it."

"Not good enough. What did he look like?"

"He didn't say, but I'd venture he was a Spaniard."

Tom's mouth went dry. He had to control himself so he didn't leap across the counter and shake the rest of the story from the man. "From Spain or Havana?"

"One would suppose the latter."

Tom's skin prickled. "This man. Was he shorter than me with dark complexion and black eyes?"

The jeweler wrapped the brooch and put it into a small mahogany box. "That describes many Cubans."

"Then he *was* from Havana."

The jeweler began to walk away.

Tom stopped him with a single sentence. "The doubloon is yours if you can tell me the man's name."

"He never gave it." The jeweler tucked the box into a safe.

Tom must know if it had once belonged to the man who'd betrayed his father. "Then tell me this man's single most distinguishing feature."

27

The jeweler eyed him. "Would you be referring to that scar in the shape of a question mark just below his left eye?"

"Mornez." The prickles turned to a wash of ice water. Ten years ago the man had hired Pa to take him to Louisiana. En route, he had incited the crew to mutiny, cast Pa off in the ship's boat, and stole the ship. Three weeks adrift had ruined Pa's health. The loss of the ship and the resulting charges of neglect had cast the family into poverty. "Luis Mornez."

"Like I said, I never knew his name."

Tom pushed the doubloon toward the jeweler, who bit the edge to be certain of its authenticity.

The jeweler smiled. "A fair trade, considering you're heading out for a wreck."

A chill shivered through Tom at the reference to a local fear that a sailor giving up gold would soon meet his end.

"I'm not superstitious." He stopped in the doorway. "I put my faith in God."

⚜

The morning after the height of the storm dawned with an unusually refreshing breeze and brilliant blue skies. The seas that had tossed Catherine and her shipmates so terribly yesterday had calmed to even swells. They'd never had to abandon ship.

She arose late that morning to find the *Justinian* limping along with crew and passengers intact. To the west, a sliver of darker color hinted at land, certainly no closer than yesterday morning. The remaining sails caught the breeze, but they were too few and ragged to pull the laden ship at any speed.

After a sleepless night and a painfully small breakfast of stale biscuit and salted pork, Catherine and Mrs. Durning surveyed the damage from just outside the main cabin. The sun's brilliant light cast everything in cheer, as if the storm had not occurred. The wreckage above deck told a different story. The ship's boat sat on deck, tangled in its moorings, never having reached the ocean below.

"Oh my," Mrs. Durning exclaimed. "Look at that mast."

The tallest mast—the mainmast, Catherine believed—had snapped off a few feet above the deck. The rigging had been cut away, and the crew was busy salvaging what they could.

"What will we do now?" Mrs. Durning's brow pinched with concern.

The second mate, whose name eluded Catherine, stepped toward them. "Put into port, ma'am. Miss." He dipped his head slightly to recognize them. "The mast must be replaced."

"Are we near Jamaica?" Mrs. Durning asked.

"No, ma'am. The storm blew us off course."

"Then where will we stop?" Catherine interjected. "And how long will repairs take?"

"Perhaps Nassau, but the captain will make that decision. If you'll excuse me, I have duties to attend to."

A cry of "ship ahoy" drew everyone's attention to the forward lookout.

The mate's brow furrowed as he clambered up the ladder to the quarterdeck, where he withdrew his spyglass.

Catherine looked again in that direction and spotted a triangular blot of black on the horizon. Black sails? Or was it a trick of the morning light? Unaccountably a shiver raced down her spine. They'd seen many a vessel during the voyage, especially since reaching the Caribbean Sea, yet this one was different. The nervous tension of mate and crew betrayed that this ship signaled trouble.

Mrs. Durning grasped her hand in a fierce grip. "It's pirates. I know it is. They can say what they want, but I've read the stories. There are still pirates in these waters." She trembled. "What would they do to us?"

Catherine had no answer, for she had read the same tales but presumed them pure fancy. What if the stories were true? "I will speak to the mate. He will reassure us."

Since the officer had not yet finished directing his men, she waited at the base of the stairs. When he made no move to acknowledge her, even after he finished giving instructions, she called up to him, "Sir!"

He glanced down. "I have duties to perform, Miss Haynes." He then called out instructions to the sailors on deck.

A few climbed the ratlines, but most manned winches. Over the course of many tedious minutes, the *Justinian* slowly changed course. By then, the sailing vessel had grown much closer. Its sails weren't black, as Catherine had first surmised, but its hull was. From this distance she could see no flag flying from its rigging. Again she shivered. The Spaniards still plied these waters, as did slavers from Africa. She could think of no reason for them to intercept the *Justinian* unless a war had begun or mischief was planned.

Regardless, the dark ship was heading straight toward them, and they could not outrun it.

"Wake the captain," the second mate barked to one of his men, who instantly scurried down the stairs and into the cabin.

Mrs. Durning squeezed Catherine's hand. "My George will take care of everything."

Catherine had once held that sort of faith in her father. Papa had always taken care of her. He'd ensured she had the finest gowns and attended the best balls for her Season. When she'd refused every suitor, he'd understood why she would not marry a man who could not inspire a love like the one Papa had for her mother.

"Oh, Papa," she whispered. Would today be her last?

Mrs. Durning patted her hand. "You still miss him terribly, but it will grow less with time."

Catherine supposed it would. After all, Maman had retreated into the fringes of her memory, though she could still recall every agonizing moment of her mother's last night. She had been sent to her room to sleep, but the black mood in the house had kept her awake. She paced the room and finally slipped out to tiptoe to Maman's bedchamber. The door was closed, and the doctor murmured words she would never forget: "It won't be long now."

She had run down the stairs and hidden in the library, as if all those books could somehow shield her from what was to come. When Papa found her later, he didn't attempt to extract her from beneath Maman's writing desk. Instead, he settled in his wing chair and picked up his Bible. Minutes passed in silence save for the turning of the page. Unable to bear it, she came out of hiding and climbed onto the chair beside him. He'd simply held her. Though he'd never said the words, she knew. Maman was gone.

Mrs. Durning let go of her hand as the captain came on deck. "What is it?"

The captain's worried expression softened. "Nothing to be concerned about, but why don't you take Miss Haynes into the cabin. She looks a bit pale."

Catherine was not about to faint, not over some unknown ship. This was clearly an attempt to get them off deck. Why? She turned back to the approaching ship. She could now see the silhouette of men on its decks. Still no flag. At this rate the unknown ship would soon overtake them. She looked up to see that the *Justinian* was not flying the ensign either. Had Captain Durning taken it down, or had it been lost during the storm?

"Was the ensign flying this morning?" she asked Mrs. Durning, who tugged at her elbow in a vain attempt to draw her into the cabin.

"Goodness, I don't know. I suppose it was. Why?"

That might explain the unknown ship's reluctance to reveal its country of origin. She leaned over the rail, squinting at the approaching vessel. It had sleek lines, beautiful really, and did not display the usual ravages that the sea took upon those ships bold enough to sail her. Surely it had endured the same storm, yet it looked as fresh and clean as if it had just come out of the shipyard.

Did Captain Durning suspect treachery? Was that why he'd suggested they retire to the cabin? Catherine hesitated. She preferred to face an enemy in open air, not cower belowdecks, but Mrs. Durning had paled so much that she might well swoon.

Catherine took the woman's hand. "Let's go inside. I would like to rest. Perhaps the cook would serve tea in the officers' dining saloon?" From that room Catherine could position herself to see the vessel's approach and ascertain whether they ought to bolt themselves in their quarters or not.

The cook grumbled at her untimely request for tea but obliged with a pot and two cups. Mrs. Durning located sugar in her husband's stores, but milk had vanished from the tea service weeks ago. Catherine relished the idea of sipping proper tea—with milk—once she reached Chêne Noir, the Lafreniere plantation in Louisiana.

Catherine positioned herself so she could keep the approaching ship within view. Mrs. Durning sat opposite her and dropped a nip from the sugarloaf into her teacup.

"That's better." Catherine sipped the tepid tea. "The sun is rather hot in these climes. I wonder how long it will take to repair the mast." She hoped the change of topic would distract Mrs. Durning from the idea of pirates.

"Mr. Durning will take care of that." Mrs. Durning dropped another chunk of sugar into her cup. "I suppose if a new mast is available, then it will not take all that long."

"I hope so." The bulk of Catherine's fifty pounds had gone toward passage and the provisions she would need while traveling. Naturally her cousin Roger had held her to the letter of their agreement, without a pence more.

"On the other hand, we should be prepared for a long stay. Mr. Durning will provide for me, of course. Do you have means, dear?"

Had her concerns been that obvious? "That will depend on how long the delay is. Did your husband ever encounter this before?"

"Once. They were dismasted off the Cape." Mrs. Durning stared into space, a plump finger tapping her chin. "Three months' delay, I believe."

"Three months!" Catherine's funds could not last three months. "I must get to New Orleans." From the city, it was a short distance to Chêne Noir, according to Maman.

"You could always seek passage on another ship. After all, you would have taken a second ship from Jamaica to New Orleans."

"The fares might be much higher from Nassau." Perhaps all she had left.

A jolt drew her attention to the window. The black-hulled ship had come alongside. She flew to the window, Mrs. Durning in her wake.

The sailing ship was much smaller than the *Justinian*, perhaps half its size or less. The sails were a somewhat dingy color, not the black that they had appeared to be on the horizon. The dark hull, however, gleamed. At the wheel stood an older man in rather ragged clothes. A pirate?

She scanned the rest of the small crew. The men ranged from a lad of perhaps fourteen to a weathered old salt, but the man who captured Catherine's attention looked to be in command. Tall and smartly dressed, he stood in direct contrast to his crew.

Mrs. Durning pressed close. "That one's too handsome to be a pirate."

Catherine couldn't rip her gaze from the dark-haired gentleman in fine trousers, leather boots, and a navy blue frock coat. Though he issued orders with precision, proving he was in command, he was far younger than she had first presumed. He looked around her age, perhaps a couple years older. His skin had been bronzed by the sun, yet he carried himself with the confidence of a nobleman. If he was indeed a pirate, she would not mind at all being taken aboard his ship.

"He doesn't look evil," she murmured.

Just then the man's gaze caught hers, and an impish grin curved his lips, as if he was accusing her of snooping on him. Not one to look away, Catherine stared back imperiously. He held her gaze a long minute before answering the *Justinian*'s hail.

His confidence took her breath away. She spun from the window and headed for the dining saloon doorway.

Mrs. Durning trailed after her. "Where are you going?"

"To find out precisely who he is."

The woman's eyes widened. "What if he isn't . . . respectable?"

"Then I shall discover that fact at once."

"But you might fall into harm. Aren't you afraid?"

Catherine mirrored the confident captain's grin. "No, but if he makes one wrong move, he will regret it."

2

Tom dragged his gaze from the gorgeous woman in the aft cabin window of the dismasted barque. He had business to attend to, and it didn't include gawking at pretty ladies. The crew of the *Justinian* had not lowered a ladder. Either they intended to refuse pilotage, or they feared him. Regardless, protocol required he make vocal contact and show his credentials to the master. By his estimation, that would be the older gentleman in the fine wool uniform.

He cupped his hands around his mouth. "Do you require assistance, Captain?"

"We do not," a rangy crewman, likely one of the mates, shot back.

"You're dismasted." It always helped to point out the obvious. "And soon to sail onto the reef."

That drew the master to the rail of the quarterdeck. "I am well aware of our condition and course."

"Then you know how treacherous the reefs are."

The master scowled. "As you can see, we're making good

progress on the fore and mizzen sail. With winds light, I foresee no difficulties."

Reluctance to accept assistance was usual. Tom seldom found an eager master unless the ship was in dire straits. That was not the case with the *Justinian*. The barque could limp into Key West on her own, but maneuverability would be lessened with the reduction in sail. One small miscalculation could send the ship onto the reef, but no master liked to be told what to do, especially from a man half his age.

So Tom tried an approach that appealed more to the man's heart than his skills. "Are any of the passengers or crew ill or injured? I can take them speedily ashore. Key West has fine physicians and a marine hospital."

As anticipated, that gave the master pause. After stiffening slightly, he consulted with the rangy mate. Perhaps someone aboard was ill.

Tom waited.

The response came as predicted. "We need no assistance."

Tom was down to his last ploy—helpfulness. Coupled with a broad grin, it generally disarmed the most suspicious master. "Closest port to your position is Key West. Shipwrights there can replace your mast. The best channel for a ship your size lies beyond a narrow gap in the shoal, unmarked. Sail past Sand Key lighthouse on a northeast bearing, avoid the reef, and search for the opening."

"I'll take that under advisement."

"If you later decide you need a pilot . . ." Movement along the rail drew Tom's attention. The pretty lady had appeared, bareheaded, on deck. The sun lit her auburn hair on fire. Unlike the usual fashion, pulled up under a bonnet or hat so no one could see it, she let the thick mane of curling locks flow around her shoulders. The sight took every thought from his mind.

"You're a pilot?" the master shouted. "Licensed?"

Tom refocused on the man. "Licensed by the federal court in Key West, Judge Marvin presiding. You may examine my credentials if you wish."

The captain still looked wary, but he ordered the ladder thrown out.

While Tom waited for the crew aboard the *Justinian* to secure the rope ladder, he glanced again at the lady. She was still looking at him. He smiled. She cocked her head, a rare assurance in her manner, as if she was in full command of the situation.

"Ready, mister," the rangy mate called out.

Again Tom had to draw his attention to the task at hand. Gazing at a pretty woman had best wait until port, though he wouldn't mind learning who she might be. A gentlewoman surely, maybe even a duchess. This was a British vessel. The thrill of possibility increased at each rung of the ladder.

The rangy crewman held out a hand to help him over the bulwark and onto deck. "Welcome aboard, sir. I'm Mr. Lightwater, first mate, and this is Captain Durning."

Tom tugged his coat into place and stuck out his hand. "Tom Worthington, master of the *James Patrick* and licensed pilot." Seeing as the *Justinian* did not require salvage, he didn't mention his wrecking license. "Pleased to meet you, Captain. Mr. Lightwater."

Captain Durning did not crack a smile. "Your papers."

Tom reached in his inner coat pocket for his leather wallet. Once more his gaze landed on the pretty woman, who had drifted near. This time she gave him an impertinent little grin.

The captain cleared his throat.

Tom opened his wallet and withdrew the pilot license and handed it to Captain Durning. The man read it with care before handing it back.

"It appears to be in order. If you are who you say you are."

That carried suspicion to a new level. Tom merely nodded, smiling. "You may certainly proceed without a pilot. If you do happen upon the reef, I am also licensed as a wrecker."

The woman laughed.

The master's complexion darkened. "I am fully capable of handling this ship."

Again Tom nodded, keeping the pleasant smile. "Indeed you are. Only a highly skilled master could come out of that storm with his vessel still afloat."

As expected, the master's outrage eased.

"As pilot, I am simply aboard to offer navigational counsel, which you may accept or reject." Tom named his fee. "You will find it the lowest rate out of Key West."

"That seems reasonable," the woman interjected, her melodic voice as captivating as her fiery hair.

The master's attention snapped away from Tom to land on her. She could not have known how ill-timed her comment was. "Mr. Lightwater, please escort Miss Haynes to her quarters."

Her eyes widened, and Tom suspected a protest was about to be unleashed, but then an elderly woman stepped to her side. The woman's stout carriage and confidence placed her as someone with authority, definitely not the pretty lady's maid.

"I happen to agree with Catherine. I, for one, do not care to end up wrecked on a reef."

Catherine. So that was the lovely woman's given name. Since she bore no physical resemblance to the older woman, Tom surmised they were friends rather than relations.

The master blanched and stammered that they were never in danger.

The matron was not appeased.

Tom stifled a snicker. That explained the woman's authoritative manner. She was the master's wife. A wife often held command, especially where the family's safety was concerned. His mother certainly had, even before Pa lost his ship.

Tom bowed before the women. Perhaps this time away from wrecking the *Isaac Allerton* would prove worthwhile after all. "Tom Worthington at your service, ladies. Pilot, captain, and wrecker."

Though the master muttered something about modern-day pirates, Mrs. Durning warbled about his fine manners.

Catherine Haynes, on the other hand, jutted out her perfectly proportioned chin. "Did you not leave off the superlative, Mr. Worthington?"

He cocked his head, keeping that grin in place. "I can't imagine what you mean."

"Ship pilot extraordinaire. As well as the least expensive and most mannered."

"I can't challenge that assessment."

"Pride goeth before a fall."

Ordinarily Tom would take offense, but he'd never enjoyed such delightful sparring. "I assume you know that from experience?"

As anticipated, that drew a scowl. Before she could level another barb, Captain Durning's bark of laughter stilled her tongue.

"I'll give you this, Worthington. You're the first man to match Miss Haynes in conversation. If you're half as skilled at piloting as you are at crafting words, you'll be worth the fee."

Tom grinned and stuck out his hand. "Agreed?"

Captain Durning shook on it.

Tom had been hired. Best of all, that would give him more time to get acquainted with the intriguing Catherine Haynes.

"Match me?" Catherine stormed into her cabin after being escorted from the deck along with Mrs. Durning. "That arrogant man, who knows nothing about me, had the audacity to suggest that I suffer from pride."

"Now, now, that nice Mr. Worthington didn't mean any such thing." Mrs. Durning closed the door to the cabin.

"Of course he did."

"In jest, perhaps."

Catherine's pique eased as she recalled the merriment in his eyes. "Perhaps, but it is not the way one ought to treat a lady and a stranger." Yet she longed to go right back on deck to parry words with him again. If Captain Durning had not insisted they retire, she would still be there.

Mrs. Durning failed to notice Catherine's conflicted emotions. "Then you will be much relieved to learn that he is not likely to join us for the midday meal."

"Oh." Disappointment crashed over her. "He would not eat?"

"He will be much occupied with directing the helmsman, I imagine."

"Yes, I suppose you are correct." Then why this unaccountable dissatisfaction? She tossed her head. "That is a good thing. After all, I cannot be distracted from my purpose, even by a handsome man."

"Indeed not, as Mr. Lightwater must have learned by now."

"One can only hope." Catherine wrinkled her nose. "But he is not handsome by any measure." The mate had been too attentive from the moment they left Liverpool and refused to take a single hint that she was not at all interested. She'd had to enlist Mrs. Durning's help. "At least I shall soon be rid of him."

"A blessing."

"Indeed." Catherine gazed out the window. "Once ashore, I must find passage to New Orleans as soon as possible."

"Oh dear. I hadn't counted on losing your companionship so soon. You could wait for the *Justinian* to be repaired."

Poor woman. She had come on this journey at Catherine's request and must have expected her company until they arrived in Jamaica. She might even have hoped Catherine would lose interest in her quest and return to England with her. That would not happen.

"You said that repairs could take months."

"Perhaps not. You heard Mr. Worthington's assurance that Key West had shipwrights ready and able to replace the mast."

That was not the point. Even quick repairs would take too long.

"I cannot . . ." Catherine floundered for words. There was no way around the truth. "That is, my funds cannot provide for a long delay. Assuming this outpost will even accept English currency."

"Why wouldn't they? British sterling sets the standard throughout the world. And we will stay aboard ship."

"I must still provide my own food."

"You will dine with us. It's the least Mr. Durning can do, given the inconvenience."

Captain Durning was not to be faulted for foul weather. Catherine would not rely on others to feed her. Now that this leg of the journey had been truncated far short of their original destination, she could well find her funds short. Aside from the cost of provisions, the passage to New Orleans could demand a higher fee.

She tried to recall the maps of the West Indies in Papa's atlas, now part of cousin Roger's library. "Key West is farther from New Orleans than Jamaica, is it not?"

"I have no idea, dear. Mr. Durning insists I have no head for navigation."

Frustrated, Catherine strode to the window. Through the opening, the sea stretched as far as she could see. Nothing but azure blue. She heaved a sigh. This storm had cost more than a sleepless night. It could jeopardize her entire future.

Mrs. Durning yawned. "I do believe I shall rest a spell. I didn't sleep a wink last night. You will be all right?"

"Of course." Catherine's attention was drawn to the shouts of men outside the window. She was vaguely aware of Mrs. Durning's departure but more concerned by the obvious sound of activity.

"Raise the jib," came the shout.

One of the vessels was raising sail, but how much more canvas could the *Justinian* carry? She was missing the tallest mast. This shout must have come from the black ship, Tom Worthington's ship.

Tom. An able name. But it was the eyes and grin that captivated her. What woman would not be impressed with such confidence and ease of manner? Tom Worthington acted as if he commanded the world.

"Aye, Captain," returned the response.

Captain? Mr. Worthington was the captain of the black ship. Why would he leave? Had Captain Durning changed his mind? Had he gone back on his word and dismissed Mr. Worthington's services? Foolishness. No captain could know these waters more than a local sea captain. Tom Worthington had said they must cross a dangerous reef. Catherine had not endured the terrors of the storm just to end up tossed into the sea due to masculine pride.

She tore out of the cabin, flew down the short hallway, and skittered up the few steps to the main deck. A sixty-day voyage was not going to end up with the ship wrecked on a reef.

⌒⚓⌒

Tom sent off Rander and the crew. "I'll join you when you return to Key West."

No small part of him wished he was heading with them on the *James Patrick* to claim his portion of the fortune to be made off a fully laden wreck. If George Alderslade was calling for help, there must be a huge and expensive cargo to be salvaged. That meant money in every man's pocket.

Except his.

Half the piloting fee would go to Rourke to pay the costs imposed on him as owner of the shipping company and Tom's boss. Normally the split wouldn't be that even, but Tom had given Captain Durning a low quote in order to get the business. He would have to give more to Rourke. Maybe he should have let the master have his way. The barque would end up lodged on the reef and require salvage.

Tom shook his head. No Christian man could place a ship and its passengers in danger. One passenger in particular might have swayed him to settle for a lower fee. Her fiery hair and mischievous smile still danced in his mind.

The sail of the *James Patrick* shrank as she hurried northeast toward Washerwoman Shoal. Tom pressed the spyglass to his eye. Even from here he could pick out the cluster of wrecking vessels. Once the swells calmed, divers would be sent down and the work would begin.

He sighed. As disappointed as he had been to receive the piloting assignment, deep down he understood Rourke's reasoning. The company owner had to send someone to pilot the barque. Naturally he'd chosen the least experienced captain in the fleet. As much as Tom wanted to salvage the wreck, Rourke couldn't delay an entire ship to wait for him. Salvage priority was given to those wreckers who arrived first. Delay cost money.

"Course, sir?" the helmsman inquired.

Soon after the ladies disappeared into the great cabin, the master followed. That left Tom alone on the quarterdeck with Lightwater and the helmsman.

"Yes, do give us the proper heading," the mate sneered.

Tom ignored the jab. Mates were as distrusting as masters.

"Northeast," Tom barked to the helmsman. To ensure accuracy, he pointed in the correct direction. "Head on the Sand Key lighthouse for now."

"And later?" Lightwater asked.

"We'll keep the light a quarter mile to larboard. I'll give a new point of reference when we're in range."

This day had been a challenge. First, Ma's letter put him in a foul mood. Then, at the cost of a doubloon, he'd come one step closer to finding the scoundrel who'd destroyed his father. Finally, this unwanted piloting job had gotten a lot more intriguing at the appearance of Catherine Haynes.

The clatter of rapid footsteps behind him coupled with Lightwater's sudden jerk to attention told him someone important had ascended to the quarterdeck.

Tom swung around, prepared to greet the captain, only to find Miss Haynes facing him. Fire sparkled in her eyes.

"You're still here," she said.

"Stating the obvious?"

She tossed off the barb. "I heard your ship cast off and one of the men call out to the captain. I assumed you were on it. You did say you were the captain."

Lightwater snickered.

If he had been one of Tom's crew, Tom would have let the man know exactly who was in charge.

"I am captain when I'm aboard." At least some of the time, but he wasn't about to let Lightwater know that.

"Then who's sailing it now?"

"Captain Rander."

"Oh." Her superior attitude thawed. "Then you are taking us to safe harbor."

"That is my job."

"Which you will, no doubt, complete without incident."

Tom had to smile. Catherine Haynes wasn't as tough as she let people think. After spending what was doubtless a sleepless night battered by the storm, she wanted assurance that she would reach land.

"That is my intent." In spite of every effort to suppress his mirth, the corner of his mouth tugged upward.

Her gaze narrowed. "Are you always this impertinent with passengers?"

"Only with female passengers who mistakenly believe they are allowed on the quarterdeck."

Her jaw dropped. She looked at the edge of the quarterdeck and then at Lightwater before swallowing. "I was not aware. I beg your pardon." She backed away.

This quieter, humbler Miss Haynes didn't stir him like the feisty one. "That doesn't mean your presence is unwelcome."

Her eyebrows jerked upward.

"It doesn't?" Lightwater exclaimed.

Tom couldn't care less about the ship's mate. He held out the spyglass to Miss Haynes. "Take a look. You can see the lighthouse on Key West from here."

She glanced at Lightwater before advancing to take the glass. "How do I use it?"

Lightwater hurried forward. "Here, let me show you."

Tom brushed the man aside. "It's my glass. I will show the lady."

Her lips curved into a coy smile, as if she had intended to drag just that sort of reaction out of both men. What a minx!

Tom wanted to fire back a retort, but at present he preferred leaning over her shoulder, almost cheek to cheek, showing her how to adjust the lens until the shore came into focus. Her hair smelled faintly of roses, in spite of enduring a long night at sea. He breathed in deeply.

"The course, Mr. Worthington," the mate snapped.

Miss Haynes handed the spyglass back to Tom. "I don't want to distract you from your duties."

Curses on that mate! He'd said that just to disrupt Tom's moment with Catherine Haynes. They were nowhere near the point when they must change course.

"Steady as she goes," he growled.

"Steady as she goes," repeated the helmsman with a snicker.

Tom glared at Lightwater, but the man clearly hadn't a caring bone in his body.

"Don't want to run aground," the mate said. "Do we, Miss Haynes?"

Lightwater had the audacity to tip his hat at her.

A smile teased her lips. "Indeed, Mr. Lightwater. Mr. Worthington. I will leave you to your navigation."

Lightwater stepped forward. "Allow me to escort you, Miss Haynes."

She shot the man a withering glare. "I am fully capable of descending a few steps, Mr. Lightwater, without *anyone's* assistance."

Tom choked back a chuckle. She had no use for the gallantry of either man. Catherine Haynes was capable of standing on her own. Lightwater looked affronted, but Tom admired that characteristic in a woman. This journey had just gotten promising.

3

Through the spyglass Catherine had made out the lighthouse before the two men got into a spitting match. Goodness! Never had she endured such a fuss, not even in her Season. Certainly not at home, even when cousin Roger was trying to marry her off.

Home. Deerford. A sudden longing ached in her breast. She would never see it again. She knew that. Her cousin knew it too. That's why he'd agreed to her terms. The tenants had wept when she told them the property had been sold. At first they resisted accepting the bit of money she'd been able to scrape from her cousin, but she stood firm. Many had clung to her, thanking her, but their eyes spoke fear. What would the future hold for an elderly widow or a young family struggling to make ends meet? She hadn't been able to assure them, and that left a sour taste in her mouth, one that no amount of masculine attention could erase.

Back in her cabin, she pulled the daguerreotype from her trunk. Papa. Maman. The sitting had taken place in the library. She had loved those books, but she would never see them or her beloved Deerford again. Like the tenants, she must move on and trust her well-being to people she had not yet met. Home would now be made in an unfamiliar land.

The daguerreotype went back in the trunk. Best not dwell on what couldn't be changed.

After attempting to stitch the sampler she'd been working on for months, she tossed it aside and stood at the window, where she could watch the open seas pass. The ship drew near a light structure atop a low, sandy island. That must be the lighthouse that Tom Worthington called Sand Key. The ship turned, and their destination came back into view.

Key West.

"What will you bring?" she murmured, though an island could hardly answer.

Again the ship turned, and the island disappeared from view. She could see it better from the dining saloon, which had windows facing the opposite direction, and she was not likely to run into either the mate or Mr. Worthington, not with the ship this close to port.

She slipped down the hallway and into the room. Mrs. Durning sat at the table, a bowl of clear broth before her.

"I thought you were napping."

The elderly woman looked up. "Catherine, dear. Join me. The cook said he made plenty, and Mr. Durning is sound asleep."

Instead of joining the woman, Catherine drifted to the windows. "You were not tired?"

"I've never been able to nap on an empty stomach." She patted the tabletop. "Join me." She then proceeded to call for the steward and order a second bowl of broth for Catherine.

"I'm not hungry."

Mrs. Durning would not hear her protests. "Of course you are. You didn't eat much more than some stale biscuit this morning. That won't give you fortitude for the day ahead."

Catherine had eaten more than Mrs. Durning recalled, but the woman had a strong need to mother her. That had been the case ever since Maman passed. With no children of her own, Mrs. Durning had taken to stopping by Deerford daily to offer her assistance and opinions. Papa had managed to turn her away while making her feel as if she had accomplished the very thing she'd set out to do. Papa was gifted in that way. Catherine had not inherited that talent.

She leaned against the window, but the island had yet to come into view. That meant it was dead ahead, and she could only see it from the main deck, where she would be subjected to unwanted masculine attention. She pressed her cheek to the glass.

"The steward will not thank you for that smudge on the window," Mrs. Durning scolded.

"I don't want to miss seeing our destination."

"Never fear. Mr. Durning said it will take a full hour to draw near, given the opposing breeze."

The steward arrived with the broth and set a place for Catherine across the table from Mrs. Durning. She sighed. If it would take that long to arrive, she might as well dine.

Over the light repast she asked Mrs. Durning what she knew of Key West.

"Only that it's a smallish yet rather lively seaside town from what Mr. Durning has heard. He has never stopped there. The *Justinian* can sail long distances before reprovisioning."

That explained his eventual agreement to take a pilot. On the long voyage Captain Durning had seldom taken the advice of others. She supposed that was due to his many years of experience. Accepting pilotage from Tom Worthington, whom he would consider barely more than a boy, must have grated on him.

"Key West is better than Havana," Mrs. Durning said with a shudder. "You can't trust those Spaniards."

Spaniard. The dark stranger from ten years past popped into her mind. At the time she'd thought him an Arabian or perhaps from India, but he might just as easily have been a Spaniard by birth. During her time keeping the accounts, she'd scoured the estate records and found only one unusual notation from that time—*DeMornay settlement*—accompanied by an extremely generous credit to the account.

DeMornay. She knew no one by that name. Not a tenant or neighbor. She'd assumed he was a London solicitor bringing news of an unexpected inheritance or grant, but what if he wasn't? The dark stranger had left with a strongbox. What if he had carried money *into* his meeting with Papa rather than from it? She would likely never know, for DeMornay was a French name, not Spanish. That notation could not have referred to the dark stranger.

She sighed. "It won't make any difference, for we're not going to Havana."

"I should hope not." Mrs. Durning drained another spoonful of broth. "At least Key West has one particularly handsome attraction."

Though Catherine knew perfectly well what Mrs. Durning referred to, she had no intention of following this line of thought. "Warmth and sun."

"You can't pretend you don't know what I mean." Mrs. Durning set her spoon down, an all-too-knowing smile on her lips. "Mr. Worthington is quite dashing, if you ask my opinion. And the perfect age. He can't be much older than you."

Catherine busied herself stirring the soup. "A year or two, perhaps."

"Quite confident and well cut across the shoulders."

50

Catherine hadn't failed to notice that either. "But he is rather bronzed."

Mrs. Durning chuckled. "All who sail are weathered by the elements."

Was that why the stranger had been so dark?

"You can tell a seafarer who stands watch by the nature of his complexion," Mrs. Durning continued. "Consider it a mark of diligence in his duty."

Catherine set down her spoon. Thinking about the past—or was it Tom Worthington?—had made her too anxious to eat even clear broth.

Through the windows, a large brick edifice came into view. She pushed back the chair just as the door to the dining saloon opened. Mr. Lightwater entered.

Her spirits sank. "Aren't you supposed to be on duty?"

His complexion was pale and pockmarked. He pulled off his hat. "Mrs. Durning. Miss Haynes." His gaze lingered uncomfortably long on her.

She turned away.

He stepped closer. "To answer your question, the watch has changed, and I am pleased to join you for the midday meal."

She stepped around him. "I have already eaten. Perhaps Mrs. Durning would enjoy your company. I am going to take some air on deck."

Before he could stop her, she slipped out of the room. Mrs. Durning would delay the mate, but not for long. Catherine hurried down the hall and up the stairs to the main deck. There, for the moment, she was rid of him.

But not the other man.

His gaze made her cheeks heat, but she would not give Tom Worthington the satisfaction of knowing how much he unsettled her. She was, after all, a gentleman's daughter. Gentlewomen did not take up with sailors, not to mention wreckers. A sea captain perhaps, if he had served long in the Royal Navy. Certainly not an overconfident American rascal who assumed she would swoon over his attention. Moreover, her purpose was set. She must go to Louisiana.

The brick edifice beckoned from the shore. Since viewing it kept her back turned to one Tom Worthington, she pretended greater interest than it had at first stirred. Now that she could see it in its entirety, its purpose became clear. It was a fort, complete with gun ports and cannon. Armament did not excite her. Its position offshore on a spit of sand was mildly intriguing.

"Fort Zachary Taylor." Mr. Worthington must have slipped down from the quarterdeck during her observations.

"Shouldn't you be directing this vessel?"

"I am."

"From here?" She made the mistake of looking at him.

His soft brown eyes twinkled with mirth and something else . . . Interest? "As you said yourself not long ago, I am extraordinarily gifted."

"That is not what I said." She broke his gaze and stared instead at the shoreline with its pretty little houses with verandas and columns and picket fences.

Instead of leaving her alone, he joined her at the rail. "I believe the word was *extraordinaire*."

"Irony, Mr. Worthington. And I did not say that you were endowed with special gifts."

"Implied."

She peeked sideways at him. Surely he was jesting.

He caught her glance, and his smile turned to a ridiculous frown.

"You are not very good at this," she pointed out.

"Good at what, Miss Haynes?"

His exaggerated dumbfounded expression reminded her so much of Eustace Kirby—excepting that Mr. Kirby had not been jesting—that she laughed.

"Aha! You are capable of humor," he said.

Try as she might, she could not make a frown stay in place. "What makes you believe I was speaking in jest? Even the most adept navigator cannot direct a vessel from the main deck."

"Oh? You're an expert in maritime navigation?" Mr. Worthington turned, cupped his hands, and shouted out a bearing.

The helmsman repeated the command, and the vessel's course shifted slightly.

"There is proof that counters your assertion, Miss Catherine."

She felt a flush of heat at the sound of her given name on his tongue, and not merely because of his impertinent social blunder. This jolt of excitement was utter nonsense. She could not dally about with a mere sailor. She had a journey to complete and a family to reclaim. Key West could not be more than a brief stopping place en route to her final destination.

"Perhaps you can be of some assistance," she said carefully.

"For you, anything."

The heat increased, and she had to resist the temptation to fan her face. Instead, she looked forward, as if the Key West shoreline fascinated her.

Aside from houses and quaint buildings, it had the usual seaport wharves and warehouses. Only the palms differed from an English seaside town, but then she was no stranger to palm trees, having seen them in Lisbon and the Azores. Of greater interest was the large number of vessels in port. Masts sprayed upward like spines on a hedgehog. Surely one was going to Louisiana.

"I'm seeking passage to New Orleans. Where might I make inquiries?"

He leaned on the rail. "I thought the *Justinian* was headed to Jamaica."

"It is. From there I had intended to book passage to New Orleans, but now we will be delayed."

"You could wait out the repairs."

She shook her head. "Too long. I can't afford the wait."

"Oh?" He straightened and surveyed her. "Are you meeting someone there?"

She hesitated. "Yes, in a manner of speaking."

His eyebrows rose. "What does that mean? Are you or aren't you meeting someone?"

"I am." She did not care to explain herself. "Simply tell me where I might inquire about booking passage."

Though he paused long enough to shout out another course correction to the helmsman, he did answer her. "Check with the shipping agents. They have offices near the wharves and customhouse. I would be delighted to escort you there, but you should be aware that travel has slowed due to the storm."

"But it will begin again."

"In time."

She did not have a great deal of time. Or money. "Do you have any idea how much passage might cost?"

"That varies, depending on the vessel and the accommodations."

"I don't need much." She could get by for a short time with modest provisions. "How long is the voyage?"

"That would depend on the ship. A fast clipper can make it in nine days."

"Nine days!" The distance from Key West to New Orleans was greater than she'd hoped. "And a steamship?"

"It would depend on the route. Many stop in Mobile and other ports. They could take just as long. For a direct route, perhaps a week."

A week. She could endure almost anything for a week.

"Mr. Worthington." The sneer of Mr. Lightwater made her cringe. "We are hiring you to pilot the vessel, not seduce the passengers."

Her already heated cheeks grew hotter, this time from anger. One thing she could not endure for another week was Mr. Lightwater.

She glared at him and brushed past before he could corner her.

⁂

So Catherine Haynes was headed for New Orleans. Tom tumbled that around in his mind as Lightwater took off after her. He'd hoped to get to know her, but one detail told him to take caution. True, Lightwater was trying to claim her, but she clearly did not like the man's attentions. Tom's concern came from another quarter. A woman traveling alone—assuming Mrs. Durning did not escort her to New Orleans—and in a hurry to get there meant just one thing.

Miss Haynes must be betrothed to marry.

She was clearly English, and her clothing was of such fine quality that she could well be titled or at least moneyed. Did the English arrange marriages? If so, New Orleans seemed a peculiar destination with its French roots.

Whatever was going on, it more than piqued his curiosity.

Unfortunately, he didn't have time to decipher the puzzle, since they had reached the harbor.

He bounded up the ladder to the quarterdeck and began directing the helmsman while the second mate gave orders to the crew on deck. Sails were trimmed or came down. Mooring lines were readied. Over the course of the next hour, he didn't have time to think about Catherine Haynes.

Only when the *Justinian* was securely moored at the O'Malley wharf and Tom had received payment for his services did she reappear on deck. This time she wore a pretty if impractical little hat that matched her gown and carried a striped parasol. Gloves covered her hands, and a dainty little bag dangled from her wrist. In the plum color, she looked the picture of the English gentlewoman. She must also be wilting from the sun's heat, for the warehouses blocked the breeze that had kept them cool at sea.

Lightwater hastened to her side. She did not look at the man or take his proffered arm.

Tom chuckled. The mate was wasting his time, but he seemed oblivious to that fact. Miss Haynes's annoyance was building. Tom hurried down the deck to her rescue.

"Ah, there you are, Miss Haynes." Tom took her hand and placed it on his arm.

Though she shot him a glare, she did not remove her hand.

"I did offer to escort you to your destination," he added for Lightwater's benefit.

She looked ready to spit out a refusal.

He cut to the point before she could speak. "Shall we begin with those shipping agents near the customhouse?"

Her frown reversed to a pert smile. "An excellent idea, Mr. Worthington."

Tom led her to the gangway, leaving Lightwater rooted to the deck, a scowl on his lips.

When they reached the wharf, she slipped her hand from his arm. "I believe I can manage from here."

"Only if you want Mr. Lightwater to come rushing after you."

She tucked her hand back around his arm. "To the custom-house."

"Directly ahead."

"The building with all the people around it?"

"I'm afraid so." Tom scanned the harbor and spotted the wrecking schooner *Florida* at a nearby wharf. Judging from the unusual crowd surrounding the vessel, it must have come from the *Isaac Allerton* wreck. "A ship ran aground in the storm just northeast of here. It appears that either the crew or the first of the salvage has reached port. Either way, it means a long wait at the customhouse."

She blew out her breath, clearly frustrated, but he saw an advantage. His pilotage fee was tucked in his breast pocket, and Rourke was gone on the *Redemption*. No one would be looking for him right away.

"We could get you situated first," he offered.

She hesitated, and a mix of emotions passed over her face.

He had to remind himself that she had not intended to come to Key West and likely knew nothing of the port. "Will you be joining Mrs. Durning at the Admiralty Inn?"

"But I thought—" She shook her head. "I need to first inquire about passage. You said there are other shipping offices."

His spirits sank. Apparently nothing would deter her from her purpose.

"There are." He swept out his right arm. "This way."

The wharves were crowded, and not just with stevedores and porters. With a salvage under way, the curious and the greedy crowded the docks, looking for what might be pilfered or pur-chased at a cut-rate price. Most Key West homes were full of salvaged cargo. From pianos to chairs to jewelry, anyone who could afford to purchase salvaged items did so. They could be acquired for a fraction of the cost.

Miss Haynes clung to his arm as people rushed this way and that, most paying them no attention whatsoever. A compact man, Cuban by looks, jostled her.

"Goodness! Are people always so careless?" She looked toward the retreating man, and her fingers tightened around Tom's arm.

He followed her gaze. "Do you know that man?"

"Impossible."

"I don't recall seeing him on the *Justinian*."

"Not from the ship." Her voice was barely audible, and he had to keep hold of her lest the bustling crowds tear her away. "From long ago. When I was a girl."

4

It could not be. Ten years was a long time, and memories often faded. Still, Catherine would never forget the stranger's eyes. Black as night with a gold fleck in the center, as if a cat stared into a bright light. At the time she'd called them "tiger's eyes" before learning that a tiger's eyes were nothing like that. Then there was the odd scar beneath his eye.

This man had passed too quickly for her to spot either distinguishing feature. Yet his stature and coloring made her pulse race. Could it be?

"I must follow him." She let go of Tom Worthington's arm and began weaving through the crowd.

The throngs that had seemed thick before now turned into a solid mass. Her parasol had become a detriment, so she folded it. Even so, at every step she was pushed in a different direction until she wasn't sure where she was headed.

"Here." Mr. Worthington grabbed her elbow. "Follow me."

Within a moment he had pulled her out of the masses and into a shaded alcove beneath an overhanging porch roof. Only then did she realize how hot the sun was. Perspiration trickled down her temples and the nape of her neck. Her heart raced, and her head seemed to swim as if she was still aboard ship. She grabbed onto a pillar, but the sensation did not abate.

"Here." Mr. Worthington eased her to a small bench. "Do you have a fan?"

"In my bag." She fumbled to open the clasp.

"Perhaps the gloves are the problem."

"Of course they are," she snapped, "but no lady appears in public without them."

"Perhaps in England, but customs are different here. No one will condemn you for removing them." He knelt before her. "Or I might open the bag for you."

She groaned with frustration. The last thing she needed was for Tom Worthington to see what she carried in her bag. Off came the gloves. Sure enough, the clasp was now easy to open. She withdrew the fan and snapped the bag shut again.

He held out a hand. "Allow me."

She blinked. "To what?"

"Create a bit of breeze with that fan of yours."

She sat up straight. "I am perfectly capable of fanning myself."

He grinned and stood. "Of course you are."

She preferred him at eye level, but her legs were too wobbly to stand just yet. So she stared at the street with its glistening sand and gravel. Tom had guided her away from the crowded wharf and across the street to . . . She glanced at the sign above the door. STEPHEN RUSSELL, ESQ.

"An attorney's office?"

He laughed. "The closest place to sit. You still have your sea legs."

"Excuse me?"

"From being aboard ship so long. The ground will feel like it's swaying."

"How did you know?" She chided herself. "Forgive me. You're a sailor."

Instead of taking offense, he laughed again. "Don't worry. It'll go away in a day or so."

"A day! How will I ever catch up to . . . Never mind." The man, whoever he was, was gone.

He crouched again so he was at eye level. "Who was that man?"

She stared at Mr. Worthington, who seemed able to read her mind. "I'm not sure—but I think it may be DeMornay."

"Mornez?"

"No, DeMornay. A French name, I believe." Was it disappointment that flitted across his face? "Have you heard the name before?"

He shook his head. "Where did you come across it?"

She fanned her face. "When I was thirteen, a dark stranger piqued my imagination. That man on the wharf reminded me of him. I saw the name in the estate's record book from ten years ago, about the same time the stranger appeared at Deerford." She forced a laugh. "I'm afraid I romanticized him into all manner of man, from avenging knight to daring privateer."

He smiled. "You were well-read."

"Deerford had an extensive library."

"Deerford?"

"The family lands in Staffordshire. Rather, what used to be our lands." She could not keep the bitterness from her voice. "My cousin sold them."

He paused long enough for that to sink in. "Then your family has other land here?"

She understood his confusion. "My mother was American, from Louisiana."

"So you are rejoining family. I assume then that Mrs. Durning is not your mother."

A laugh burst out. "You do realize how preposterous that is. Aside from the complete lack of resemblance, we do not share a name."

"She might have remarried." But he was grinning, as if relieved that she was not related to Mrs. Durning.

"No. Maman died when I was twelve." She could not keep down the sigh. "And Papa last September."

"Thus the mourning attire."

She looked down at her impractical gown. "Thus the dark colors. I had hoped it would deter Mr. Lightwater."

"I suspect nothing that simple will keep him at bay." Mr. Worthington scanned the thinning crowds. "He may find us if we do not move on. Take my arm, and I will lead you to the closest shipping agent."

Seeing as the dark stranger was likely little more than a play of her imagination and Mr. Lightwater might this very moment be closing in on her, Catherine let Tom Worthington guide her two doors down to a cramped office with grimy windows.

She hesitated to enter.

"I can go in with you," he suggested.

Catherine breathed out in relief. She hadn't yet acquired steady legs, but she had found a friend. Perhaps she could also find quick passage to New Orleans.

Something about the way Miss Haynes uttered the name *DeMornay* had sent shivers down Tom's spine. At first he told himself it couldn't be the man he sought. *Mornez* was a stretch from *DeMornay*. Then she mentioned that she'd seen him ten years ago in England.

62

Ten years had passed since Mornez had hired Pa to sail him to New Orleans. Moreover, Pa insisted the man had come to Boston from England. The similarities were too great not to consider that DeMornay and Mornez might be the same man. Tom wanted more, but she offered nothing else.

He turned his attention to assisting her to the nearest shipping office. He didn't think much of Baldwin Fromp as a shipping agent. The man's rumpled coat looked like he'd slept in it for weeks. Tea and tobacco stains dotted his shirt. Dust coated every surface of the office except Fromp's chair, which is where the man was when they entered the tiny office.

Miss Haynes held the fan to her nose.

He hoped it was scented, because the office reeked of snuff, sweat, and odors he couldn't quite identify.

"Good day." Fromp tugged his coat straight over his portly midsection and with a groan rose to his feet. "Anything I can do for you?"

She straightened her back. "Passage to New Orleans."

Fromp blinked in surprise that she had answered.

Tom should have told her to let him speak.

Doubtless sensing money to be gained, Fromp rubbed his hands together. "Now let me see. New Orleans. Packet or steamship?"

"Give me the price for each."

Fromp took a longer look at her. No doubt he'd taken in the quality of her clothing and the distinctly English accent. Not to mention the elegant parasol.

Tom cleared his throat to remind Fromp that he was here on the lady's behalf. "And the schedule. Last I heard no one's sailing."

"True, true," Fromp muttered, "but they'll be heading out soon. Got a steamer due in any day now from New York."

"They'll be slowed," Tom interjected.

Fromp glared at him before refocusing on Miss Haynes. "As I said, the *Lady Jane* is due in soon." He rustled some papers until he found what he wanted. "Ah yes, as I thought. Headed for Mobile and then New Orleans."

"Are there any ships going directly to New Orleans?" she asked.

Tom eyed her. She was in a hurry indeed. Why, if she was only joining family? No, there must be more involved. Tom hoped the same cousin who had sold their lands in England had not sent her to marry.

Fromp shuffled through more papers. "Uh, not that I know of, but there's always the odd ship that comes in without notice." He frowned. "Most are heading the other direction, though. Stopping here after New Orleans. You might have to wait."

That clearly did not please her. "I will ask another agent."

"You won't get a different answer," Fromp said.

"Then how much is passage on the *Lady Jane*?"

Fromp named a figure that made her blanch.

"For third class?" Tom gave Fromp a look that said he'd better not pad the fee.

"That'd be half the price, but a lady like you wouldn't want to travel with that riffraff, not without a strong escort." Fromp glared back at Tom.

Miss Haynes wavered. Apparently she'd planned to travel unescorted, a thought that made Tom nervous. Too much could happen to a beautiful woman traveling alone without protection.

"All ships can't cost that much," she whispered.

Fromp shrugged. "Can't say. Each company sets its own rates."

Something like desperation set her expression. "I will keep asking then."

Without waiting for him, she pulled open the door and darted from the office. Tom followed and closed the door behind them, an idea forming in his head. If she could wait and he could explain the problem to Rourke, maybe he would have just the solution. But it would cost. Perhaps a great deal.

The other shipping agents gave the same answers as the first. Perhaps in this small port they banded together to set fees and regulate transport, such as it was, for Catherine could not find any passage beyond the *Lady Jane*. That vessel planned a two-week stay in Mobile to off-load cargo. Catherine might as well wait here for the *Justinian* to be repaired.

Frustrated, she hurried back toward that vessel, Tom Worthington on her heels. She had hoped he would help her, but he hadn't convinced a single agent to lower his fees or bring a vessel here sooner. It was unfair to think he could change either, but her dwindling funds put her in a precarious position. She couldn't afford a long delay.

"Where are you going?" His easy tone matched his loping gait.

She, on the other hand, could barely speak between gulps of air. "To the ship."

"But you can't stay aboard."

She halted. "Why not? I have paid for passage all the way to Jamaica. Apparently that is the only way I will reach my destination."

"They still won't let you stay aboard during repairs. That's why I asked if you were staying at the Admiralty Inn. See?" He nodded toward the wharf.

Captain and Mrs. Durning stood there beside a pile of trunks. Three of them were Catherine's, along with the crated portrait of Maman. Mrs. Durning waved at her. The captain acknowledged Catherine and then headed for the stevedores.

The woman clapped her plump hands when Catherine arrived. "I wondered where you went. We have been put off, dear. Quite shocking, but there it is. Nothing to be done but to buck up and make the best of matters. Mr. Durning will stay with the ship, naturally, but no passengers are allowed on board."

"Why?" Catherine asked, when what she really needed to know was *where* they would stay. Tom Worthington had mentioned an inn, but that would cost precious money.

"Mr. Durning says it's too dangerous, and we wouldn't sleep a wink with all the pounding going on."

Catherine briefly wondered if the captain simply wanted to avoid his wife's oversight during the repairs, but she shook the thought away. Even now workmen crawled over the *Justinian*.

"Then repairs will be completed quickly." And she would reach New Orleans after only a small delay.

Mrs. Durning fanned her plump face, which was dotted with perspiration. "I do hope so. This infernal clime is more than a lady can bear."

"Perhaps you would be more comfortable at the Admiralty Inn." Mr. Worthington bowed before them. "I would be glad to hire a porter and escort you there."

"Walk?" Mrs. Durning's fan paused.

He smiled. "It's a very short walk, but I can arrange for a hack if you wish."

Something about Mr. Worthington softened the older lady. Catherine had noticed it that morning.

With the sun now dropping quickly toward the horizon, they had best find lodgings as soon as possible. Given the numbers that had crowded the wharf earlier, there might not be many rooms left at what was likely the best inn on the island.

Catherine's fears proved well-founded. After delays to arrange for a porter and waiting for a hack, they found the inn full.

"I'm sorry, ma'am," the innkeeper managed to state without looking the least bit sorry. "All we got left is the admiral's quarters at two dollars for the night."

"Two dollars!" Catherine and Mrs. Durning exclaimed at the same time.

"Will you accept British sterling?" Catherine added.

"Silver? Aye," the innkeeper grunted. "But I gotta warn ye that the room's got just one bed."

"Poor quarters for an admiral," Catherine remarked.

"Take it or not." The man shrugged. "Makes no difference to me."

Catherine managed a weak smile as she turned toward Mrs. Durning. "Would you be willing to share the bed?" She hated to imagine what manner of rodent might crawl about such a place after the lamps were extinguished.

"Of course, dear, but that is not the problem."

Tom Worthington sidled near the innkeeper and said something to him in too soft a voice for Catherine to hear. She guessed he was trying to get a lower price, but the innkeeper staunchly shook his head.

Even half that rate would deplete her savings in no time, and she would have to pay for the privilege of listening to Mrs. Durning's snores.

A pleasing aroma drifted from the vicinity of the dining room, and Catherine's stomach rumbled. She hadn't eaten much more than stale biscuit and a few spoonfuls of clear broth all day. This smelled like a fish stew she'd once enjoyed on the coast.

"What will we do?" Mrs. Durning blinked back tears. "Mr. Durning only gave me a few shillings. By the time I return for more, the room will be gone."

Catherine swallowed the bitter taste in her mouth. "I will pay the cost for tonight. In the morning we will seek a better situation."

Mr. Worthington returned. "I suggest private lodging."

Mrs. Durning gasped. "In a stranger's home?" She looked out the open door to the neighboring houses. "There couldn't possibly be room for two additional ladies in any of these."

Catherine had difficulty imagining it too. The houses were not large, certainly not the size of Deerford with its two sitting rooms, two parlors, study, library, dining room, and six bedchambers. These were more like tenant cottages. Even the ones with a second story could have at most three bedchambers, and those would likely be filled with children.

"I know just the place," Mr. Worthington said. "Mrs. Elizabeth O'Malley is known for her gracious hospitality. You would be most welcome."

Catherine eyed the darkening doorway. She could not impose on a stranger so late in the day. "Perhaps tomorrow. For tonight we will take this room." She turned to the innkeeper, determined to succeed where Mr. Worthington had failed. "However, since we must share a single bed, I expect a lower rate."

The innkeeper blinked, apparently unused to a woman speaking her mind.

"I assume the rate includes meals," she added.

He paused for a few moments before recognition dawned on his face. "You're asking if meals is included. Didn't understand, what with that accent and all."

Indeed. He was the one with the atrocious accent. Instead of pointing that out, she smiled.

He didn't. "Meals is extra."

Catherine gritted her teeth and forced that smile a bit longer. "We would be greatly beholden to you, sir, if you might include supper and breakfast." They could survive without the midday meal if necessary.

His gaze narrowed. "Now then, seems to me that you're the one needin' a room and I'm the only inn that's got one. Law of supply and demand."

Meaning he could charge a pirate's ransom. "Our Lord gave us another law. To love your neighbor as yourself. Surely you can find it in your heart to help two women unexpectedly stranded on this fair isle. I eat no more than a bird."

"A pelican?" the innkeeper snorted, his gaze darting to Mrs. Durning.

"A wren."

Mr. Worthington outright laughed. "Come now, Sullivan, both you and I know you're overcharging. Give it to the ladies for a dollar—with meals."

"One dollar without meals," Sullivan countered.

"I accept." It wasn't ideal, but she would make do. She had some food left in her trunk, and Mrs. Durning could get meals from the cook on the *Justinian*.

Mr. Worthington chuckled after she'd registered and paid the fee. "You have a way with people."

Catherine wasn't certain if that was a compliment or not, considering she'd failed to persuade a single shipping agent to budge on his rates and couldn't winkle a single meal from the innkeeper.

He drew them away from the registration desk. "I still think you should consider meeting Elizabeth O'Malley tomorrow. I would be glad to make introductions, and she would welcome company with her husband gone. You will find her two children well-mannered for their age."

"How young?" Mrs. Durning asked.

"Around five and three years of age."

The matron brightened. "Perfectly delightful ages. I would appreciate the society. Perhaps we should call on her."

Mr. Worthington directed the porter to carry their trunks to their room. "You will adore her. Everyone does." His eyes twinkled as they settled on Catherine. "She's my captain's wife."

A wrecker's wife. Catherine held out little hope for the type of society that Mrs. Durning anticipated.

5

N o." It took Captain Rourke O'Malley much less time to come to a decision than it had taken Tom to formulate the question.

When Rourke returned to town at the end of the following week with the first load of salvage, Tom had been ready. At least he'd thought he was. Once face-to-face with the man who had rescued him from a near-fatal duel and had given him a new direction in life, he'd stammered out his request to forgo salvaging the wrecked ship. The answer was swift and decisive.

Tom wouldn't let a single refusal stop him. More than a woman's passage stood at stake.

"No gentleman would let her travel alone," he pointed out.

"Perhaps, but this is someone you barely know. Moreover, you would be throwing away a sizable fortune, enough to set yourself up in business ashore." Rourke leaned close. "This is the big wreck, Tom, the one we've all dreamed about. If you can't convince her to stay, you'll need to let her go."

"I can't."

Rourke looked at him long and hard. "Are you in love with her?"

Tom choked and coughed. "In love? We just met." This nagging desire to protect her couldn't be love, even though he had paid her a call each day.

"Some do fall in love right away. It was that way for John and Anabelle."

John was Rourke's top captain and lifelong friend. He had married Elizabeth's former maid and half sister after a daring escape from slavery in Key West.

"It's not that way," Tom mumbled, uncomfortable discussing his feelings. "I just can't stand to think of her traveling alone."

"Then persuade her to wait."

"She needs to get to New Orleans as soon as possible."

"Why?"

Tom hesitated. He couldn't air his fear that she might be betrothed, because he had no confirmation of the reason for her haste. Neither could he mention that she too chased a dark man who could very well be the one who'd destroyed his father. He had no proof of connection, just a suspicion.

"She said she's rejoining her mother's family," he finally said. "I didn't want to pry. Maybe someone is ill or there's trouble that only she can resolve. Regardless, she's in a rush to get there. This week of waiting for a ship has driven her to desperation. I'm afraid she will accept the first affordable passage, regardless of safety."

"I appreciate your good heart, Tom, but this is best left alone."

Tom couldn't bear letting go of her or the best chance he'd had in years to find Luis Mornez. "How long is the salvage going to take?"

Rourke's intent gaze met his without blinking. "Until it's done."

He didn't know. No one knew. Catherine Haynes could be gone by then, an innocent walking straight into trouble.

"She won't wait until we're done."

"Then you have a decision to make. Are you a wrecker or not? I don't need to remind you that stepping away from your duty will haunt you the rest of your career."

Tom had spent all week weighing the cost. The last of his savings would go toward passage just to see Miss Haynes walk away from him into the arms of her family, likely without a second glance his way. Unless her DeMornay was the very same man he was seeking. The chances were slim, but he couldn't let the opportunity go.

The corner of Rourke's mouth twitched. "She must be pretty."

Tom felt heat creep up his neck. "Some might think so."

"Some?"

He shrugged, pretending that fiery auburn hair and those sharp green eyes didn't send a thrill through him. "She's English. Acts like nobility."

Rourke chuckled and clapped him on the shoulder. "Then I pity you, poor man."

Tom let out his pent-up frustration in a sigh. He had a decision to make.

လ⁓

At the end of the week, Captain Durning joined his wife at the Admiralty Inn. That put Catherine out of her room and onto the hospitality of Tom Worthington's friend Elizabeth O'Malley.

Tom, as she was beginning to think of him, had introduced Catherine and Mrs. Durning to the lady two days after their arrival. Mrs. O'Malley had proven every bit as gracious as Tom had promised and soon put Catherine at ease. Mrs. Durning had found the children a bit too exuberant for her taste, but Catherine enjoyed the lively atmosphere. It reminded her of the tenants' children, and a sadness crept over her that refused to leave. She had failed them, and now her quest to join her mother's family—which had sounded so perfect two and a half months ago—was flagging too.

This morning she stood on the veranda of Mrs. O'Malley's peaceful house. A visit was entirely different from asking for lodging, even though Mrs. O'Malley had made the offer. Catherine lifted her hand to knock but hesitated. The house was too quiet, given the children. Perhaps Mrs. O'Malley was not home. She turned to leave, but the front door opened.

"Kin I help you, miss?" A Negro maid stood in the doorway, her apron white against her coal-black skin.

Catherine was not accustomed to Negro servants, there being none in the vicinity of Deerford. Moreover, Mrs. Durning had whispered after their previous visit that the maid was likely a slave. That made her more than a bit nervous this morning.

"I'm sorry. I wished to call on Mrs. O'Malley. Is she home?" Beads of perspiration formed on Catherine's brow.

"Come in." The maid stepped aside to let her enter the modest yet comfortable home.

Once inside the door, Catherine heard the unmistakable laughter and giggling of small children.

"I'll fetch Miz Lizbeth. She be in the nursery."

Catherine shrank. Not only was she begging a room, but she had called at too early an hour. "I can return later. Pray tell me when would be most accommodating."

"Now, don't you fret none. I'll fetch Miz Lizbeth."

Catherine gave up and ran through her speech in her head, all the while fussing with the clasp on her bag. She had barely enough money for passage to New Orleans, least of all room and board before securing a berth. Mr. Fromp had assured her that the *Baltimore* was due next week and might have room for her. If she could scrape by that long, she might have enough for the fare without selling the last of Maman's jewelry, a set of pearl earrings.

"Miss Haynes." Elizabeth O'Malley swept down the hall with arms open. "Do come into the parlor and have a seat. I'm delighted to see you again and hope all is well."

After pleasantries were exchanged, with each woman insisting the other use her given name, Catherine broached the painful business. "I would only need a room until I secure passage, which might be as soon as next week if the *Baltimore* arrives as scheduled."

"Stay as long as you wish." Elizabeth called for the maid and instructed her to prepare a room. "The back room would be best. Put Jamie in the nursery."

"Oh dear. I don't want to displace anyone."

Naturally, Elizabeth waved off her concern. "They prefer being in the same room, but I must warn you that the nursery is next to your room and they might well giggle past their bedtime."

"That is no bother." Catherine opened her bag. "I will pay the same rate as the inn."

"Nonsense. You are our guest."

"But I am disrupting your daily life."

Elizabeth waved her hand. "Don't give it another thought. Part of Key West tradition is offering hospitality to stranded travelers. Neither my husband nor I would have it any other way. You will stay with us."

Catherine was accustomed to giving, not receiving. Even the sum she'd managed to extract from cousin Roger had been granted only because it was legally due her. The pittance she'd managed to give the tenants had come at great cost. If Maman's family did not take her in, she would have nowhere to go and no means for either room or board.

"Thank you." Gratitude shouldn't hurt, but oh, this was so difficult to swallow. "I will help as much as I can, purchase food and necessities."

"I assure you that isn't necessary. We own a mercantile, and my husband catches much of what we eat. I hope you like fish." She smiled. "Our diet is not varied, but the Lord blesses us with plenty."

Catherine was not accustomed to such open expression of faith. "I thank you. And your husband—is he home? Tom led me to believe he was at sea."

"He is here tonight, though I expect he will return to the wrecked ship tomorrow or the next day."

"Does he come and go frequently?"

Elizabeth laughed. "It might seem that way. Sometimes he does, but other times he is gone for weeks. That's the way it is in wrecking." She strolled into the neighboring room, where a tea service sat on the sideboard. "Would you care for tea?"

"Why, yes. Thank you, but I should send for my trunks."

Elizabeth poured two cups of tea and added the milk and sugar Catherine requested. "Let's leave that for the men. I expect Tom will return with Rourke."

Catherine started. "Does Mr. Worthington stay here too?" She had never dreamed he might be under the same roof. The idea that they might meet again was surprisingly welcome.

Again Elizabeth laughed. "Tom stays at the boardinghouse, but he often shares meals with us, especially when Rourke is here."

"He seems most helpful."

76

"That he is."

Catherine had hoped for more. "He took me to each of the shipping agents and made certain they did not overcharge."

"Tom likes to make himself helpful." Elizabeth paused and Catherine sensed a caution, but the lady only shook her head. "You mentioned a ship due in next week. Where are you planning to sail?"

"New Orleans. My mother's family has a plantation outside the city."

"Louisiana." Elizabeth's whispered reply came as she slowly set her teacup back on the saucer.

Her sigh, almost mournful, raised Catherine's curiosity. "You know someone there?"

Elizabeth took a long sip of tea. "My nurse." Her eyes misted. "My father sold her to a planter in Louisiana some ten years ago."

Ten years ago. Everything seemed to have happened at that time.

"I'm sorry."

Elizabeth smiled wistfully. "Me too, but that is old news. Very old. You are rejoining family. What joy that must be after your season of sorrow."

Catherine squirmed. She hated to admit that she'd never met them.

Elizabeth ended all chance of avoiding the subject. "When did you last see them?"

"We have not met." When Elizabeth's eyebrows lifted, Catherine added, "It is a very long distance between England and Louisiana."

"Naturally."

Though Elizabeth appeared willing to let the explanation go at that, Catherine felt compelled to explain further. "My mother eloped with my father while visiting England on her grand tour."

"How very romantic."

"It was." Now her own eyes misted. "Papa adored Maman. Her death changed him." She sighed. "At least they are together now."

"That must be a comfort to you. I'm certain your mother's family looks forward to your arrival."

Catherine couldn't admit to the trepidation that had been building the nearer she got to Louisiana. "It will be a memorable meeting."

"Who will travel with you? Has your family sent someone here?"

Catherine fidgeted with the empty teacup. "I planned to make the voyage on my own."

When shock did not immediately greet that statement, Catherine looked up at Elizabeth. The woman's mouth was pursed as if she was deep in thought.

"I could caution you, but I'm certain others have done so already."

"Indeed," Catherine admitted.

"An older lady would be ideal, but I know of no one planning to travel in that direction." Her brow knit in a frown for a moment before easing. "Of course! A gentleman might escort a lady if done with the utmost discretion. Why, Tom escorted me to Key West when the *Victory* foundered."

Though Catherine was intrigued by the fact that Elizabeth had once been on a wrecked ship, she was too surprised by her naming of Tom to think of anything else. "Tom Worthington?"

"Yes, the very man." She sobered. "Except he was much younger then."

Catherine wasn't sure how to read her tone. "Is he not to be trusted?"

"Oh, you can trust Tom. When he says he is going to do something, he will do it." Elizabeth sighed.

"But?"

"He carries a weight on his heart, one that he refuses to reveal, even to Rourke. My husband pulled him out of a foolish duel that would have cost Tom his life."

"A duel? Surely those are outlawed."

Elizabeth smiled softly. "Key West is so far from the rest of the country that sometimes the law is ignored. In this case, it all happened so quickly that the town constable would not have had a chance to step in. Fortunately for Tom, Rourke was there. He took Tom aboard his ship and curbed his temper, but I'm afraid that anger still lurks beneath the surface. He would not harm you, but there is something that eats away at him."

Catherine recalled the peculiar look in Tom's eyes when she mentioned the dark stranger. The figure that had flashed past her in the crowd had fit her memory closely enough that she had thought it was DeMornay. Might Elizabeth know him?

Catherine swallowed. "Do you know anyone named DeMornay on the island?"

Elizabeth slowly shook her head. "That name doesn't mean anything to me. Are you expecting to meet him here? Rourke told me your visit to Key West is unexpected."

"It is, but I saw a man on the wharf who reminded me of someone I met ten years ago in England. It defies reason to think it could be the same man, but I had to ask."

"Ah, ten years ago. That was a difficult time here. A terrible hurricane destroyed most of the buildings in October of that year. Shortly afterward I was sent to Charleston. What time of year did you meet him?"

Catherine thought back to the record book but could only recall the year. She tried to picture the time in her mind. She had been wearing her light frock, the pale yellow muslin that Maman had bought her in Paris. "Summer, I should think."

"So, before the storm. I fear that I noticed only Rourke." A pleasant rose color dotted Elizabeth's cheeks. "I fell in love with him when I was just sixteen, though I'd known him for years. He saved my life. More than once."

There was an intriguing story behind that statement, but Elizabeth did not elaborate and Catherine would not pry. Her thoughts remained on the stranger from her past. What had he carried away in that strongbox? Papa had regretted losing what was hers. She'd thought he meant Deerford, but what if it was something else? What if the large influx of money had been brought by the dark stranger?

Elizabeth was peering at her. "You remembered something?"

Catherine set aside her empty teacup. "I'm not certain. It's all terribly confusing."

The maid stepped to the doorway and nodded.

Elizabeth rose. "Let me show you to your room. Here perhaps you can find a little peace."

Catherine would not find that until she set foot on Lafreniere lands.

⌀

Fromp gave Tom the bad news. The *Baltimore* had arrived in port early and had room for one passenger. The price, however, was greater than he had quoted Miss Haynes earlier that week, and the man would not budge.

Just as well, for Tom did not care to send Catherine off alone. *Catherine.* The fact that he'd begun to think of her with such familiarity quickened his heart. But setting her loose in harm's way brought it to a halt. He hoped she would find the fare as outrageous as he did. On the chance she did not, he checked with the first mate to see if they needed a deckhand.

They would take him, but only for a full circuit back to New York. Tom couldn't give up his position here for what could amount to half a year, and he sure didn't want to leave Catherine alone in New Orleans.

That left him with just one course. He must persuade Catherine not to sail on the *Baltimore*.

Tom formulated his plan on his walk to the Admiralty Inn. Once there, he learned Catherine had already departed.

"Where did she go?"

"How'm I supposed to know?" the innkeeper snapped. "I don't keep track of where everyone goes. She paid 'er bill, that's all I care about. That 'n' fetching 'er trunks." He motioned to the stack near the door. Three large trunks as well as one oddly shaped crate.

"All of that?" Tom had assumed the huge pile of trunks on the dock when they'd come ashore had mostly belonged to Mrs. Durning.

"Aye. Enough ta fit out a house. Some women got no sense."

Tom was about to retort that Catherine had more than the usual sense when he realized the opportunity sitting in front of him. "I will have the trunks delivered if you can tell me where she is staying."

The innkeeper shrugged, but the grating voice of Mrs. Durning gave him the answer.

"She went to that lady friend of yours, Mrs. O'Malley, hours ago. She wouldn't say as much, but I'm certain she intended to accept the offer of a room, now that Mr. Durning has joined me here."

Tom swung around with a smile. "Thank you, Mrs. Durning.

You have been most helpful." He dipped into an exaggerated bow, and she warbled about it being nothing.

Since Tom was going to Rourke's house anyway, this turn of events had worked out perfectly. Elizabeth O'Malley was a romantic. Perhaps he could enlist her help in convincing Catherine to wait until he could escort her to New Orleans.

He rubbed his hands together. "Do you have a porter and wagon available for hire?"

The innkeeper seized this chance for a little more income and set off to have his man hitch up a wagon.

Within the hour, Tom had helped the porter carry each trunk into the O'Malley house and down the hall to the very last room. Catherine directed which one to set to the side for her personal use. The rest, along with the crate, were stacked against the wall.

The porter mopped his forehead. "The lady sure travels with a lot o' luggage."

"I am not traveling, sir," Catherine announced. "I am relocating from England to America."

"Yes, miss." The man backed out of the room. "My mistake."

Tom grinned. "You certainly set him in his place."

Instead of laughing like he'd expected, Catherine frowned. "That was not my intention. I simply can't abide that people leap to conclusions."

Tom bit his tongue. Everyone made hasty assumptions from time to time.

"If you will excuse me," Catherine said, "I wish to change for dinner."

Tom was about to remark that he found nothing wrong with her plum-colored gown when he realized that this gave him an opportunity to speak with Elizabeth O'Malley alone. After she called for the housekeeper, Florie, to assist Catherine, Tom followed Elizabeth to the parlor. There Jamie was running and hiding behind the furniture while little Sarah stood in the center of the room with a look of confusion on her face.

"Playing hide-and-seek with your brother?" The elegant woman bent over to whisper something in her daughter's ear.

The little girl squealed and toddled off to the very chair where Jamie was hiding.

"I left Rourke at the warehouse," Tom said. "I don't expect him home early. It's going to take a while to unload."

"I imagine so."

"Might I have a word with you?"

Elizabeth gave him an inquisitive look. "What is it?"

Tom's insides knotted. How to explain? "It's about Catherine. Miss Haynes." He felt the heat creep up his neck.

"She is a lovely woman. And very determined."

"Exactly." Tom had to hurry. Catherine might return at any moment. "I fear she will travel alone to New Orleans."

"You may be right."

"I spoke to your husband, asking if he would give me time off to escort her there, but he would not."

"I see." She paused to direct the children on another round of hiding and seeking. "No doubt he relies on your expertise."

Tom appreciated Rourke's confidence. No one had found him indispensable before. Even Ma, who'd depended on his income, didn't fuss when he had nothing to send her. Now that she was remarrying, she didn't need him at all.

"He did say it is a valuable salvage," she added.

Tom knew all this. "Can you persuade him?"

"Me?" Her eyebrows rose.

"He hangs on your every word."

She laughed then. "Thank you, but I know better. I also know that Rourke would not deny you face-to-face and then change his mind with me."

That route was cut off. Tom blew out his breath.

"How can I protect her?"

Elizabeth touched his arm. "Go with her on whichever ship she chooses."

Hadn't she heard what he'd just said? "Rourke won't let me."

"Then you have more persuading to do."

6

Persuade whom?" Catherine stepped into the parlor. "I don't suppose you're speaking of me."

After a hurried glance at her, Tom's face flushed beet red. He then studiously examined his toes.

Elizabeth took each fussing child by the hand. "Please excuse me. It's time for a nap."

Moments later Catherine was alone with Tom. Outside the wide-open, floor-length windows, a steady flow of pedestrians passed by. Anyone who looked could see them.

"I, uh, stopped by Mr. Fromp's office," Tom said. "There is one berth available on the *Baltimore*." He then named the fare.

Catherine cringed. "You must have heard incorrectly. That's double the rate he quoted me. I will go there at once and clarify the matter." She turned to do just that, her silk skirts rustling.

"Catherine."

The use of her given name startled her. She could not get accustomed to the familiarity between acquaintances here. On the other hand, Tom Worthington had become more than a mere acquaintance. Still, it was much too soon to greet each other by their given names.

"Miss Haynes." He cleared his throat, but his gaze drifted over her gown, a frothy mint green that highlighted her eye color. "Mr. Fromp gave me this." He reached into his inner coat pocket and withdrew a small sheet of paper, which he handed to her. "The only room is first-class promenade deck."

It was a printed schedule of fares for the East Coast Steamship Company. Catherine had examined enough schedules of late to make short work of this one. Tom was not exaggerating. The fee was impossibly high for the only available cabin.

"Are there any other ships expected?"

"Not for at least a week."

Catherine groaned. First the *Lady Jane* and now the *Baltimore* had been beyond grasp. "Will I ever find passage?"

"You will."

Catherine struggled to share his optimism. "It's so frustrating."

"Do you need to be there by a particular date?"

"No." Did she see Tom relax? Still, she couldn't admit her financial situation. "I don't want to be beholden to Mrs. O'Malley longer than necessary."

"You won't." He grinned. "She loves company and often takes in ladies who need a place to stay."

That made her feel a little better. "I will do my best to help her while I'm here."

Tom swallowed, looking nervous. "I have to join Rourke—Captain O'Malley—on the salvage operation when he takes the *Redemption* back to the wreck site."

Unaccountable disappointment welled. "I see. How long will you be gone?"

"It's difficult to know. Even Rourke—Captain O'Malley—doesn't know. There are a lot of wreckers involved. It might go quickly, or the wreck could be in such a precarious spot that it'll take longer. We don't want anyone getting killed."

She shivered at the thought of men trapped belowdecks in a sunken ship. "No, we don't."

He looked uncomfortable again. "There is one other matter." He cleared his throat. "Will you wait for me?"

Her jaw dropped. "Wait? Why would I do that?"

His face blotched red. "Then you do have a traveling companion. Mrs. Durning, perhaps?"

Catherine shook her head. "She will join her husband on the *Justinian* and sail to Jamaica."

"Then who will escort you?"

All of Mrs. Durning's admonitions came back in a rush. In her haste, Catherine had not taken into account the propriety of traveling without proper escort. "Perhaps there is another lady requiring passage to New Orleans." Elizabeth had considered ladies of her acquaintance. Yet no ship to date had offered more than one berth.

He stood tall. "I would be honored to see you safely there."

His offer sent a flood of warmth through her, followed at once by all sorts of objections. He was a bachelor of marriageable age. She found him more than a little attractive. Though she trusted his ability to protect her, he could not serve this function.

"I thank you, but you must realize how improper it would look to travel with an unmarried man." She couldn't bring herself to state the obvious limitations when each ship offered just one berth.

The red blotches grew more pronounced. "I intend to purchase separate passage."

It was her turn to flush. "Of course, but there is only one berth on the *Baltimore*."

"True, but I spoke to the mate about hiring on as deckhand."

"Deckhand? But you're a captain." Her embarrassment turned to awe. "You would do that for me?" To step away from his job and take on that of a menial deckhand was unthinkable. He must be giving up a fortune, not only in the difference of wages but also in the spoils from salvaging the wreck. "Forgive me, but I can't accept. Go with Captain O'Malley."

He took her hand, and a pleasurable warmth radiated up her arm. "I will hurry back."

His eyes begged for confirmation that she would wait, but she could not promise.

Once Tom left, and with him the flush of excitement, Catherine wondered why he was so determined to escort her. They barely knew each other. Propriety mattered to friends and acquaintances who might be impacted by another's rash actions, but not to comparative strangers. Tom Worthington had been willing to abandon Captain O'Malley and a fortune in salvage just to escort her to New Orleans. It made no sense.

She could never allow him to leave behind his livelihood for her sake, just as she could not have let the tenants go without assistance. As near as she could tell, he had no relations on the island.

Elizabeth confirmed it Sunday evening, after her husband and Tom set sail for the wreck. "He is from the Boston area. Nantucket Island, though he seldom talks about it. His father passed some time ago."

"Then we share that in common."

Elizabeth looked up from her needlework. "I am sorry for your loss. Though my mother passed on six years ago, her memory still weighs on me."

"Maman still lingers in my thoughts," Catherine admitted, "though she has been gone eleven years now."

"You have no sisters or brothers?"

Catherine shook her head. "Maman died after a stillbirth. The baby would have been my brother."

"Your father must have been devastated."

Catherine thought back to those times. "He kept to himself much of the time, at least at first, but he was always close to me."

"You loved him dearly."

"I loved them both. I hope to recapture that with Maman's family."

Elizabeth's eyes glistened. "It will never be quite the same. No one can match the love of a mother and father."

"But at least they are family. I had hoped to reach the plantation by the middle of this month."

"You must find passage, regardless of Tom's wishes. I will make further inquiries to see if anyone in my acquaintance is traveling to New Orleans soon."

"Thank you."

Though Catherine knew in her mind that she must go, her heart ached at the thought of leaving Tom. She'd fought the attraction, but imminent parting only intensified it. From the first time they met, he had stood by her, always ready to assist in whatever way she needed. She relied on him. She trusted him. She had not trusted another man since Papa.

She sighed. "Tom is a good man."

Elizabeth smiled. "Yes, he is. Loyal and trustworthy."

"Good virtues."

"Splendid ones in a prospective suitor."

"Suitor?" Catherine felt the heat rise to her cheeks. "I cannot contemplate marriage." Yet hadn't she already judged him superior to Mr. Lightwater and Mr. Kirby in every respect? "I must first rejoin family. Then perhaps my thoughts can turn in that direction." The thought of family had once been dear but now crushed her spirits like a black storm cloud, for Tom would not be there.

"I understand." Elizabeth pulled scarlet thread through the fabric. "You must realize that even if Tom escorts you to your family, he wouldn't stay. He's not a planter. He has the sea in his blood. I'm married to such a man. Nothing can keep them from the water."

Deep inside, Catherine knew that. She must regain her life at Chêne Noir, though Tom could never bear to live there. Best to cut the ties between them now, before they got too strong. She must leave while he was busy salvaging the wreck, thus avoiding the heartache of parting.

How she had wept as the carriage carried her away from Deerford. She'd looked back as long as she could, trying to imprint every feature of the house and grounds in her memory. Though this parting wouldn't be that severe, her heart had borne too much sorrow already. She must leave now.

"I will speak with the shipping agents in the morning." She caught Elizabeth's gaze. "Do ask if anyone you know will be going in that direction."

❧

"Send down the hook," yelled an exasperated Jules from the water below.

Tom yanked his attention back to the task at hand and lowered the line with the hook secured to the end.

Upon arrival, he'd transferred to the *James Patrick*. There he'd seen firsthand how battered the wrecked *Isaac Allerton* was from its encounter with the reef. The crew had cut away the broken masts and managed to get it off the reef, only to have it sink in five fathoms of water. Only the strongest divers could manage that depth for any length of time. Jules was one of them. The scrawny lad swam like a porpoise.

"Pull!" yelled another diver who'd just surfaced.

The crew on Alderslade's vessel, anchored on the other side of the *Isaac Allerton*, heaved on the line the diver had just secured to the wreck. Minutes later, a plank popped to the surface, and a cheer went up among the gathered fleet, as it had each time the maneuver succeeded in the past eight days. The moment the plank emerged, divers plummeted downward, eager to secure one of the now-freed crates for their vessels.

Jules was the first to reappear. "Heave!"

Tom joined the rest of the men on the *James Patrick*'s deck. The weight on this one meant Jules had secured the hook to cargo, not another plank. Soon they'd have spoils to fill their holds. Since the *James Patrick* had the smallest holds in the O'Malley fleet, it would head back to port first.

Tom would see Catherine soon. If she hadn't left. That thought knotted his innards every time. Even if she survived the passage unscathed, what would happen to her once she arrived? Could she get to the family plantation? Who would meet her? No one would know she'd been delayed in Key West.

"Harder!" Rander yelled.

Tom snapped back to the present.

The line wasn't budging.

"It's hung up," Jules yelled from just inside the bulwark, where he was dripping seawater all over the deck. "Hold fast and I'll get it."

"No!" Tom let go of the line and raced to stop Jules from attempting the dangerous dive. If the cable snapped and the heavy crate fell or shifted, Jules could be crushed or pinned. "Stop!"

But the lad dived into the sea.

Tom looked back at Rander, who understood the danger. The man had gone pale. Tom gnawed on his lip. Times like these made him question the risks they took. He'd once been as brash as Jules. Then he'd seen a diver trapped inside a hulk. Dead before anyone could get him out. Wrecking could pay handsomely, but it came at a high cost. No wonder men like Rourke now commanded ships and ran mercantiles rather than risk the dangerous dives. Wives could end up widows. Like Ma.

Tom's insides knotted even tighter. Pa hadn't taken unnecessary risks. He'd accepted a well-paying passenger on board. Mornez. Pa hadn't questioned the man's story. If he had, he might have discovered everything Mornez said was a lie. Instead of profit, the thief had taken Pa's ship and livelihood.

Tom eyed the line, still holding taut, and then peered at the ocean. The murky green water had gotten stirred up again by strong winds from the southwest. He scanned the entire area. Jules should have surfaced by now.

"See anything?" Rander called out.

Tom shook his head. "I'm going in after him."

He kicked off his shoes and stripped off his coat and shirt, but before he could climb onto the gunwale, a sharp *thwang* sounded. The men cried out. Tom turned to look back, and the severed line struck his temple.

The blow took him off his feet. He toppled over the rail and plummeted into the sea below.

7

Catherine's days had settled into a routine. In the mornings, she inquired of the shipping agents about passage to New Orleans, thus far without success. In the afternoons, she watched the children so Elizabeth could make calls or host her teas attended by a smattering of ladies and gentlemen, none of whom would be considered high society in England but all of whom held some regard in Key West. Catherine found the older women dull, Mrs. Cunningham insufferably arrogant, and Dr. Goodenow pleasantly interesting, but her favorite by far was Mrs. Prosperity Latham, who radiated generosity, peace, and goodwill.

On the second Monday after Tom's departure, Mrs. Latham wandered into the nursery. "I can watch the children if you would like to take tea."

Catherine rose from the little table where she was attempting to interest the children in drawing so they wouldn't wake the baby. "Thank you, but I would rather stay here."

"Me too." After checking on her sleeping daughter, Mrs.

Latham bent to kiss her two toddlers. She whispered encouragement over their artistic efforts, then addressed Elizabeth's son. "Good afternoon, Jamie. What are you drawing?"

"Papa's ship."

"So it is. And you've drawn a lovely flower, Miss Sarah." Elizabeth's daughter beamed up at her.

Catherine could not imagine how Mrs. Latham spotted a ship and a flower from the scribblings. "A flower?"

"Of course." Mrs. Latham outlined the figure with her finger, drawing a squeal of delight from Sarah. She then smiled softly at Catherine. "I am highly skilled in deciphering sketches."

Catherine sighed. "I suppose it comes with practice."

"That it does."

The baby fussed from the cradle.

Mrs. Latham wandered to the rocking chair. "Do you mind if I sit with my little one?"

"Not at all."

The woman gathered her baby from the cradle and then sat down to rock her. After a little fussing, Constance drifted off to sleep. "It has been a long day, but you don't want to hear about me. I understand you're from England."

"Staffordshire."

"This must be a tremendous change of climate. It was for me. I came from Nantucket, far north of here, near Boston."

"Nantucket?" Catherine had heard that before. "The same place as Tom Worthington?"

"Indeed, though we did not know each other. I only know of him through Elizabeth. She holds him in high regard."

That was good to hear. Catherine hadn't been certain after her last discussion with Elizabeth. "He is quite solicitous."

Mrs. Latham chuckled. "Elizabeth believes he is taken with you."

That explained his insistence that he escort her to Louisiana. Pleasure curved her lips before she recalled that a relationship between them could never be as long as he was wedded to the sea. Her future was at Maman's family plantation. There she would have family. But the thought wasn't as comforting as it used to be.

A commotion from the front of the house put an end to her thoughts. Catherine hurried to the hallway to see what was happening.

Captain O'Malley stood at the door while the doctor donned his frock coat and top hat.

"What is it?" Catherine asked when Elizabeth came down the hall toward her.

"It's Tom. He's been injured."

"How? When?"

But Elizabeth had hurried back to join her husband.

Everyone shouted over each other, asking questions. The doctor and the O'Malleys were too intent on what must be done to answer.

"Bring Tom here," Elizabeth insisted. "He can't recover in a boardinghouse. Who would look after him?"

Her husband added, "I've sent Jules to fetch the wagon from the mercantile. We can use that to bring him here."

Catherine's heart pounded. If a wagon was required, then Tom was gravely injured.

"I'm going with you to the ship," the doctor added as he and Captain O'Malley hurried out the door. "Maybe there's something I can do to treat the wound before we move him."

Catherine started out the door after them, but Elizabeth held her back.

"We have much work to do." Elizabeth turned to her guests, who crowded, wide-eyed, in the parlor entrance. "I'm afraid we must end our tea early."

"Of course," murmured one of the older ladies. She and her friend fetched their bags and parasols and quickly bid farewell.

Mrs. Cunningham sniffed. "Such things are to be expected in dangerous occupations. Stewart insists the days of wrecking will come to an end once all the lights are installed on the reef. Then we won't lose so many men."

Catherine reeled. "How many men die from wrecking?"

"Several a year," Mrs. Cunningham reported with what sounded like glee. "Stewart says with all the wreckers working this shipwreck, there are bound to be fatalities."

Catherine could not breathe. Her heart beat wildly, and she had to lean against the wall for support. She felt a comforting hand on her arm. Prosperity Latham squeezed gently.

"Good afternoon, Mrs. Cunningham," Mrs. Latham said. "It was a delight to see you again. Don't forget your parasol."

She held out the object, and Mrs. Cunningham took it with another sniff.

"I gather that lieutenant of yours is still working on the fort?" the insufferable woman asked.

Prosperity Latham answered in the affirmative as Elizabeth led Mrs. Cunningham onto the veranda and down the steps to the street.

"At last." Catherine sighed. "I couldn't bear another moment in that woman's company."

Mrs. Latham laughed. "You knew no one like that in England?"

"Yes," she had to admit, "but not any who insisted on lingering during a crisis."

"I'm afraid that some people are drawn to tragedy, perhaps thinking they can help."

Mrs. Latham was being too kind. Mrs. Cunningham would not have lifted a finger to help. She wanted to appease her curiosity so she could tell all her acquaintances what had happened.

Elizabeth climbed the stairs to the veranda. "Prosperity, I'm glad you're still here. We need to prepare a bed on the sleeping porch."

On hot, still nights, the family slept on the back porch. Since Catherine's room was well shaded, she stayed there. She could not imagine sleeping out of doors would be good for someone injured.

"I will sleep on the porch. Tom can have the room I'm occupying." After all, it had been partly her fault that he'd been injured in the first place. If she had accepted his offer to travel with her on the *Baltimore*, he would not have gone out wrecking.

"That's very generous," Mrs. Latham said.

Elizabeth nodded her agreement. "We must strip the bed and remake it. Florie!"

The maid popped out of the nursery. Catherine expected Elizabeth to instruct her to make the bed, but instead she asked the maid to stay with the children.

"Catherine, you will need to pack anything you might need over the coming week or so into a trunk. We will have the men move your trunk to our bedroom. With Rourke at sea most days and off to the mercantile the others, you can dress there." Elizabeth turned to Mrs. Latham. "We will make up the bed on the sleeping porch while Catherine strips the one in her room."

The two women hurried off to the back porch while Catherine moved to her room. *She* must strip the bed? And likely remake it. She had never made a bed in her life. The housekeeper or maid had always taken care of that.

As she stuffed her nightgown and other personal items into her main trunk, she attempted to come to terms with the fact that she was far out of her element. What if Chêne Noir was like the O'Malley household? What if she must take care of the house herself? Maman had led her to believe there were many servants, but that was more than twenty years ago. Much might have changed. This new life might be nothing like Deerford.

Perhaps this whole voyage had been a mistake.

Tom couldn't see straight, and his head ached worse than anything.

"Lift him carefully," said Dr. Goodenow, who'd examined him and wrapped a cloth around his head. "No jostling."

"I can walk." Tom pushed to his feet, but his legs wobbled and gave way.

Strong hands caught him before he fell back onto the *James Patrick's* deckhouse, where he'd sat since the crew had hauled him out of the water back at the wreck site.

"Not so fast," Rourke said.

It frustrated Tom that the captain had been forced to leave the wreck site due to Tom's inattention. If he hadn't been watching the surface of the water instead of the line, it wouldn't have hit him. If he'd dived sooner, the snapped line would have missed him. Instead, according to Rander, the end with the swivel clunked him in the temple and sent him over the side.

"Rander, you take one side and I'll take the other," Rourke instructed. "All right, Tom, we're going to walk you to the gangway and onto the wharf. Jules has a wagon waiting there."

"I don't need all this fuss," Tom groused. "In a few hours, my head will clear."

"Or you'll slip into unconsciousness and never wake up," the doctor said.

Tom blinked rapidly, but the blurry vision wouldn't clear. "I'm not leaving this world." His voice sounded thick and mumbled.

Rander and Rourke lifted him, and somehow they dragged

him across the deck and off the ship. Every step made his head pound. And the wagon was none too comfortable either.

"To my house," Rourke commanded whoever was driving, "and take it slow. We don't want more jostling than necessary."

Tom didn't hear anything else the men said. They were taking him to Rourke's house, where Catherine was staying. He closed his eyes and stopped resisting.

Catherine met the group of men at the front door. Elizabeth directed them up the steps and down the hall. Her husband and another sailor carried Tom into the house. The patient did not cry out in spite of the jostling. To all appearances, he had lost consciousness.

They placed Tom on the bed in the back bedroom, and then the doctor reexamined him. Catherine waited in the parlor with everyone but the captain, who remained with Tom and the doctor. No word came during long minutes of waiting. Each person held his or her breath and occasionally glanced toward the hall. Quiet prayers were said.

After the clock struck the hour, Catherine hopped up and paced to the windows, open to let in the cooling breezes. Dusk had begun to settle over the town.

She gripped the frame. "He would never have been on that ship if I hadn't refused to let him escort me to New Orleans."

"Nonsense." Elizabeth joined her at the window. "Tom is a wrecker. They salvage ships and know the risks they take." She placed her hand over Catherine's. "There is no good to be gained by claiming fault for what was clearly an accident."

Yet she could not shake the guilt. "He must survive, and when he does, I will accept his offer."

"I gather you are not speaking of a marriage proposal."

"No!" Catherine realized how her words must have sounded as heat flooded her cheeks. "I meant his offer to escort me to my destination."

Elizabeth patted Catherine's hand as Dr. Goodenow entered the parlor. All turned their attention to him.

The physician donned his top hat. "His heart is steady and his color good, but with the head injury we cannot know the extent of the damage until he awakens."

"He is still in danger, then?" Catherine asked.

"Fluids might yet accumulate on the brain. That would be very serious. Call for me at once if there is any indication of swelling about the head, and I will let more blood."

She felt ill. "Is there nothing we can do for him?"

The doctor spoke instead to Elizabeth. "Your husband is with him now. Mr. Worthington must be watched at all times. Keep his head cool. Use compresses soaked in a mixture of half vinegar and half water. His feet must be kept warm. When he awakens, he may have a light diet. Most of all, the house must be kept quiet."

"The children," Elizabeth said. "They are rather exuberant."

Mrs. Latham offered to take them with her.

"Nonsense. You have three of your own. Jamie and Sarah would be more comfortable with their aunt Anabelle."

Catherine had yet to meet Elizabeth's sister.

"I can fetch her," Mrs. Latham said.

Elizabeth shook her head. "I'll send Florie with the children." She glanced outside. "It's still early enough."

The doctor had donned his black coat. "I would be glad to accompany them."

"Thank you, Doctor, but it is out of your way. Rourke can go with them."

Catherine at last saw where she could help. "I will sit with Tom, then."

Elizabeth nodded her gratitude before seeing the doctor out. Catherine walked down the hallway, now longer than it had ever seemed before. The children were quieter than usual, perhaps sensing the struggle that Tom faced. Would he recover?

Catherine's hands shook as she pushed open the door to the bedroom.

Captain O'Malley rose to his feet. "The doctor left?"

She nodded. "Elizabeth needs you. I will sit with Tom."

He readily agreed. Once he left the room, silence descended. Tom looked normal in the low light of dusk, except that his eyes were closed. She settled into the chair at his bedside, still warm from the captain's presence.

Only a sheet covered Tom, who was still fully clothed except for his shoes. His hair stuck out at odd angles. She reached to smooth it and discovered it was caked with salt. His clothing had the greasy feel of saltwater-soaked cloth. Once the captain returned, Tom ought to be changed into clean clothes. Then again, he had no clothing here. Perhaps Captain O'Malley might lend him a nightshirt.

Every bit of that was trivial compared to Tom's well-being. Catherine gently touched the bandage on his head. Swelling could prove fatal. The doctor had not said so, but it was understood.

"Get well, Tom," she whispered. "You must get well."

In a storybook ending, his eyes would have fluttered open just then. This evening they did not move at all. Tom had gone deep into himself. She prayed he would return.

8

Catherine woke with a start. Had she heard something? The nearly full moon lit the room with a silvery glow. Tom's features looked pale as marble. Unmoving. Frozen.

She leaned over him to listen for a breath. At first she heard nothing, then slow, shallow breaths greeted her ear.

Thank goodness!

The compress had vanished, likely onto the floor. Catherine didn't dare light a lamp, lest it disturb Tom, so she tiptoed to the washstand and located another cloth. This she dipped in the basin of water and vinegar mixture and squeezed. Before applying it, she touched a fingertip to his forehead. Warm but not hot. She applied the compress.

She did not know the hour, but the house was quiet. Captain O'Malley and Elizabeth must be asleep by now. So too Florie, who insisted on sleeping in the cookhouse, though Elizabeth had made a room for her in what was once the butler's pantry. "Weren't no air," the maid had complained. She'd used it only once, when a torrential downpour would have soaked her even under the cookhouse roof.

At this hour, Catherine could do nothing but watch and pray. Yet her thoughts kept drifting to all that had happened in the last three months. Key West was far from Deerford, yet a long journey still awaited her before she reached Louisiana. On such a night she wondered if she would ever see Maman's plantation.

Tom tossed his head to the side.

She reapplied the compress. "I should have let you escort me to New Orleans on the *Baltimore*." It would have cost more than she could afford, but she would be there now, and Tom would not have been injured.

Raindrops sounded outdoors. She went to the window to close the shutters only to once again discover she'd been fooled by the rustling of palm fronds. A trick of the ear.

"What do I do, Papa?"

In the stillness of night, she did not know.

Tom tossed and turned, drawing her attention from unsolvable problems. She returned to his bedside and refreshed the compress. He sank back into deep sleep.

She liked the rhythms of Key West and the friends she had made here. Elizabeth O'Malley and Prosperity Latham exuded grace and hospitality. They were truer friends than any she had known at home. She could envision living among the palms and cocoplums, but restlessness still tugged at her soul. She must see Maman's family and find out, if she could, what her Papa's last words had meant.

Louisiana. The very name whispered with exotic intrigue. It was not like France. Maman had made that very clear, saying that New Orleans and the great river were entirely unique. For years Catherine had dreamed of seeing this fantastical place of

Maman's stories. Now she would, and there she would make a new life with family. Family. With Maman and Papa gone, she needed that more than anything else.

Again the palms rustled in the breeze that swept into the room and caressed her cheek. Soon. Very soon.

She gazed at the sleeping patient. "I will let you escort me to Louisiana when you recover."

His eyelids did not so much as flicker.

⌀

Though Tom regained consciousness the following day, he could not walk without dizziness and remained bedridden. Catherine busied herself with the day-to-day business of the household. Jamie and Sarah always needed something, often simple attention. Elizabeth had many a caller, most of whom Catherine avoided.

She could not avoid the person who knocked on the door a week after Tom's accident. Florie was out to market and Elizabeth busy, so Catherine answered the door.

"Good morn—" Her greeting cut off at the sight of a tall, elegant Negress standing at the door. "Morning." Catherine felt her face flush. "That is, welcome."

The stunningly beautiful woman's expression did not waver. "I'm paying a call on my sister."

"Florie is at market."

The woman's eyes were direct and clear as she said carefully, "My sister Elizabeth."

Catherine managed to stifle a gasp. Once again she had leapt to the wrong conclusion, but who would think otherwise? Still . . . if they were sisters, then they shared a parent. This woman's mother was likely a slave in the household, meaning Elizabeth's father . . . The thought made her nauseous.

"Please inform her that Anabelle is here."

"You're Anabelle?"

The woman smirked. "You expected a white woman."

Oh, how her cheeks burned. "I'm sorry."

"I'm not. It is a fact. My father admits I'm his daughter. Now I only lack my mother."

Catherine led Anabelle to the parlor while her mind sifted through these details. "Where is your mother?"

"Louisiana." The bitterness oozed from her voice like black mud. "She was sold to a planter there."

Elizabeth's former nurse must be Anabelle's mother.

Catherine managed a shaky breath. "How horrible."

"No one considers that a slave has feelings."

This was the cruelty of slavery preached in British churches even now, when every enslaved person in the empire had been set free. Until now, Catherine had not come face-to-face with anyone affected by it. Cousin Roger had torn the tenants from their homes, but to rip mother from child was unbearable.

"I'm so sorry." Words failed to convey enough solace. Her hands shook as she poured a cup of tea for the visitor. "Have you ever heard from her?"

"My mama can't write."

Again Catherine's cheeks heated with embarrassment. How little she knew of the way things operated in this country. "Forgive me."

Anabelle inclined her head just as Elizabeth burst into the room. "Sister! I see you have finally met each other." She embraced Anabelle.

Only then did Catherine see the resemblance. She swallowed hard, wishing to be far from this family gathering. "I will watch the children."

"Nonsense. Florie is back. Sit. We'll all take tea." Elizabeth hurried to pour two more cups and then settled onto the settee. "Tell me how John is faring."

The next half hour was full of tales from the salvage operation. Catherine's mind soon drifted, for Tom was not there—he rested in the rear bedroom. Instead, she pondered what Anabelle had said. Her mother had been sold to a Louisiana planter. Catherine would soon be in Louisiana.

"I will ask about her."

Anabelle and Elizabeth turned to her, the conversation abruptly halted.

"About whom?" Elizabeth asked.

Catherine flushed, not realizing she'd spoken the thought aloud. "I will ask if anyone knows where your mother is, Anabelle. I am going to Louisiana."

Anabelle stared.

Elizabeth smiled graciously. "It is a large state, and Mammy went there many years ago. She might be anywhere now."

"Even home in glory," Anabelle said solemnly.

They were right. A woman without rights could vanish and never be seen again. She'd seen it happen to the unfortunate in Staffordshire. Tragedy, such as the loss of a husband or parents, often sent the bereaved wife or daughter far from home. Just like her. Catherine shivered. In this light, Maman's glittery stories looked tarnished.

❧

"You want to do what?" Tom's eyes widened when Catherine mentioned that she intended to inquire about Anabelle's mother.

It had taken two more days before Tom ventured far from bed. This afternoon, he lingered on the back veranda of Elizabeth's house, where the coconut palms and lime trees shaded the yard. Though his recovery had been slow, he'd seemed more his normal self this afternoon, so she'd broached the subject.

"I intend to ask if Mammy lives in the area."

Tom shook his head. "If that's the only name you have, it's hopeless. Many Negro nurses are called 'Mammy.'"

"Elizabeth's father, Mr. Benjamin, said she would most likely have his last name."

"Unless the new owner changed it." Tom sank against the back of the seat. "It's a hopeless task."

"With God, nothing is impossible."

"That's what you will need, then. An act of God."

"My, aren't you a curmudgeon."

"A what?" He sat up, eyes flashing.

"Ah, that's better. I knew there was some spirit left inside you."

He scowled. "I've been injured. A little sympathy is in order."

"You've had sympathy." Catherine was beginning to think he was taking advantage of the situation. "Elizabeth tells me you will return to the salvage operation on the next ship that returns."

His scowl deepened. "That's what everyone says."

"I heard the ship is arriving now."

He shot to attention. "Which one?"

"Which one of what?"

"Which ship?" His every muscle tensed.

She couldn't resist teasing. "There is more than one?"

He heaved a frustrated sigh. "I've told you dozens of times that the O'Malleys have three ships in the fleet. Is it the *Redemption*, the *Windsprite*, or the *James Patrick*?"

"How would I know?"

"I thought you went into town each day to check with the shipping agents."

She hated when he caught her, something he was far too adept at doing. "I can't possibly remember each of the ships. Moreover, I'm asking for passage to New Orleans, not about your shipwrecks."

"Wrecking vessels." His jaw tensed. "They're called wrecking ships, not shipwrecks."

She knew that, but she loved to irritate him. It brought back the spark in his eyes. "Shipwrecks. Wrecking ships. Whatever they're called, one of them was sighted heading this way." A thought crossed her mind. Tom needed to get out of this indolent state. A walk to the harbor would do him good. "Let's meet it."

To her surprise, he resisted, claiming fatigue.

"I thought you were a wrecker," she countered. "A strong and courageous man."

That brought another scowl to his face and his feet to the ground. "Don't question my courage."

Minutes later, they left the relative calm of Elizabeth's house and entered the frenzy of the harbor. Several ships were at the wharves unloading cargo.

"Your ship is here?"

Tom shook his head. "I don't see any of the fleet, but we're far from the O'Malley wharf." He tugged her in the opposite direction, where the newer warehouses stood.

Here the wharves were just as busy. Stevedores and porters milled about along with sailors and the curious, who'd come to see what treasures had arrived in port.

"It's the *Redemption*." Tom pointed toward the open water. "See? She's just reached the harbor entrance."

"It looks like it's at anchor."

"Waiting out the ship that's currently unloading. They're working the *Allerton* wreck too. There's talk it'll be one of the richest wrecks in Key West history." The old gleam flickered to life in Tom's eyes.

Catherine smiled to herself. This walk had done precisely what she'd hoped it would—energize a man who'd been stranded ashore. In the little time she'd known Tom, she'd come to recognize his restless nature. He was indeed searching, and she doubted any woman could fulfill that yearning.

That thought gave her pause. The time they'd spent together during his recovery had been pleasant, and she'd come to appreciate not only his wit but also his knowledge. He was well-read, having digested Shakespeare and Swift as well as the Americans Melville and Hawthorne. He had a lively mind but an even more restless spirit.

Even now he hurried her toward the O'Malley wharf, weaving through the crowds with expertise that left her winded. Her grip on his arm slipped, and then she lost it completely. He looked back, but the crowds surged between them.

"Pardon me." She sidestepped a brawny man backing toward her with a cart and ended up jostling someone else. Flustered, she reached to straighten her hat.

"Jewelry," a nearby woman exclaimed to her friend. "We must insist our husbands purchase all they can afford."

Necklaces and rings held little interest for Catherine. The only jewels that meant a thing to her were the ones her mother had worn. Those were nearly all gone now, sold or buried with Maman.

She spun around, searching for Tom. He was tall. If only she was a little taller, she could spot him above the crowd. Someone grabbed her arm, and she whirled around, ready to battle a pickpocket or nab the elusive stranger.

Instead, Tom pulled her close. "I almost lost you."

"The crowd . . . I couldn't hold on."

"It's my fault." He held on tightly now. "Let's head toward the customhouse where it's a bit less frenzied."

She gratefully followed, eager to get out of the fray. His hands were strong and his guidance sure. Within moments they'd emerged from the hordes and stepped into a clearing near the customhouse.

"I've never been so grateful for a little space." She breathed in deeply. "I'm not accustomed to such crushing masses."

"Would you care to sit a moment?"

As wonderful as that sounded, she would rather stay secure in Tom's arms. It wasn't just the protection he afforded but the confidence and the delightful sensation that there was no place she would rather be. In fact, one look up into those brown eyes, dancing with mirth, made her heart leap.

Elizabeth suspected he was taken with her.

In that moment, when Catherine's gaze met his, she could not refute it. Her lips tingled with anticipation, shocking though it would be to put on such a display in public view.

She dragged her gaze from his. "Perhaps I should rest." How it hurt to say that!

His thumb stroked her wrist once, then again. "Of course."

He tucked her hand on his arm and led her to the little bench outside the lawyer's office. Unaccountable disappointment dogged each step until he settled beside her.

"I'm a bit fatigued also," he admitted, though the twinkle in his eyes said otherwise, not to mention the way he held her hand.

She looked away and fanned her face with her free hand lest he see how much his nearness was affecting her. She could not afford an emotional attachment. She would leave. He would stay.

She withdrew her hand from his grasp. "Perhaps we should— Mr. Fromp?"

The plump shipping agent approached them as rapidly as his short legs would carry him.

"Miss Haynes. There you are."

He cut rather a comedic figure. If in a court of law, she would have expected to see him with the barrister's wig slightly askew. Today his plump cheeks glowed red, and perspiration ran off his forehead in rivulets. Between gasps and groans, he mopped his face.

Tom rose and helped her to her feet. "Do you have word?"

"A berth," the shipping agent gasped. "On the *Rebecca*."

Her pulse stirred. Soon she would reach her new home. "What is the fare?"

"Always the fare." Fromp shook his head as if chiding her. He then named a price somewhat less expensive than on the *Baltimore*.

She did not hesitate. "I will take it."

Fromp beamed. "I thought you'd say that and took the liberty of booking it for you."

Tom squeezed her arm. "Is there a second berth available?"

Fromp's gaze narrowed. "Didn't know you were looking for two rooms." A quick flick of his eyes made the disreputable connection.

Catherine felt her cheeks heat and stiffened her spine. "We are not traveling together."

"We are traveling on the same ship," Tom added.

She shot him a scathing look. "I believe we have already had this discussion."

He smirked. "I believe you already gave your answer the night I lay injured."

Her jaw dropped. He'd heard her tell him that he could escort her to New Orleans? "Words spoken in haste under stressful circumstances."

Fromp cleared his throat.

Tom abandoned the spat with her. "Tell me there's another berth."

"Third class," Fromp said. "But the ship leaves at dawn tomorrow."

Catherine gasped. That gave her little time to pack.

Tom didn't hesitate either. "I'll take it. We will meet you in your office in, say, an hour?"

The men settled on the timing, and then Fromp went into the customhouse to take care of business for one of his clients' ships.

Only then did Catherine point out what had occurred to her while the men talked. "You are expected on the *Redemption*."

His jaw tightened, and she knew she'd struck a blow.

"I am free to do as I wish," he finally muttered, his brow drawn low.

While her heart danced at the idea that Tom would be with her for the voyage, she could not let him give up the life he loved and a small fortune just to see her safely home.

"I will ask if anyone else from Key West is making the voyage."

He folded her hand in his. "There's no need to ask. I am."

9

Since Tom had never taken a room anywhere but at a boardinghouse, he hadn't accumulated many possessions. After he retrieved a few items at the O'Malley house, it took him less than an hour to pack. Then, by the light of a single candle, he wrote a letter to Rourke explaining as best he could why he had to leave.

Rourke would be disappointed, and that hurt worst of all. Tom didn't want to disappoint his captain. The man had given him a job. Even more, he'd given Tom faith and hope for the future. That future now included Catherine. Somehow. He couldn't put the pieces of the puzzle together yet, but no other woman had tugged so strongly on his heart. He must ensure her safe arrival in Louisiana. Even at the cost of his place in Rourke's fleet.

At least Ma no longer needed him. Tom clenched his hand until it ached. She would be married by now, Pa long forgotten. He flexed his hand. There was nothing he could do about his mother's decisions, but he could make sure Catherine came to no harm.

Tom sealed the note with wax from the candle on the writing table. Since the *Redemption* had not docked and wouldn't until late morning, he would leave the note with Elizabeth when he stopped by to escort Catherine to their ship.

His conscience pricked. Leaving Rourke's employment was bad enough, but not giving him the news face-to-face smacked of cowardice.

*   *   *

Catherine regretted leaving so hastily that she could not bid farewell to all the generous people she'd met in Key West. Captain O'Malley had not returned home. There was no time to pay a visit to Prosperity Latham.

Catherine had had just enough time to see Mrs. Durning, who warbled on about how much she would miss her company and was quite in tears before they parted.

"I will be beside myself with boredom." The elderly woman dabbed at her eyes. "Mr. Durning is so busy running the ship. I shall miss your companionship."

Catherine regretted not paying more attention to the woman, who had given up the comforts of home to travel with her across the Atlantic. In addition to finishing the voyage to Jamaica, Mrs. Durning must repeat the exhausting transatlantic crossing sooner rather than later. Catherine suspected the captain would hurry their stay in Jamaica in order to recoup both the time and the money the storm had cost.

Now, in the glow of the parlor lamp, Catherine embraced Elizabeth, her eyes misting at the thought of losing her new friend. "Please tell everyone how sorry I am that I cannot properly say good-bye."

"Of course I will." Elizabeth held on tightly. "We've all known this day would come, though I'll admit I selfishly wish you did not have to leave." She mustered a smile. "Of course you must go. Your family awaits you."

Catherine hoped her letter had arrived and Elizabeth's words would come true. Often she'd envisioned the family embracing her. Uncle Henri must look like Maman, though perhaps more stoic. His wife and any children still at home would gather around, eager to meet her. She hoped her grandmama still lived. Neither Maman nor Papa had mentioned any deaths in her family, and Catherine had found no correspondence from America in the house.

Moments later, Tom arrived to escort Catherine to the *Rebecca*, a side-wheel steamer that trudged a steady route between Charleston and New Orleans with stops in St. Augustine, Key West, and Mobile. In its belly it carried freight, but the upper decks were outfitted for passenger service with cabins, a dining saloon, a reading room for the ladies, and a smoking room for the gentlemen.

After the lengthy boarding was complete, the ship pulled away from the wharf and soon churned past the *Redemption*, which was still awaiting a berth. Tom guided Catherine to the opposite side of the deck, perhaps unwilling to watch his friends pass by. Barely outside the harbor, she spotted the lean lines and black hull of Tom's ship approaching from the south.

"Isn't that the *James Patrick*?"

Tom frowned. "They're back soon. Maybe the salvage is going more quickly now."

"Maybe." She squeezed his hand. Seeing the ship where he'd been hurt must bring up mixed feelings. "Do you wish you were with them?"

"No." He smiled at her. "Never."

For a moment his regard warmed her heart, but all too soon melancholy stole over her as she watched Key West fade into the horizon behind them. She'd grown attached to the place and couldn't imagine never again seeing the friends she'd made there. However, her future awaited. Maman had painted a beautiful picture of life on the plantation. That would become her home.

The *Rebecca* was not a fast ship, and it stopped at every trading post along the way. The *Justinian* could have made the passage more quickly. Catherine's initial excitement soon faded beneath the interminable boredom of sea travel.

Since her cabin was cramped and the woman sharing her room annoyingly talkative, Catherine spent much time on deck or in the reading room, where most of the occupants never picked up a book. Whispered conversation, embroidery, and cards more often occupied the ladies gathered there. A few wrote letters. Catherine carried a book but hadn't read more than a few pages before one of the conversations caught her attention.

"The handsomest man I've seen in ages," one matron declared. "Perfect for my Clara. Why, with his ample height, she need not fear towering over her beau." She sighed. "If only his skin wasn't so tanned by the sun. It's almost as if he isn't the gentleman he appears to be."

Catherine realized the woman was talking about Tom. Though confined to third class, he made a point of joining her whenever she strolled on the promenade. That man had an uncanny ability to know where she was at all times. More than once she'd wondered if he spent his days following her. Maybe it would be fun to see him squirm under the attention of an eligible young lady and her eager mother.

Then again, the thought of another lady capturing his attention made *her* squirm. Though she'd taken care to keep their relationship no more than friendship, part of her did wonder if a sea captain would make a good husband. Then she thought of Mrs. Durning's long months and years alone and cast the thought from her mind. She wanted more. She needed a solid foundation that could only come from family.

Even so, she could not bear seeing another woman with Tom.

Naturally he would return to Key West once they reached New Orleans. Yet she'd only accepted that with her mind, not her heart. Watching him go would hurt more than it should for an acquaintance of a mere month. Mr. Kirby certainly hadn't inspired such emotions. With the journey soon drawing to an end, she must come to grips with the inevitable breaking of the bond that had grown between them.

Catherine closed her book and slipped out of the lounge, not wanting to overhear any more praise or speculation about Tom. None of them deserved him.

She stepped through the door onto the promenade, where the breezes were fresh. As usual, Tom joined her within the first few steps.

"Do you wait outside every door for me?" she jested, even while admiring the curl of his hair at the nape of his neck and the impeccable condition of his suit despite third-class conditions.

He grinned, sending a flood of joy through her. "You can't escape me. I'm everywhere."

How she loved to tease him. "You insisted on escorting me, not hounding me."

He pretended to be affronted. "Surely you don't find my presence intolerable."

That was the problem. She not only didn't find it intolerable, but she found herself looking for him with eager anticipation. When he did not appear at once, disappointment drove her to seek him out. He should not know that, however. A man should never know how strongly he affected a woman.

They'd been at sea for nearly ten days. The warm waters

filled with sea turtles and porpoises had given way to deeper waters, cold and blue, before warming again to turquoise as they drew near land.

"I understand the stop in Mobile will be brief," she said to distract herself from the far too personal subject of how she felt when she was with him.

"That's what I heard."

"Then we won't have time to go ashore."

Tom shrugged. "What does Mobile have that can't be found in Key West? For that matter, what could New Orleans have to best that fair island?"

"My family."

A playful grin flitted across his face. "I thought the plantation was located upriver from the city."

Catherine ignored his attempt to split hairs. "Close enough. Maman said it was less than a day's carriage ride from the city."

"Not far at all then. Do you intend to hire a carriage?"

She hadn't thought that far ahead. "I suppose I shall. Unless the family is in the city."

"Oh?"

"They shouldn't be. If I remember correctly, this is harvesttime. The family would be on the plantation. Maman said they spent much of the winter in the city."

"Whatever for?"

"I imagine it's like spending the Season in London. For entertainments and so forth."

"Oh."

Again she realized just how far apart their worlds were. Tom was a sailor's son. He knew nothing of balls and theaters and outings to the museums and parks.

"Perhaps things have changed since then," she murmured.

"Perhaps not. The plantations still use slave labor."

Catherine stared at the passing sea. She hadn't wanted to deal with the subject of slavery. After all, she'd been raised to abhor it. But that didn't change the fact that her family's plantation likely swarmed with slaves. How would she reconcile her convictions with the truth of her family's livelihood?

"Perhaps I can change that," she said. "I will speak to Uncle Henri. It is a matter of economy. At Deerford I kept the accounts. I may see a solution that he has not."

"Do you think he will listen?"

How could she know? She had never met the man. "I can pray on it."

His jaw worked. "I hope everything turns out the way you want."

Something about that felt final. Again she was reminded that he would leave her as soon as they landed. "Come with me to Chêne Noir."

Her impulsive suggestion was met with an upraised eyebrow. "For how long?"

That was the question. She shivered and rubbed her arms.

He unbuttoned his coat and placed it over her shoulders.

"Thank you," she murmured as she breathed in the scent of him. She could not let him go, knowing he would never return. "Until I reach the plantation house and meet my family. Is that too much to ask?"

"No. Not at all. I will do it."

The raw warmth in his voice nearly undid her. She blinked furiously as relief coursed through her. "Thank you." The whispered gratitude was not enough. "It means a great deal to me."

"I know."

She had to change the course of conversation before she lost control of her emotions. "We have spoken only of me on this voyage. What of you? Did you receive formal schooling?"

119

"Through the primary years. The rest I picked up on my own. You see, I started working summers on fishing boats when I was thirteen and took to the sea in earnest when I turned fifteen." Anger twisted his features for an instant.

"You're bitter about that. Were you forced to sail?"

He shook his head and attempted a smile, but his jaw was still tense. "I wanted to go."

She didn't believe it. He wasn't telling her everything. Something had happened to force him from school and onto the ships.

"Do you have regrets?"

He shook his head again. "Sailing is a noble profession. Hard but noble. Especially under Rourke." His expression softened.

"You respect Captain O'Malley."

"Everyone does. He's rescued many a man and led them to Christ. I think it's his mission. Anyone who works for Captain O'Malley must adhere to Christian principles, read the Bible, and observe a Sunday time of worship."

That sounded unusual for any ship's crew, least of all on a wrecker, which had a reputation for attracting rascals. "Admirable."

"He gives men a second chance."

The way Tom said that confirmed he'd been the recipient of one of those second chances. She couldn't help but recall Elizabeth's mention of a duel. Tom had once been a very different man, one he showed no inclination to reveal.

⌘

As New Orleans drew closer, Tom grew acutely aware that his time with Catherine was drawing to an end. He would accompany her to the plantation, but once she met family, he must leave. In her excitement, she would forget their time together.

He listened as she speculated about her family. Even the few hours in Mobile had been spent wondering how the grand homes there compared to New Orleans and her beloved Deerford. Each statement widened the chasm between them. Catherine was from English gentry. Not titled but landed. Her mother's family had a large sugar plantation in Louisiana as well as a house in the city.

After Mornez stole Pa's ship, Pa had to sell their house and the warehouse to satisfy creditors. Broke and shamed, the entire family went to Nantucket, where Pa crewed on a fishing boat, Ma and the girls worked at the cannery, and Tom took to the sea. Not quite three years later, Pa died, leaving Tom to support the family. Until now. Had Ma remarried to spare him from that burden?

The thought shook him.

"Are you angry with me?"

Catherine's question pulled Tom from his thoughts. He forced a quick smile. "Not at all. I was just thinking."

"I see. Do you think it fruitful to dwell upon something that upsets you?"

He didn't have an answer that she would approve of. "I suppose not, but I do hate to say farewell."

She laughed, warming the chill from his heart. "You truly weren't listening to me."

He had to admit he'd been preoccupied. "And that is a crime when such a beautiful lady is at my side."

She sighed, clearly unimpressed. "I will credit your lack of skill with compliments to spending your formative years at sea."

He mockingly bowed. "My gratitude for your leniency, my lady."

Again her laughter pealed out. "Now you're treating me like a medieval duchess." Her eyes flashed. "Trust me. I'm not."

"You are more than a duchess to me."

Color suffused her cheeks. "If you keep this up, I won't want to let you return to Key West."

"I wasn't aware you had any choice about that." Still, the thought that she'd grown to desire and appreciate his company made him stand a little taller. He looked into her startling emerald eyes. "I will be here for you as long as you need me."

Did she just catch her breath? She looked away, her gaze fixed on the choppy sea. "That is a grand promise."

"One I aim to keep."

She turned back to him. "Who are you, Tom Worthington, that you would set aside your livelihood to help a comparative stranger?"

"Someone who has come to care for you."

Again she looked away. "You know it's impossible."

"I don't believe in impossible."

She bit her lower lip. "I don't know how they would feel about you."

"Your family?"

She nodded. "We've never spoken, not even in writing."

"Never?" The revelation stunned him.

"And I can't be certain they know that I'm arriving."

Tom swallowed. "They don't know?" He might bring Catherine back to Key West after all.

"I sent a letter, but I might arrive before it does. One can't be certain." She heaved a sigh. "I'm not even sure if Grandmama is still living."

"But you're certain the family still has the plantation."

"Why wouldn't they? The land has been in the family for generations. It would never be sold. Maman told me that. Every generation inherits part of the land. Some must belong to me now. A small corner, if they know of me."

"They don't even know you exist?"

"I'm not certain. They cut off contact with Maman after she eloped."

Tom could not believe it. "You left your home to go to a family that doesn't even know you exist?"

"That does sound peculiar."

"Peculiar? It's extremely risky. What do you plan to do if they don't believe you?"

"I have my baptismal record."

Tom blew out his breath. "I hope it's enough."

"Me too." Worry deepened in her eyes. "I'm certain in my heart that they know of me. I've often wondered if the stranger who came to speak with my father was sent by Maman's family."

"The man you call DeMornay?"

"Perhaps. It was the only unusual notation in the accounts from that time. Papa received a large sum of money, and the man did carry a strongbox."

That did not sound like Mornez. He did not give. He stole. Perhaps her DeMornay was not his man after all. Even so, Tom would protect her until he was certain.

10

From a distance, New Orleans shimmered in the morning sun like the fabled city of Atlantis. As the *Rebecca* drew closer to its bustling wharves, Catherine realized the city sat below river level, shielded from Atlantis's fate by thick levees.

A rush of sentiment for Staffordshire washed over her. The familiar fields and hills. She knew the song of the thrush and skylark. She could name most wildflowers. Not so here. Everything was unfamiliar. Even the sun did not appear the same. It blazed white, searing the flesh like iron from a forge. She did not know New Orleans, and nothing Maman had told her could prepare her for this day.

"Where will we go?" she whispered.

Tom stared at her. "You don't know where the plantation is located?"

"I do, but where will I hire a carriage? The wharves are so crowded."

A portly gentleman in an expensive suit cleared his throat. "If your plantation is upriver, it's best to take a ferry rather than a carriage."

Catherine swallowed, not exactly certain why a boat would be better.

Tom latched on to the suggestion at once. "Do they run regular?"

"Like clockwork. My wife and I aim to be on the first one, providing the porters get our trunks off the ship in a timely manner."

He and Tom further discussed schedules and where to find the boat.

"I'd give the porters some extra coin, if you know what I mean," the man told Tom with a nudge. "Unless you got your own darkies waitin' for you."

Catherine bristled at the derogatory term. "We do not."

Tom gave her a look that made her flush. Her uncle must have many Negro slaves on the plantation.

The man didn't notice. "Mind my suggestion then," he said before walking away to join his wife.

"Insufferable!" Catherine muttered. "To speak of human beings in that manner."

Some standing within earshot cast her a sharp glance.

Tom shook his head. A low whistle came from his lips as the ship thudded to a stop alongside the wharf. "Welcome to Louisiana, Miss Haynes. I hope we won't be run out of the state before we've even disembarked."

Even without bribing the porters, Catherine got her trunks loaded on the small paddle-wheel ferry before it cast off for points upriver. Her stomach roiled, though she wasn't certain if it was from excitement or fear. Would Chêne Noir be as different from Deerford as Louisiana was from England? The ache for home returned, but she squared her shoulders. Home was family, and Chêne Noir offered an abundance of that. It would become home.

She clung to the railing and sent a prayer heavenward.

"I won't leave you until you're safely in your family's hands." Tom instinctively knew her thoughts. He squeezed her hand. "And you're certain you no longer need me."

Catherine could not imagine when she would not need Tom. He'd become a steady presence in her life.

They watched the shoreline pass. The riverbanks were both muddy and lush. The trees lining the bank, the clouds, and even the flies seemed languid in the midday heat.

Catherine waved a fan before her face, but it did nothing to thin the thick air or ease the perspiration running down her brow. "It's even hotter here than Key West."

"We have the trade winds." Tom scanned the shoreline and then took out his spyglass. After staring intently at something on the riverbank, he put it away.

"What did you see?"

"Nothing much." He affected an overly carefree stance that she'd begun to realize was his way of warding off unwelcome questions. "I've never been here and wanted to see what the piers and boats look like."

"Well, there is no shortage of those."

Landings appeared frequently on the shore. As for boats, she couldn't count the number plying the waters, not to mention those anchored and tied to the shore. Tom had taken out his spyglass only once before.

"Are you looking for something specific?" she asked.

His shoulders stiffened slightly before he leaned his elbows on the railing. "Just curious. The river is incredibly wide. It seems slow moving, but perhaps that's an illusion."

The illusion was the way he'd ducked out of answering her question.

"Black Oak and Titchwood coming up," announced the man who'd taken their fare.

"Black Oak?" Catherine asked, then realized that was English for *Chêne Noir*.

The man must not have heard her because he moved right past.

"That didn't take long," Tom said, extending his arm for her.

Catherine accepted it. Several people moved toward the spot where the gangway would be lowered. Might one of them be a relation? Most were simply dressed, of modest income, but an older couple boasted tastefully reserved Paris fashion.

Catherine urged Tom toward them.

The woman wore a burgundy silk gown and bonnet with matching ribbons and trim. The gray-haired gentleman wore a dark gray suit. The attire must be oppressively hot, unlike the light fabrics Elizabeth wore, yet neither showed the slightest sign of perspiration.

Catherine blotted her face before approaching them. "Pardon me, but I wondered if you know of Chêne Noir."

The woman shuddered and looked to her husband, whose expression tightened.

"I haven't heard it called that in many a year," the man said.

"It goes by Black Oak now?"

"Indeed."

"Then you are familiar with the place."

The wife tugged on her husband's arm, as if urging him to abandon the conversation. "We are nearing the dock."

"One moment, dear." He patted her hand before turning his attention back to Catherine. "I haven't been there in years."

"Then there are no balls or soirees?"

The woman's eyes rounded, and she shook her head.

The man cleared his throat. "Times have changed at Black Oak." He then let his wife drag him to the rail.

What had happened? Was the plantation no longer in family

127

hands? Catherine caught her breath. That could not be. Surely Maman's family would have broken the silence about something that momentous.

The echoes of Papa's final words sounded in her head. *Forgive me for losing what was yours.* Had he meant that Chêne Noir no longer belonged to Maman's family? If so, then she was in terrible straits. She hadn't enough money remaining for passage back to Key West, least of all England.

Bile threatened to rise, but Catherine fought it. She came from strong stock, able to endure any setbacks. She would persevere— if indeed the worst had happened. But she did not know that at all, and there was no sense leaping to conclusions.

She rejoined the older couple. "I'm sorry to bother you, but might I ask if Black Oak is still in Lafreniere hands?"

The woman looked startled. Again she glanced to her husband and waited for him to explain.

"Pardon the personal question, but are you by chance British?"

Catherine nodded, though she had no idea what that had to do with her question.

"I thought as much." His gaze held a measure of added compassion. "Then you might not have heard that Henri Lafreniere passed on this summer."

She gasped and pressed a gloved hand to her lips. "Then who . . . ?"

"I believe his oldest son, Henry, is overseeing the plantation. He lives in the city as far as I know. The younger son, Emile, is in the Army up north somewhere."

"Grand—his mother?" She did not yet want to reveal her identity to utter strangers.

"Passed on some years ago, not long after her husband."

A wave of sadness rolled over her. She would never know Grandmama. "Are any of the family there?"

The gentleman's wife found her voice. "Not a one."

"The elder Henri's wife?"

"Gone. There hasn't been a woman in the place in years."

Catherine stared. "Then who runs it?"

"The plantation manager, of course," the gentleman said.

"Do you know his name?" Tom interjected.

The woman clucked her tongue. "You don't want to go there. Not with DeMornay in charge."

A chill ran through Catherine, but she could not be deterred. "But I have come so far, all the way from England."

The woman peered at her. "The Lafrenieres are French."

"They're American," Catherine corrected, "though one member of the family settled in England."

"Impossible," the woman exclaimed.

"A fact. Lisette Lafreniere."

The woman gasped. "But she's dead."

"Yes, she died eleven years ago."

"No," the woman insisted, "she died immediately after arriving home from her grand tour of Europe, back—oh, it must have been twenty-five years ago. A tragedy, losing such a young life."

"That's not possible. My mother died when I was twelve years of age."

"Your mother?" The woman looked again to her husband.

Though he said nothing, his kindly gaze took on distinct interest.

His wife's brow had furrowed. "Are you saying that you're Lisette Lafreniere's daughter?"

"I am."

The woman shook her head. "But there's a tomb for her in the family crypt. I've seen it myself."

Catherine's ears began to ring, and her vision narrowed. Could this be true? The family had not only blotted Maman from the record but had buried her fourteen years before she actually died. Who was in that tomb?

"It must be empty," Catherine insisted.

"We attended the funeral," the woman informed her. "The body was too mutilated for laying out, but there was a casket. Why go to such expense if there wasn't someone to bury?"

Catherine's throat constricted, and she struggled to draw a breath. Someone was clearly mistaken. It must be this couple. Catherine could not believe Maman had misled her and Papa all these years. Had Maman not told her endless stories of Chêne Noir filled with minute detail? Surely she was a Lafreniere. Uncle Henri could confirm it.

Except he was dead. Catherine gripped the rail. Everyone who knew Maman was gone. None of the family was at the plantation. She could not expect a joyous reception.

The boat bumped against the dock. They'd arrived.

⁓

Though Tom asked if Catherine wanted to return to the city, she refused. She must at least see Black Oak.

The Grahams, as the couple was named, took Tom and Catherine by carriage as far as the plantation outskirts, but Catherine had to pay a man at the landing to deliver the trunks later. At first the wagon driver refused, but then Judge Graham pressured the man to take the trunks to the end of the carriage drive in front of the plantation house. The ornery driver finally agreed, but at a steep price. His reluctance made Catherine wonder.

Something was wrong at Black Oak, and no one would tell her what it was. Unless she asked.

"Why are people afraid to go on Lafreniere land?"

Mrs. Graham looked away and kept her gaze fixed on the passing scenery.

The judge took his time to answer. "You'll discover soon enough that visitors aren't welcome. Use caution and keep Mr. Worthington close at hand."

"I won't leave her side," Tom assured the judge.

Catherine drew in a shaky breath. This was not what she'd imagined. Even if the family was surprised, they would surely erupt with joy as they hugged and kissed the cousin they'd never met.

Tom took her hand in his. The gesture bolstered her confidence. With Tom at her side, she could withstand anything. Perhaps the judge and his wife were mistaken. Surely things were not as bad as they'd portrayed. Though with none of the family there, she might not be invited into the house, least of all asked to stay.

The judge seemed to read her mind. "If the need should arise, you can find us in the town of Titchwood, down this road to the right a mile or so. We're in the white house next to the courthouse."

Catherine thanked them, though she hoped she would not need to accept that offer.

The carriage rolled to a stop.

"This is the edge of Black Oak. You can see the namesake tree there, marking the property line."

Catherine looked in the direction he was pointing. A huge, gnarled tree overshadowed all others. "That's a black oak?"

"Look close and you'll see where a fire took out part of it years ago, before my time here. The scar remains."

Catherine bit her lip to still the trembling.

"Which direction do we go?" ever-practical Tom asked.

"Follow the river road until you reach the carriage drive heading away from the river," the judge said. "It'll be the first one. That will take you to the house."

After Tom helped Catherine from the carriage, she offered to compensate the Grahams. They declined.

"I wish you well," Mrs. Graham said, crossing herself in the Catholic manner. "And may God protect you."

"He will," Tom answered, "as will I."

Catherine had never been so grateful for his presence. Since he'd been involved in a duel, he must know how to use a pistol or a blade, though she'd seen no sign of either on his person or in his meager belongings. Moreover, those belongings would not arrive at Black Oak for a couple of hours. Tom's help was welcome, but she would also need God's protection.

After thanking the Grahams and watching their carriage roll inland toward Titchwood, she and Tom continued on the rutted road that paralleled the Mississippi. The early afternoon sun beat down relentlessly. From the road, she could not see a house. Sugarcane towered high on the right. Lafreniere sugarcane. She took some satisfaction in that. It was tall and thick. To her untutored eye, it looked robust. Perhaps a profitable harvest could be reaped this year. It had been many years since Deerford had turned a profit on its acreage.

On the left, trees offered occasional shade from the sun, so that was where they drifted. Tom strolled nearby, and Catherine couldn't help wishing he would offer her his arm. She had not worn sturdy shoes, and her feet began to ache a short distance down the road. They walked awhile in silence. Catherine mulled over the judge's comments and everyone's reluctance to set foot on Black Oak land. She would erase those apprehensions.

"A ball would do."

Tom started. "A what?"

"A ball. A dance. You have heard of them."

"Of course I have. I'm not a bumpkin just because I hail

from Nantucket. Before that we lived in Boston, the very center of the Northeast."

It took Catherine some time to understand. Geography had never been an interest, but it was clear he'd taken affront and was boasting about the cultural prominence of his birthplace.

"You were born in Boston?"

He nodded, his expression suddenly somber.

Odd reaction. She couldn't help but wonder what had happened there. Something must have driven him away from the seaport. "But you left. Did you go to Nantucket for whaling?" Catherine did recall that island was known for its whaling industry.

"No." He plodded on without further explanation. "I don't see a house yet. Did Judge Graham say how far it was?"

"He didn't." Catherine sighed. "I wish I could have persuaded the wagon driver to take us as well as the trunks. I can feel every stone through the thin soles of these slippers."

"He would have charged even more." Tom returned to her side and offered his arm, which she accepted. "That man was taking advantage of us. Why? Because of some superstition or unnatural fear?"

"Everyone seems to be afraid of Black Oak."

"You heard what the judge said, that visitors aren't welcome. I almost expect to be greeted by a gunshot."

Catherine stared. "Surely they wouldn't shoot at us, not in the middle of the day. If you ask me, it's simply fear of the unknown."

"And you don't subscribe to such fear?" The humor had returned to Tom's voice.

"Why should I? Most often a ready explanation will soon reveal itself." At least she hoped that would be the case. "I don't believe the family would have wiped away all memory of my mother. That part must be rumor. Family ties run deep in Lafreniere blood. Uncle Henri wouldn't deny his own sister."

Tom had the courtesy to wait for her to get her thoughts out.

"True, she eloped with Papa against family wishes," Catherine continued. "They cut off contact, but it seems preposterous to claim she'd died after her grand tour." She stopped before revealing to Tom what Papa had confessed to her. To what purpose? She didn't understand it yet herself.

"If your mother died years later in England, then who is in the tomb?"

Only one explanation came to mind. "Perhaps the casket is empty. The Grahams did say that there was no viewing."

"But why?"

That was the question. Why claim Maman had died years before she did? It made no sense, unless . . .

Tom finished her thought for her. "They wanted to ensure she had no claim on them."

"Surely not." Yet she was beginning to think that might have been their reasoning. With a funeral and grave, few would believe an Englishwoman's claims. That did not bode well for Catherine.

Perhaps it was the heat or fatigue, but her legs had grown weak and the land seemed to pitch and sway like the deck of a ship. Tom directed her into the shade and suggested she rest on a stump.

She shook her head. "I feel better now. It's just that the memories came flooding back. I remember Maman laid out in the casket, looking like one of Madame Tussauds' wax figures. Mrs. Durning insisted I touch her hand." She shuddered. "I was afraid, but I did as I was told. Her hand was cold. At the time I hated Mrs. Durning for making me do it, but I came to understand why. She wanted me to know without a doubt that my mother was dead. The mind can be a terrible thing."

He gave her a quizzical look. "How so?"

"It makes up all manner of deceits in the night." She began walking again, still with one hand on Tom's arm. "I used to think I could hear Maman in the wind or feel her when I came near her writing desk. All nonsense, of course."

"You missed her." Their stroll was languid, taking into account the heat and patchy shade.

"I did." Catherine sighed. "I still do, but I won't find her in a tomb, either here or in England. She's with Jesus." She noticed him flinch slightly and wondered why. Sorrow or discomfort? "Maman always told me that a Lafreniere is strong and can stand on her own."

"And a Haynes?"

"Even more so."

"Then you're prepared for whatever we find. If it comes to the worst, we can beg a night's lodging with Judge Graham and his wife."

"And send the poor wagon driver back to the landing with our trunks."

Tom laughed. "That's my Catherine."

His Catherine? The words caught her off guard, but not nearly as much as the carriage drive that opened to their right. Long and straight, it led away from the river and was shaded by large oaks. At the end stood a two-story house elevated on large piers. Wrapped around the house was a veranda, much like those on the homes in Key West, but this house was larger and the veranda was anchored with thick columns rather than elegant spindles.

"This must be it," Tom said. "The judge said it was the first carriage drive."

No sign marked the entrance, but she had to believe this was Chêne Noir. It would have fit Maman's description except that

135

the trees and grounds were overgrown and the house did not gleam white in the sun. It looked . . . dilapidated.

Her hand shook as she pressed it to her mouth. This was not the proud family plantation she'd envisioned. No hum of activity buzzed in the fields. She saw no one at all. Yet this is where the judge said they must turn.

She stared ahead, shocked, yet knowing the truth. "It must be."

11

For ten years Tom had dreamed of finding the man who destroyed his father. Now he was mere minutes from discovering if that villain was Catherine's DeMornay. Never in all his imaginings had he dreamed Mornez would live on a plantation in ruins. The sugarcane wasn't well tended. The house was in shoddy condition.

For a moment he doubted they would find anyone here. As they drew closer, it looked more and more like the place had been abandoned. The whitewash had peeled and faded, leaving splotches of grayed and weathered wood. Gauzy curtains fluttered between some of the veranda pillars. They must be there to shade from the sun or protect against insects, but for whom? He had yet to see a single soul.

Tom needed only an instant to know if the plantation manager was Mornez or not. The scar beneath his eye would broadcast the truth. If this was the villain who had destroyed his father, what would he do? It would depend on what he found. If Mornez was as broken and ragged as this plantation, then Tom might be able to pity him. If not . . . The hilt of Tom's blade bit into the small of his back.

He'd intended to demand restitution, by knifepoint if necessary. He hadn't considered that the man might have fallen into madness or disappeared entirely. Either would account for the poor state of the plantation. Neither would help Catherine.

She stumbled, and he caught her before she fell. "Are you all right?"

"Yes. Of course." But she did not sound well. She sounded worried.

He was anxious too. This day might be his last, but it would be worth it if he took Mornez with him. That's what he'd drummed into his head the past ten years. Now that a resolution was mere steps away, he wasn't as confident.

"Promise me," she whispered. "Promise you will let me do all the talking."

Her? She'd paled so much she looked like she would drop into a dead faint at any moment. They'd reached the main house, still without seeing anyone.

"All right, but at the first sign of trouble I'm getting you out of there."

"There won't be trouble." She stood a bit taller. "They're family."

"Who buried your mother years before she died."

"They didn't bury her alive." Her voice strengthened, rising to the challenge.

"They might not welcome your arrival." The first step creaked under his weight.

She paused.

No one came out to greet them. No one worked in the yard. Unusual for a plantation that must have hundreds of slaves. The place seemed deserted.

The long flight of stairs led to what must be the main story. Beneath the broad porch, a carriage was parked out of the sun's glare. Its leather seats were cracked and it looked gray under a coat of dust, but it appeared serviceable. Above, the curtains swayed as if someone was watching their approach. He half expected the muzzle of a rifle to appear from behind a curtain.

"Good afternoon," Catherine called out. "Is anyone here?"

The hum of grasshoppers was the only response. Tom slid the dagger to his side and fingered the hilt. It wouldn't do any good against a gun, but he could defend Catherine in hand-to-hand combat.

They ascended a few more steps.

"Hello? It's me. Catherine."

Tom tugged on her sleeve. "They might not know you exist."

Her face flushed. "Lisette's daughter," she added.

Still no response. Nothing but the creaking of the steps and the overpowering hum of insects.

They'd reached the top step. Before them, the deep veranda boasted all manner of chairs, benches, and tables from one end of the house to the other. Many double doors stood wide open, allowing what breeze there was to flow into the house. The contrast between midafternoon sun and shadow made it impossible to see into the rooms.

Catherine stepped toward the first open door.

Tom touched her arm. "Let me go first."

She didn't protest.

He stepped ahead one stride. Catherine grabbed the crook of his arm. He gently moved her to the other side so his right hand was free to grasp the dagger. He stepped forward again.

"Halt!"

They both jumped at a woman's voice.

"Who done come here? Git away wid you," the woman said stridently.

Gradually Tom's vision adjusted so he could see into the

room directly in front of them, a parlor from all appearances. A tall Negress stood just inside the open doors. Wild, gray-streaked hair sprang out from under her head kerchief, but her jaw was set. She would never let them pass.

"Git away." The woman waved a broom in his face. "Massa ain't seein' no visitors."

"But he must." Catherine let go of his arm and stepped closer to the woman. "I've come all the way from England to meet my family."

"Yo' family?" The woman hesitated only a moment. "Ain't no family here. Git away."

"But the journey was long. A storm dismasted my ship, and I had to weather over in Key West for weeks."

The woman lowered the broom a little. "Key West?"

"Yes," Catherine continued. "I've come a long way to meet my family. I understand Uncle Henri passed away. I regret never meeting him, but surely my cousin Henry would like to meet Lisette's daughter."

"He not here," the woman shouted. "Now git out."

"Wait, Aurelia." The deep masculine voice came from shadows too dark to penetrate. "I will meet them."

The woman lowered the broom and slipped away as a short yet brawny man stepped before them. His hair gleamed black, and his skin was the dark mahogany of those from Havana. A hat shaded his eyes.

Tom squinted, trying to make out his features.

The man stepped out of the shadows. "Tell me your business."

Catherine froze, her mouth agape. Tom followed suit, for beneath the man's eye was a scar in the shape of a question mark.

DeMornay?

Catherine had begun to believe the name meant nothing, but here stood a man who fit her memory of the one who had visited Deerford ten years ago.

She stared at his black eyes and dark skin. He had a muscular build yet wore the fine clothing of a gentleman of means. His hair was neatly trimmed around ears that had almost no lobes. When he stepped into the sunlight, the small scar beneath his eye became more prominent.

"You are . . . ?" she whispered, unable to get more out.

"The plantation manager," he said with a dazzling smile and a bow. "Mr. Louis DeMornay. And you are not American."

"I'm English. You visited England once?"

"Alas, no. I have lived in the great state of Louisiana all my life."

She felt Tom tense and glanced over at him. His jaw was set. He looked upset. Yet she was confused.

"But—" she began. The estate records had listed a DeMornay but no first name. Moreover, fine lines webbed this man's face, and his hair was peppered with gray. Perhaps this DeMornay was a relation of the man who had visited Deerford. "Then you have family here."

"Not any longer, but please do come in out of the hot sun, Miss . . . ?"

"Haynes. Miss Catherine Haynes. Henri Lafreniere was my uncle." But she had a feeling he'd heard everything she had told the housekeeper.

"Welcome, Miss Haynes." DeMornay ushered them into the salon.

A large fireplace dominated the room, which was sparsely furnished. The once-elegant settee and chairs were gathered in such a way as to facilitate conversation near the fire. On this hot day, none was lit. The room, plastered and white-washed with crown molding and chair rail, recalled Maman's stories despite the tinge of gray that hugged every corner and crevice.

"The current master, Henry Lafreniere, is away at present," DeMornay said, "but I'm certain he would not want me to turn away his cousin. Aurelia!" He clapped his hands.

The Negress slid into view. This time her head was bowed and shoulders drooped, all defiance gone. If not for the wild, gray-streaked hair, Catherine would have thought her a different woman. Aurelia. It was an exotic name for a woman caught in slavery.

"We will take refreshments on the loggia," DeMornay ordered. "Then prepare the mistress's room for Miss Haynes. Supper will be served on the gallery at the usual hour." His gaze drifted back to Catherine. "I trust you will stay."

"Of course."

When he spoke her name, she watched for any sign of recognition, the slightest twitch of a muscle or flutter of an eyelid, but saw none. If this DeMornay had transacted business with Papa, he was not the one who'd left Deerford with a strongbox under his arm. In spite of the scar. Or had that merely been a figment of her imagination?

DeMornay fixed his gaze on Tom. "And this man is your fiancé?"

It was a reasonable assumption, considering the distance she'd traveled. Would her cousin think the worst of her for traveling with an unmarried man? Without a doubt Mr. DeMornay would pass this information to her cousin.

Tom looked DeMornay in the eye. "Miss Haynes hired me for protection during the journey from Key West."

That was not strictly true. She had given him no money,

though she intended to buy his return fare. But it did seem to appease DeMornay.

"Then you do not require a room." DeMornay's pleased expression told her just how happy he would be to see Tom leave.

"He must stay tonight at least," she interjected. "Until he can secure return passage."

DeMornay stared at her for some moments before nodding curtly. Turning to Aurelia, he instructed a second room to be prepared. "Put him in the garçonnière."

Maman had told her of that separate building for housing the boys and guests. Catherine had a distinct impression that DeMornay wanted to put Tom as far from her room as possible. The idea of being separated from him left her decidedly anxious.

"He may stay in the house. We are friends."

DeMornay did not budge. "The garçonnière."

The housekeeper looked at Catherine, her expression urgent as if she was trying to convey something without words. But what?

"Go!" DeMornay demanded.

The Negress flinched as if struck.

Catherine got a sick sensation in her stomach. What was going on here? The housekeeper's pleading look and DeMornay's strong reaction told her all was not well at Chêne Noir.

"Thank you, Aurelia," Catherine said to the beleaguered housekeeper.

DeMornay frowned. Once Aurelia had departed, he reprimanded Catherine. "You clearly have no experience with darkies. They require a firm hand. I suggest you leave their administration to me."

Tom joined her. "I suggest you speak with respect around your mistress. You are just the overseer, *Mister* DeMornay."

His gaze never flickered. "I am the manager. As such, I am in charge of the entire property, including the house."

That brought yet another question to Catherine's mind. "I was surprised we saw no one working the fields. It is harvest-time, isn't it?"

"There is no need to trouble yourself with the operations of the plantation. That's why I'm here." DeMornay smoothed the lapel of his coat.

"Since I am of Lafreniere blood, I cannot help but be concerned. I understand accounts, Mr. DeMornay. I managed my father's estate during his decline. I would appreciate an answer."

"Of course." His smile was cold. "As is usual practice, the harvest begins at the farthest extent of Lafreniere land, near the sugarhouse and not visible from here."

"I see." Yet something about his manner raised her hackles. "Then we shall tour those fields tomorrow."

"There is no need."

What was he hiding? "I cannot remain idle. I must see every aspect of the operation." She looked around the quiet room. "Is none of the family here?"

DeMornay shook his head. "In the city. Your cousin runs his business as well as the plantation from there."

Though the Grahams had inferred as much, she still found it peculiar.

Tom put her thought to words. "Don't you find that unusual? I wouldn't want to entrust my entire livelihood to someone else."

DeMornay's smile froze. "You are outspoken for a hired man, Mr. . . . ."

"Worthington. Tom Worthington." He spoke it with undue force, and Catherine feared he would come to blows with De-Mornay.

"From Key West," she said, hoping to defuse the tension.

"You've been there?" Tom asked.

DeMornay examined his fingernails. "Can't say that I have."

"My father has. Many times." Tom's color had heightened. "He was also named Thomas. His ship was the *Rachael Deare*."

"Ah, then you come from a maritime family. Perhaps a sailor yourself?" DeMornay's smile carried no warmth.

Tom clenched his fists. "That's right."

"Then you understand how a ship's owner might remain ashore while his captain and crew sail the vessel. Some plantations are the same."

Catherine didn't understand. "But Maman described the family living here."

DeMornay turned his attention back to her. "That might have been true at the time. I was not here then."

"Where were you?" Tom interjected.

Catherine held her breath. From the moment they'd arrived, Tom had displayed animosity toward Mr. DeMornay. Why? What was this man to him? She was the one searching for the man who had left Deerford with a strongbox, yet Tom seemed to have taken her quest upon himself. He couldn't know that she was not certain the plantation manager was the man she sought. Though many details fit, especially the scar, others did not. Tom, in his misguided gallantry, seemed ready to battle the man. She tried to ease his concern with a smile.

Tom didn't stop glaring at the manager.

DeMornay's smile showed a set of even teeth, slightly yellowed. "As I said, I have lived in Louisiana all my life. Most recently in New Orleans."

His gentlemanly manner stood in such contrast to the Grahams' fear of even setting foot on Lafreniere land that Catherine felt a prickle of concern. Something was off, but what? Or rather, who?

Someone passed outside the room, dark as a shadow. Catherine turned to look but saw nothing.

DeMornay motioned toward the back of the house. "Tea and lemonade are served. Would you prefer to freshen up first? I assume you have trunks?"

"They are coming by wagon," Tom snapped.

Why was he being so impolite? To make up for Tom's bad manners, Catherine tipped the scale in the other direction. "They will arrive by the end of the afternoon. I'm certain Mr. Worthington would be willing to help unload them. We are ever so grateful for your hospitality."

DeMornay's smile still lacked warmth, and when it was followed by an unbridled assessment of her attire and figure, the hairs on her arms stood on end.

"Your journey has been long for your skirts to have gathered that much dust," DeMornay said. "I will have Gibson and Walker bring the trunks to your room so you might change. Until the baggage arrives, we will rest in the shade of the loggia."

Cousin Roger could not have done a more thorough and concise job of setting her in her place. She was to look pretty and not voice opinions or ask questions. She must remember that DeMornay was simply the plantation manager. She was a blood relation.

"I prefer to see the house. Perhaps a tour?"

He hesitated. "I will show you the house later. For now, we will get to know each other a bit better."

Tom inconspicuously squeezed her elbow. She looked up at him. He shook his head ever so slightly. Was he congratulating her on standing her ground or warning her not to follow DeMornay?

She was no good at deciphering unspoken thoughts. Neither could she give voice to the fact that her stomach had knotted. So she took Tom's arm and followed DeMornay through the back of the salon, through a dining room, and onto a rear-facing veranda. Cups, glasses, and small plates already adorned a dining table there. Below and to each side of the house stood two pigeonniers, while directly behind were the remains of the parterre garden.

"It's overgrown," she cried out. "The beautiful parterre. Maman loved it so." The moment of heartbreak was followed by Haynes resolve. "I will bring it back to its glory."

"A worthy goal for another day." DeMornay pulled out a chair facing the ruined garden. "Please sit."

She reluctantly sat. Tom selected the chair at her side. DeMornay sat at the head of the table, a place of honor that ought to have gone to family. Judging from Tom's frown, he'd noticed also.

Rather than stir up a fuss, she guided the conversation in another direction.

"My uncle did not leave a widow?" Though the Grahams said she'd passed, Uncle Henri might have remarried.

"She died many years ago."

"Then he was the only family here?"

"Excepting visits from his sons—your cousins—and their families."

Tom leaned back, his gaze never leaving DeMornay. If Catherine had been in her Season, she would have taken offense at his utter lack of attention toward her.

Aurelia arrived with a pitcher of lemonade and another of tea, both sweetened to perfection. The cool liquid soothed Catherine's dusty throat and jangled nerves.

DeMornay scooted his chair slightly so he had a direct view

of her. "We did not receive word of your arrival, or we would have had a room prepared for you."

"I did write, but the letter must have gotten waylaid or slowed by the storms." Since he didn't appear to believe her, she added, "The decision was sudden. My father died."

"Ahhh." DeMornay ran his finger around the rim of the glass, making a high-pitched ringing sound. "Your mother did not travel with you?"

"She died some years ago, but you must know that. I understand there's a tomb for her. Lisette."

"Of course. I forgot."

Tom looked like he was going to scoff aloud. She gestured for him to stay quiet, though she'd had the same reaction. If the judge and his wife knew of the grave, so should the plantation manager. Moreover, he alone hadn't questioned her claim to be a Lafreniere. Why not? If her letter had not arrived, as he'd just stated, he should question her, especially since Lisette Lafreniere's tomb here listed a date of death that would make it impossible for Catherine to be her daughter.

"How long have you been at Black Oak?" she prodded.

DeMornay's gaze swept over the grounds. "It must be fifteen years at least. Perhaps closer to twenty." He closed his eyes briefly. "Ah yes, I began working here after the panic of 1837 put me out of work."

Catherine wasn't familiar with American history, but Tom seemed to accept the explanation.

Again DeMornay ran his finger around the glass rim. The eerie sound rang in her ears.

"Miss Haynes, you have not said how long you plan to visit."

There was the key question, the one she'd been avoiding. "I-I-I hoped to stay." She hated that her voice trembled.

DeMornay's eyebrows shot up. "Stay? But this is no place for a belle like you. You need the liveliness that the city can offer. I can have Walker take both of you downriver so you can visit with your cousin."

It was a perfectly logical response, though a bit too eagerly offered. "Not quite yet. Maman spoke often of Chêne Noir." She hesitated, waiting to see if he reacted in the same way the Grahams had.

He did not. No puzzlement. No questions. No sign of fear.

"I fell in love with the plantation from a tender age," she added. "I must see it in its entirety, from the pigeonniers to the sugarhouse."

"Ah, the tour you mentioned." DeMornay did not appear pleased.

Tom must have noticed, for he cast her a knowing look when DeMornay took a sip of his tea.

"Perhaps morning would be best," she suggested. "Surely it's not as hot at an early hour. Once I see the plantation, I will know what needs to be done to bring it back to glory."

DeMornay stiffened ever so slightly before his guarded smile returned. "You have lofty dreams."

"After handling the accounts during my father's illness, I learned how to wring water from a rock, so to speak."

DeMornay's eyebrows rose. "A helpful skill, but your cousin might have something to say about it. He is the owner."

"With his brother." She stopped short of adding her own name to the list of heirs. If Maman was right, she should have a share, but that needed to be discussed with her cousin, not the manager.

"Of course." DeMornay suddenly rose. "We will contact Henry, but at present I have something to show you, something that could affect your plans. Follow me."

Part of her hesitated at this sudden change of direction, but the greater part wanted to learn more about the plantation. Tom shot her a concerned look. She ignored him. She had come all this way to reclaim her family. She couldn't let a wayward feeling and an overprotective man dissuade her.

12

Tom did not trust DeMornay, not one bit. When the man took Catherine into the study, Tom attempted to follow and was blocked by a firm hand to the chest.

"This is a family matter," DeMornay had the gall to say.

What hurt worse was that Catherine didn't contradict De-Mornay. She allowed the man to escort her into the study and close the door in Tom's face. What hold did DeMornay already have over her that she would agree to such a thing?

Tom paced outside the room. One cry from her and he would smash down the door. Or he could climb in through a window. The room must have windows. He headed toward the veranda. Since it wrapped around the house, any windows would open onto it. Fingering his dagger, he made his way through the interconnected rooms to the front of the house.

Regardless of what DeMornay had said, he was the fiend who'd stolen Pa's ship. The scar proved it. According to Pa, Mornez—or DeMornay, as he now called himself—had coerced the crew to mutiny. They broke into the gun locker and took the ship. Pa had no weapon to defend himself. DeMornay then set him adrift in the ship's boat. Pa's survival was a testament to his fortitude, but it took a terrible toll on his health. The courts then awarded creditors everything Pa had left. The shame and struggle broke him until he simply gave up.

Tom gripped the hilt of the dagger. He would avenge his father, even if it cost his life.

"Psst."

The shrill sound pulled Tom from thoughts of revenge. He looked around for the source and saw nothing.

"Here."

He saw the gauzy curtain sway slightly. Someone—a female, judging by the voice—wanted him to join her. He ripped back the curtain.

No one was there.

The hair rose on the back of his neck. Everything about this house was unsettling.

"Come," the woman urged.

This time he realized the whisper came from the opposite direction—inside the house. Double shutters, such as those common in Key West, were open to allow the breezes inside. Each room had at least one shuttered door. This voice came from the room beside the main salon.

DeMornay said that none of the family was here. It must be a slave or servant. Servants knew things, heard things.

Tom slipped into the room. It took a moment for his eyes to adjust to the lower lighting. It was a simple bedchamber, made up for guests. Perhaps for Catherine. Standing on the other side of the room was the speaker. Aurelia, DeMornay had called her. When not in the manager's presence, she stood as tall and proud as Anabelle.

A shiver ran through him. Aurelia couldn't be Elizabeth's nurse, even though the woman had been sold to a planter in Louisiana. It was impossible.

"What's your full name?" he asked, recalling that Elizabeth's nurse should bear the Benjamin name.

"Aurelia."

"Mammy?" he whispered.

"I ain't yo' mammy. I ain't nobody's mammy." Her eyes darted back and forth. "I tole you to leave. Git her and git out."

"Only when I get proof." He would not seek vengeance until he was certain.

"Proof of what?"

"Proof that DeMornay stole my father's ship." This was Tom's chance. "Ten years ago. The *Rachael Deare*. Did you ever see it?"

"I ain't seen no ship."

"She was a schooner with clean lines and full sail and a cargo of stoves, copper kettles, and household goods. Did you hear of it? She was bound for Mobile but likely ended up in New Orleans."

"I ain't never been to New Orleans." Aurelia's gaze darted toward the doors opening to the rear.

"I need to know," he urged in a whisper.

Her gaze didn't meet his. "Won't get nothin' more'n trouble if you stay. Take her and leave."

Tom refused to retreat. His father must be avenged, but there were many ways to see justice served. Tom need not end up on the gallows if he could prove that DeMornay was the thief. A scar was not enough. He needed proof that the theft had occurred. Finding the ship or some record of its arrival would be enough to bring to Judge Graham.

If the ship had been sold, which was likely, then he needed to find record of the goods arriving. Stolen goods would not have passed through the customs collector or any official. They would have been sold to unwitting parties. The stoves had serial numbers. He had copied the bill of lading from the shipping office, but it was in his bag, which had not yet arrived. If one of those stoves had ended up here or he could find record of their sale and could match it to the bill of lading, then he would have his proof.

"Where are—?" he began to ask, but Aurelia had vanished, slipping away as silently as the breeze.

He would have to find proof on his own. That meant staying. Somehow. Catherine and DeMornay would fight it, but he could convince her. Perhaps it was time to tell her the other reason why he'd come here. She had lost a father. She would sympathize with him, provided DeMornay hadn't already convinced her that Tom was a villain.

The man had recognized the Worthington name. DeMornay managed his reactions well, but Tom had seen the brief widening of the eyes. He knew who Tom was. He would suspect Tom planned vengeance. No doubt this private meeting with Catherine was intended to convince her that Tom was dangerous or untrustworthy.

Danger did lurk, for if Tom could prove that DeMornay had stolen Pa's ship, he could wrest control of Black Oak from the man's clutches and get it back where it belonged—in Lafreniere hands. That would win Catherine to his side.

It could also push her to stay here the rest of her life. Though a river coursed nearby, Tom was no river pilot. He was never more alive than on the open seas. A plantation felt like prison. Cursed dilemma!

Muffled voices broke into his consciousness. They had left the study and were headed his way.

He slipped onto the veranda.

DeMornay's low voice carried through the rooms. "You will have everything your heart desires."

Don't believe it, Tom wanted to cry out. *It's all lies.*

He must protect her.

Pa was dead, but Catherine lived. He could not allow another light to be snuffed out by Louis DeMornay.

Oh, Mr. DeMornay had a silver tongue and a gentlemanly manner, but something about him left Catherine unsettled. Perhaps he smiled too much and was too solicitous. Certainly his claims were unbelievable. He opened account books before her that showed a tidy profit, far more than Deerford had ever turned.

Yet her childhood home had always looked well-kept. Their housekeepers had kept it meticulously clean. Her parents had filled the shelves and walls with beautiful things—vases and paintings and figurines. This house was barren. It looked . . . picked over. Perhaps her cousin had taken everything to the city. That would make sense if the family had abandoned the plantation house like DeMornay said. Even the study was severe. Half-empty bookshelves. No portraits. Nothing to tell the visitor that the home had a legacy. The only peculiarity was an empty birdcage, its gilded door open as if waiting for a bird to arrive. This was not the house Maman had described.

"As you can see, my oversight has benefited your family quite handsomely." He closed the ledger. "And now it benefits you. As manager, I am at your disposal. Your wish is my command."

That was a ridiculous assertion, given Henry Lafreniere owned the plantation. "My cousin might object."

"We will send word to him that you have arrived. I'm certain he will want to meet you."

It was Catherine's dearest hope. "He has children?"

"A handful."

His vague answer unsettled her. As manager, he should know everything about his employer's family. Unless they never came to Black Oak.

"My cousin owns Black Oak." Speaking the words aloud cemented their finality. "To remain here beyond a few days, I must secure his permission. Do you expect him to visit during the harvest?"

"No." DeMornay steepled his fingers.

It was so reminiscent of cousin Roger that she flinched.

DeMornay misinterpreted her reaction. "I'm sorry to disappoint you. I will send word, of course, but there's no need to wait. I can have the carriage readied to bring you and Mr. Worthington to the city before nightfall."

Why did she get the impression he was trying to get rid of her?

"Thank you, but not tonight. Aurelia has already prepared our rooms, and I look forward to the tour of the plantation." Catherine moved to the door. "We could begin now."

She twisted the knob. It did not move. Was it jammed? She tried again.

Nothing.

DeMornay rose. "As you wish. The grounds first, before nightfall."

He approached the door and snapped back the latch. What had he meant by locking the door? Chased by shapeless fears, she hurried through the doorway.

He followed. "Rest assured, under my guidance you will have everything your heart desires."

The words rang hollow. She fled before them, through the dining room and the salon. Maman had described these rooms so well that she knew where each one lay in relation to the other. DeMornay trailed after her.

"My heart desires to tour the plantation." She stepped onto

156

the front veranda and drew a deep breath. "We shall begin at once, as soon as I find Tom—that is, Mr. Worthington."

That proved an easy feat, for Tom appeared before her, hand at his hip, as if grasping a pistol or knife. He had been prepared to defend her. That knowledge filled her with a warm affection that shook away the lingering dread.

She smiled with relief. "Mr. DeMornay has agreed to show us the grounds and house."

DeMornay approached from behind and placed a hand on the small of her back. The intimate gesture sent a jolt up her spine and drew Tom's brow into a scowl.

She stepped to Tom's side and took his arm. That touch raised an entirely different reaction, one of confidence and security combined with anticipation—the very same reaction she'd felt at their first meeting. She trusted him. The realization stirred something inside. She did trust him. More so than anyone since her father.

"You may lead, Mr. DeMornay, and we will follow."

The manager didn't betray disappointment that she'd left his side, though his smile grew a bit more rigid. "Of course. However, if Mr. Worthington wishes to return to the city tonight, I can have Walker bring him to the landing. There should be a down-bound ferry yet this afternoon. Just wave and they will stop for you."

"Thank you for your consideration," Tom said with a great deal more politeness than she would have shown, given DeMornay's obvious attempts to get rid of him, "but I wish to remain with Catherine until she no longer needs me."

He squeezed her hand, and she felt a surprising thrill at the consideration he'd shown her. He could return to Key West at once, but he would stay until he was certain she was all right.

DeMornay persisted. "There might not be a down-bound ferry tomorrow."

"I will take that chance."

She looked up to see Tom gazing at her. His look echoed what she'd already felt. He would not abandon her.

"I am grateful for Mr. Worthington's presence." She beamed at him. "He is a dear friend."

That clearly did not make DeMornay happy, and this time he didn't bother to hide his displeasure. "With the harvest under way, we will be too busy to entertain."

"Of course," Catherine said. "We will occupy ourselves throughout the day and join you for supper."

Instead of soothing DeMornay's concerns, that deepened his scowl. "In England, do you often receive unexpected guests?"

"In England it is usual to extend hospitality to travelers, whether friend, family, or stranger. Often my father invited those passing through to spend the night with us."

"Perhaps that is why you are here, Miss Haynes," DeMornay said, "and not home in Staffordshire."

The blow was precisely executed and sent Catherine reeling. Had she truly been the cause of Deerford's demise? Cousin Roger had implied it. DeMornay now echoed that. But she had done all in her power to wring a profit from the leases—without burdening the tenants. Mr. DeMornay might claim financial superiority, but at what cost? He paid no wage to his labor. He did not care for the estate. He knew nothing of Deerford or indeed of Staffordshire.

She caught her breath.

Staffordshire. She had not once mentioned where Deerford was located. There was only one way DeMornay could know it was in Staffordshire. He'd been there.

13

Naturally the tour of the house and grounds revealed nothing. Tom stuck close to Catherine's side, doing his best to keep some distance between her and DeMornay. The man brushed past many of the structures, casually pointing out the pigeonniers and garçonnière along with the necessary buildings like the cistern, washhouse, and cookhouse. The stables and the overseer's house were separated from the main grounds.

"That's where you live?" Tom asked.

"I did until Mr. Lafreniere asked me to move into the main house."

Tom had to admit the man could easily explain away anomalies. "And the servants? Do they stay in the main house also?"

Catherine shot him a sharp look.

But DeMornay revealed no surprise at his question. "Their quarters are just beyond the overseer's house. You can make them out through the trees."

Though dusk was beginning to fall and obscure the views, Tom could pick out the low, weathered wood building.

"How many servants on the plantation?"

Catherine squeezed his arm as if he was being the impertinent one.

DeMornay didn't hesitate. "Only essential household servants stay here at present. The rest have joined the field workers at the quarters situated near the sugarhouse. That's where we're harvesting right now."

Catherine craned her neck, looking upward at a dovecote. "Does the plantation keep pigeons?"

"Not for some years."

"It also appears the garçonnière hasn't been used for a long time." She squeezed Tom's arm again. "It was used for guests and to sequester the boys when they got near manhood. Maman said the boys always managed to make mischief, and they would often sneak out to secretly meet with their loves."

Tom imagined sneaking out to meet Catherine tonight, and his pulse raced. Was she hinting that they should plan this?

DeMornay lifted an eyebrow. "I trust Mr. Worthington is grown enough not to attempt such a thing."

Catherine grinned. "If Tom were still in his youth, he would find a way. He is resourceful and will let nothing stop him."

Her smile melted the anger that had been building in his heart. Catherine admired him. She was willing to vouch for him in front of the enemy, though she did not yet realize that DeMornay was the enemy.

The man found no humor in Catherine's statement. Instead, he guided them to the nearest pigeonnier. She left Tom's side to take a closer look.

"The entrance is narrow," DeMornay pointed out, "and the interior is likely filthy. Even though it hasn't been formally used as a dovecote, some birds do still nest there."

She drew back. "Then we shall skip it."

DeMornay placed Catherine's hand on his arm. "We should

return to the house. The sun is getting lower, and you will want to freshen up before supper. Your trunks might have arrived by now."

Tom's scowl did nothing to pry Catherine from the man's clutches. He suspected the only time and place he could meet with her in private was by moonlight, like those boys of old. Catherine had been trying to tell him that, but now DeMornay would be on the watch. They must act carefully, and that meant getting away from the man long enough to make plans. If they could explore the plantation without DeMornay's constant presence, Tom would find the evidence he needed to go to Judge Graham.

But first he needed to get her alone.

Thankfully the house tour revealed where her room was located. Though DeMornay did not point out where he stayed, Tom suspected the man had chosen a bedroom near his study, which he had carefully avoided during the tour. Likewise he had kept the door to the master bedroom closed, saying it was where her uncle had passed and thus was not fit for exhibition.

Tom didn't know how the natural end of life on earth turned a room into a mausoleum, but Catherine didn't question De-Mornay's omitting it from the tour. With each room Tom looked for a way to get her alone. At each step he ran into DeMornay.

The man clearly didn't trust him. DeMornay would never be put at ease—and thus prone to make an error—until he thought Tom gone. But that put Catherine in harm's way. Not that Tom thought DeMornay would do her bodily harm, but he would have full opportunity to work his persuasive skills without Tom to contradict him.

When they returned to the salon, the long-sought opportunity arrived.

Aurelia stepped from the shadows. "Massa, Angel and Hunter done disappeared."

DeMornay frowned. "You're supposed to keep track of them. What sort of mother are you?"

"I fears dey fall into some kinda trouble."

Catherine's eyes widened. "We must find them. Can't we send someone?"

DeMornay's gaze narrowed. Apparently he did not like anyone to step into what he considered his business, something Catherine did not recognize.

"I can help search," she offered.

Aurelia sucked in her breath and cowered, as if fearing a blow from DeMornay.

Irritation and even anger built beneath DeMornay's calm surface.

Tom couldn't resist putting another gaping hole in it. "I will join you. Let's go, Catherine. Where were they last seen, Aurelia?" He took Catherine's hand.

"Dey likes to play in de cane."

Naturally. The tall sugarcane would completely hide them and anyone else who wandered into it.

Tom tugged on Catherine's hand, but she hesitated.

"There's a lot of sugarcane. Do they have a favorite spot?"

Aurelia hesitated, her eyes turning briefly to DeMornay. "Out back. Past our room."

"I'll send Walker," DeMornay said stiffly. "We will not impose on our guests for two misbehaving darkies."

Catherine tensed, and Tom saw the revulsion on her face. She didn't like this any more than he did. After working with the captain of the *Windsprite*, Tom had come to respect the former slave's skill and knowledge. Moreover, Anabelle was as educated as any woman in Key West. The common refrain that the Negro didn't possess the capacity for learning was contradicted by those two. He shuddered at the thought of them under the control of someone like DeMornay.

"Shouldn't we send more than one man?" Catherine asked. "Everyone should search."

Aurelia looked at the floor, at the wall. She wrung her hands, twisting her apron around them.

Tom wouldn't have thought that odd if she hadn't stood so tall and proud earlier when she warned him. That's why he needed to talk to Catherine alone. That's why he had to get her out searching the fields with him.

"We will help Walker," he stated.

DeMornay darkened, and Tom instinctively braced for a rebuke. Aurelia stepped out of reach. That was the reaction of someone who feared physical punishment. Tom didn't doubt DeMornay whipped the slaves. That he would flog a woman made him especially angry.

"Come, Catherine." He would not let DeMornay stop him.

She took his outstretched hand, and he led her from the house, hoping he hadn't just brought Aurelia more trouble.

⚜

The pigeonnier was eerie at night, but it was the place Tom had suggested in a whisper during the moment DeMornay instructed Walker. The strapping black man had found the children within minutes and sent them off to their quarters before Catherine could pull Tom into the sugarcane. Walker then informed them that their trunks had arrived.

Catherine would have chosen the cane for their midnight meeting, but agreeing on a location proved impossible in such a short space of time. It took only moments before DeMornay's attention was back on them, and he did not leave her side until she retired for the evening.

To her relief, the bedroom door had a latch. She'd drawn it at once. Then she'd spent the remaining hours until the house quieted plotting her escape. Since the veranda, or gallery as Maman had called it, surrounded the house, she could slip out of the room without walking through the interior.

When the moon lit the landscape and the sounds of night shimmered in the air, Catherine stepped over the short sill onto the veranda. To avoid the study and the rooms that DeMornay might occupy, she took the rear steps down. Her calfskin slippers barely made a sound.

Slight movement in the yard caught her eye. She stopped and watched, but it did not happen again. It must be Tom. Quite likely he was making his way to their meeting spot.

She hurried to the side of the house and the pigeonnier. The half-moon gave enough light to make out her path, though she must race through several areas where the long shadows stretched.

Before making the run across the yard, she took a deep breath to still her nerves. No one would harm her. She was of Lafreniere blood. They would honor and protect that. Still, she hurried across the open space, hoping her foot did not land in a hollow.

Seconds later, she reached the pigeonnier.

"Tom," she dared to whisper.

No answer. No human sound at all. Had she been wrong? Had the movement been a dog or servant? Had she misunderstood where he wanted to meet?

She tested the door. It was unlocked. But it would be terribly dark inside.

Fear could make a person give up before she reached her goal. Catherine would not give up. Tom had looked upset earlier. Something was wrong, and he needed to speak to her in private. She also needed to tell him that DeMornay had lied. He had been to Deerford. She was sure of it.

She unlatched the door, took a deep breath, and stepped inside.

Utter darkness greeted her, and she had to wait for her eyes to adjust. Gradually she was aware of faint light filtering from the openings near the top of the pigeonnier. This place felt foreign, even more so than Key West, which had a homey feeling with its close families and interconnected relationships. Here everything felt disjointed and vacant. Lonely. Was that why Henry had moved to the city and Emile joined the Army?

"Tom?" she whispered.

No answer.

She must have arrived first.

Unless he was deep inside. Surely he would have heard her, though. Wouldn't he?

"Tom?" This time she spoke a little louder.

The door opened behind her, and she let out a gasp. A hand covered her mouth. An arm reached around her. A man's arm. She struggled.

"Shh. Stop it."

Tom. She breathed out with relief and stopped struggling. "You frightened me."

He released her, but she didn't move away. His strength was a comfort in the darkness, and tonight she needed it.

"I need to leave," he said softly near her ear. "Come with me. Let me keep you safe."

Panic set in. "Leave? You're leaving Black Oak? But you said you'd stay as long as I needed you. I need you."

"I know." He stroked her cheek with his thumb. "That's why I want you to come with me."

"But why can't you stay?"

"I need to find something." There was a desperate edge to his voice.

"I don't understand. Find what?"

"Proof. Evidence."

Now she truly was confused. "Proof of what?"

His hands gripped her shoulders, and she felt the desperation in them. "Proof that DeMornay is the man who destroyed my father."

"What?" Was that the secret Elizabeth had sensed weighing Tom down? Tom's father was dead. That much she remembered. Also that Tom was prone to temper. "What do you intend to do? Challenge him to a duel?"

"No. Find proof of his crime and bring him to justice." Tom kept his grip on Catherine's shoulders though she pulled away slightly. "Through the law."

He felt her relax, thank the Lord, and released her. He needed her. In the long hours between supper and the appointed hour for their meeting, he'd realized that only Catherine stood a chance of finding evidence in the plantation's records. Provided DeMornay had left any. It might be the smallest anomaly. Tom didn't understand ledgers, but Catherine could read them. She'd managed her family's estate in England.

Something had clearly gone wrong there if she was here looking for help from her mother's family, but he had a feeling it had nothing to do with her abilities. Catherine Haynes was quick of wit and intellect. She could find discrepancies. Yet he wasn't quite as certain she could withstand DeMornay's assault. The man's sickening attentions to her were bound to wear her down.

At supper, DeMornay had pulled out his finest clothing, the

best table service, and impeccable manners. He could converse on any topic, and she'd smiled more than once. The man ignored Tom, of course. He clearly wanted him out of the way. Tom shared that sentiment, but first he needed to discover if his father's ship was moored nearby. Most likely the man had sold it. Tom hoped otherwise.

In the dark shadows of the pigeonnier, Catherine drew in a breath. "What did he do?"

"Stole my father's ship and its cargo."

"And that destroyed your father?"

Tom hadn't wanted to relate the whole tale, but to gain her assistance he spilled the entire painful story.

"Pa was half the man he'd been before the incident," Tom finished. "Ma nursed him back to health, though she could not revive his spirit. The courts destroyed that by taking everything, including our house, to satisfy creditors. That's when we moved to Nantucket Island."

"To start anew."

"To escape the stares of pity. Pa worked on a fishing vessel."

"It was something," she said.

"He'd been a master, captain of his own ship." He reached for her shoulders again but dropped his hands before making the mistake of gripping her. "Don't you understand? He had to haul nets and gut fish. Pa. A captain."

"I'm sorry." The softness of her voice showed she truly was.

"It ruined him. He died a broken man."

"Oh, Tom." Her hand cupped his jaw. "I'm so very sorry. It must have been devastating."

Tom didn't want to admit the depth of his pain. He also didn't want her hand to leave his jaw. When she pulled it away, he grasped it firmly. "It was . . . difficult, but thanks to you I'm beginning to see that life can go on."

"Because of me?"

"Your fortitude in the face of losing your parents. To travel halfway around the world is astonishing."

She drew in a sharp breath. "That reminds me. I'm now certain DeMornay is the man who visited Deerford when I was a girl."

"How?"

"Something he said. He let slip that Papa's estate was in Staffordshire, but I don't recall ever mentioning that. Did you?"

"No." His pulse accelerated. "That could mean that your DeMornay and my Mornez are the same man."

"How?"

"The scar beneath his eye. Both DeMornay and Mornez had exactly the same scar as this man."

She seemed ready to question that conclusion but instead returned to his story. "Do you have proof that DeMornay took your father's ship?"

"That's what I need to find. Why I need to leave. Come with me. Now that you know he lied, there's no reason to stay."

"But there is. First of all, this is the only family I have left." She revised the statement. "The only family who might want to see me. My cousin Roger, who inherited Deerford, was only interested in marrying me off so I would be out from underfoot."

Tom had heard of such things in storybooks, but to hear that it had happened to Catherine shocked and angered him. "Such men don't deserve positions of authority."

Her sigh of agreement dispelled his anger.

"Secondly," she said, "if we both leave, DeMornay will suspect we know his secrets and are going to warn my cousin Henry. He wants you to leave, but I believe he wants me to stay. If we're both gone, he could vanish again, and you'll never get justice for your father."

"And you'll never get the family you crave. You're a brave woman." This time he cupped her chin.

The moonlight spilled from high above, silvering her features so she looked like a marble statue. But his fingers said otherwise. This was a warm, breathing woman. One so beautiful she took his breath away. He longed to kiss her, but Catherine was not the sort of woman to stand for impulsive actions. She needed to be courted properly. His heart gave a twinge. Her suitor ought to be in her social class. He never could be.

She stepped back, and her breath was shaky. "Speaking of family, if you go to the city, will you find Henry Lafreniere and tell him I want to meet him? I'm beginning to doubt that DeMornay has any intention of contacting him."

"Of course I will, but will you be safe?" His pulse pounded, highlighting the threat.

"He won't harm me. He wouldn't dare. Perhaps I can be of use to you in your quest. You said you need proof. What are you looking for?"

It took effort to bring Tom's mind away from Catherine's soft lips and back to avenging his father. He drew in a deep breath and let his thoughts settle. "Look at the plantation accounts if you have a chance. See if there is anything unusual—a large amount received, for instance, within the last ten years."

"Such as for the sale of a ship?"

"Or its cargo. Stoves and other household goods. I have a list of serial numbers." He pulled from his pocket the list he'd copied from the bill of lading.

She took it. "You expect him to keep a list of stolen merchandise?"

"Check the stoves on the plantation. See if any of these items are in the house or on the grounds."

"You think my family would harbor stolen goods?"

"No." He sensed the outrage in her voice. "Not intentionally. I suspect DeMornay lied to your uncle and everyone else."

"And the crew from your father's ship?"

"Likely long gone." Tom hoped they weren't dead.

"Is that why you must leave?"

The whispered question trembled slightly. This time when he reached for her, she fell into his arms.

"Only for a short while," he whispered into her hair, drinking in the scent of her. "I must search for Pa's ship and ask questions. Moreover, DeMornay won't open up until he's certain I'm gone. He knows my name."

"He knows you're here to hurt him."

"He suspects it. I must appear to leave, but I won't be far." He kissed her cheek and tasted salt. She was crying. "Don't worry. He won't hurt you. I'll make sure of it."

She leaned into him. "I hope you're right."

So did he.

14

In Tom's arms Catherine felt secure, something she hadn't experienced in a long time. His story unsettled her, though. If DeMornay was capable of stranding a man for his own gain, what would he do if he found her looking through the ledgers? He'd seemed open enough when he showed her the accounts, but he hadn't let her peruse them. Had he carefully selected which pages to show her?

Tom left after breakfast with a great show. He begged her to join him for the voyage back to Key West. Even though she knew the plea was made up for DeMornay's benefit, her heart yearned to do just that.

A sleepless night had not improved her perception of the plantation. The servants—few as they were—moved silently through the house. No laughter or chatter anywhere. The yard was empty save for the girl, Angel, who'd hidden in the sugarcane yesterday. Today she carried a pail of milk to the cookhouse, trailing after her mother. Aurelia unnerved Catherine, perhaps because of her wild eyes and fearful manner.

Catherine idly sipped tea and stared at Tom's empty chair.

"There is no need to regret Mr. Worthington's departure," DeMornay said. "You are home now."

Then why didn't it feel like home? Perhaps because she had nothing to do. She took another sip. Perhaps it was time to make a purpose for herself, regardless of Mr. DeMornay's feelings.

"Where are the harvesters working today?" she asked. "Can we see them from the loggia?"

"Doubtful." He stood. "There's no need to trouble yourself with such matters. The sun is shining too brightly here. You should go indoors so your complexion isn't ruined."

Catherine hated the way he and her cousin Roger treated her, as if she was fragile or addlebrained.

She made no move to leave. "Since my cousin isn't here, I will take charge of seeing that the family lands are properly maintained."

DeMornay's lips thinned. "Your cousin might disagree. He has placed full trust in me. I suggest you do that also." The ingratiating smile returned. "If you wish to discuss this with him, there is still time for you to reach the ferry landing. I can have the carriage readied."

He wished her gone also. Perhaps Tom was right, and DeMornay had something to hide.

She did her best to appear as naive as he thought her to be. "That won't be necessary. I shall occupy myself with embroidery and reading until the midday meal—unless I can be of service managing the household."

"Aurelia has been in charge of the house for ten years. She can manage quite well." He swept a hand toward the interior. "The house is at your disposal."

But not the study, as she learned later when attempting to enter the room. The door was locked and the shutters latched from the inside. DeMornay did not trust her. She would have to think up another way to see the accounts. In the meantime, her only avenue of exploration was to search for items on Tom's list. The list included serial numbers, but where did one find such a number on a stove? She had never used a stove.

Just like in Key West, the kitchen was located in a nearby outbuilding to keep the oppressive heat from overwhelming the house. At all hours, smoke curled into the thick air. The stoves must operate all day long. To find a serial number, she would have to search the stove in the dead of night without arousing anyone's suspicion.

It was impossible. She blew out her breath.

This was not her quest. She had come to Black Oak to find family, not resolve Tom's need for revenge. She would make a reasonable attempt to find something on his list and consider her duty done. Then she would go to the city to see cousin Henry. Perhaps he would give her authority to manage the plantation. She could bring it back to prosperity.

She spent the remainder of the day looking through every room. Not one item on Tom's list was located in the house. Either Tom was wrong or DeMornay had sold everything elsewhere.

After supper, she retired to the task of unpacking her trunks. The gowns fit beautifully in the ornate mahogany armoire. All the items of her personal toilette found a place on the dressing table. But there was nowhere to hang Maman's portrait or the daguerreotype of her family.

"Papa," she whispered as she cradled the image, "why couldn't you have stayed with me longer?"

But then she would not have met Tom and Elizabeth and all the good people in Key West. She also would not be here alone in an unwelcoming place. If only Tom had stayed. She sighed at the memory of his touch. The whisper of his breath against her cheek had sent a delightful fluttering through her. He insisted he would protect her, but that was not possible from the city. She rubbed her arms against a sudden shiver.

"Tom, oh Tom, where are you?" she whispered.

The evening breeze tickled her skin, but it didn't delight like Tom. She closed her eyes, dreaming of him. But dreams could only go so far.

"Lord, watch over him. Keep Tom safe, and bring him back to me."

The prayer made her feel better.

After she propped the daguerreotype on top of the dressing table, Aurelia arrived and prepared her for bed. A glass of warm milk would send slumber her way.

Still, sleep refused to settle over her that night. Restless, she paced the veranda outside her bedroom. The house was silent and dark except for the slatted light from the back room on the opposite side of the house. The study. DeMornay was awake.

She could ask if he had any connection with Tom's father, but that would only put Tom in peril.

Instead, she slid on her calfskin slippers and padded around the veranda to the lit window. The unfamiliar hum of insects rent the air with a shrill cacophony. No light emanated from the cookhouse or slave quarters. All slept except her and DeMornay.

She shivered, though it was not cold. She sought the garçonnière, wishing Tom was there.

After waiting long minutes beside the window, she dared to look through the narrow space between the two shutters. Perhaps a quarter-inch gap gave her a slender glimpse of the room. DeMornay sat at the desk, making entries in what appeared to be a ledger. He would make a few random strokes with the pen and then blot. A stroke here or there and then blot. The pattern repeated, and he turned the page. This time he made but two strokes before blotting and turning the page. Peculiar. He was not writing. He must be adding information.

Then she recalled his unwillingness to let her turn a page. What if he was changing the entries? What if cousin Henry only thought the estate was prospering when in fact it was in ruins? She shook her head. The thick air must be addling her brain. Anyone with eyes could see that the plantation was not prospering. If Henry Lafreniere ever visited, he would realize it too.

She rubbed her arms.

All was not well at Black Oak.

She stepped to the other side of the double shutters. The veranda wrapped around the entire house, so to return to her room, she could follow it around back and enter the house from the loggia. First she took one last look at the shutters. Here the edge gapped half an inch from the wall. She could see the shelves clearly as well as the empty birdcage.

Something caught the corner of her eye.

She peered through the gap again. Centered on a shelf was an object she hadn't noticed the first time she was in the study. Had it been there, or did DeMornay bring it out afterward? Memories raced through her mind.

Could it be? She pressed closer to the opening. The edge of the shutter partially blocked her view. Even so, she could not mistake the presence of a strongbox. Was it the one the stranger had carried from her father's house ten years ago? If so, it doubly confirmed that DeMornay had lied to her.

Did the lies stop there? Her heart pounded.

What if she was wrong? She'd been able to see only part of the strongbox through the narrow gap. She edged a little to her left, trying to get a clearer view. By slowly pulling on the shutter, she eased the opening a tiny bit wider. There . . . yes, there it was—the strongbox!

Something on the shutter clunked. She sprang back, and the shutter popped open. Lamplight spilled over her.

"Who's there?" DeMornay was at the window before she could flee.

His gaze landed on her.

Caught!

⌘

"I could not sleep," Catherine told DeMornay after he ushered her into the study.

He acted oddly unconcerned at finding her outside his window. "You should have knocked on the door. I would have relished the chance to converse with someone as lovely as you."

Though the words extended grace, the glitter in his eyes and his steepled hands reminded her too much of her cousin Roger.

"I did not want to disturb you."

"This is your home." He swept wide his hand, encompassing the entire width and length of the house. "I am simply the plantation's manager. If you have questions about anything, you only need to ask."

That was not what he'd said yesterday. What had brought on this change? Tom's departure?

She decided to test DeMornay and wandered about the room, taking in every item. Yes, that strongbox looked very much like the one she recalled the stranger carrying from Deerford. Of course, it did not have any identifying marks on the exterior. She would have to examine it carefully, inside and out, to see if there was anything in it to tie it to Deerford. That, however, could wait.

She faced him. "I would like to see the account books for the past year."

Unlike cousin Roger, he did not respond with shock or dismay. "They are not yet complete. I was just adding some figures that are now finalized." He turned the open ledger so it faced her. "Have a look."

At once she could see that this method of accounting bore little resemblance to what she was accustomed to at Deerford. Cryptic column headings gave her little indication of what the scratched numbers beneath referred to.

"FNS?" she asked.

His smile grated on her. "Female Negros."

The S stood for *slave*, she presumed. "Then MNS are the men. FIN? And FCN?"

"Female infants and children."

She ran her finger down the columns. The numbers for the children remained fairly steady, but the numbers for the women and men rose and fell over and over.

"Why the change in numbers?"

His smile hardened. "An English gentlewoman couldn't possibly understand the complexities of American plantation labor or the record keeping involved. We must report all servants to the federal government." The last was stated with marked distaste.

"Servants?" She couldn't help noticing his choice of word.

"Planters, harvesters, grooms, housemaids, cooks. The full range. Depending on the season, the number of field hands will change dramatically."

Though that made sense, it wasn't what she'd expected or understood about slaveholding plantations. "You lease field hands from other planters?"

"Sometimes."

"Is it less expensive than housing your own?"

He laughed. "How perceptive you are! I can't help but wonder why such a bright mind is here rather than managing your father's estate."

"He passed away, and it was bound by prior settlement to fall to my cousin."

"Ah. So you came here while another manages your childhood home. Your father did not provide for you?"

That was getting too personal. "He did, but I longed to rejoin Maman's family. She spoke so often of the plantation."

She did not tell him that Deerford had been sold. By now, the house—her house—was likely razed. In place of the elegant country house, a hideous factory would rise. The tenants had been thrown out. Her father had poured his lifeblood into them. She closed her eyes against the memories.

"Forgive me. I did not mean to raise a painful subject." He stood close. Too close.

She took a breath and stepped back. "It is over. This is my home now."

Again, he did not betray surprise. Instead, he bowed slightly. "It has never known a more beautiful mistress."

Unpleasant prickles danced along her spine, and she took another step back. DeMornay left her unsettled, as if she were on the shifting deck of a ship. She could not judge from what direction the next wave might strike. She wanted to run, to seek refuge. If only Tom were here. But she was alone with only God to protect her.

She feigned bravado. "I shall retire now. Sleep presses in upon me at last."

"As you wish, mademoiselle."

Maman had been the last person to use that term. Her playful voice tugged at the back of Catherine's memory, light and filled with happiness as she pulled Catherine into one Paris shop after another. The voyage had been a grand adventure, just Maman and her. Mother and daughter flitting from one delight to the next. It had been their last. The dreams of Chêne

Noir had proven just as fleeting. Only Maman had the right to call her *mademoiselle*.

She squared her shoulders. "Miss Haynes, please."

Again the little bow. "As you wish."

Once he was in New Orleans, it didn't take long for Tom to learn enough about DeMornay to wish he'd never left Catherine in the man's hands, but none of it got him one bit closer to finding his father's ship. For two days he searched but could find no hint of the *Rachael Deare*.

On the third day, he stumbled upon an old salt whose penchant for rum loosened his lips. When Tom bought the spirits, Mr. Boyce admitted he'd seen the stolen schooner.

"The black ship," the sailor stated. "That's the one ye mean. Whatever ye do, steer clear o' the black ship."

Tom had found this balding salt by passing on word he was looking for a ship. Most took it to mean he wanted to join a crew. Boyce understood that Tom wanted to find a particular clipper ship, faster than the wind.

"She moves by night," Boyce continued, his words remarkably clear in spite of the rum. "Lies hidden by day."

"Where?"

"Somewhere upriver." A wave of his hand indicated a generous stretch.

"Where upriver?"

The man whistled through the gap caused by the loss of a front tooth. "That'd be the question now, wouldn't it?"

Tom leaned close so no one else could hear. Most were reluctant to speak of DeMornay or claimed not to know the man while not once meeting Tom's eyes. Lies. And fear. These men feared DeMornay, as well they should. Cunning deception clung to the man like a well-fitted coat. Even now he was likely wooing Catherine to his point of view. Tom had left the list of goods from the bill of lading in her hands. If DeMornay discovered it in her possession . . . Tom swallowed. He didn't want to think what the man would do to her. He must finish this search so he could protect her.

"Where upriver?" Tom glared.

Boyce tapped his cup, and Tom ordered more grog, though he hated what spirits did to a man. He would never put himself in that position again. The ill-conceived duel had been borne from the fruits of drink. Rourke had rescued him from certain death and taught him never to succumb to that temptation again.

The tavern girl filled Boyce's cup and once again asked if Tom would be joining in.

"No, thank you."

She looked disgruntled until Boyce asked her to leave the bottle.

Tom saw nothing good coming from that much liquor. "A cup is enough."

"I gots a mighty thirst, son," Boyce said. "Can't seem ta find my voice without somethin' ta wet the pipes."

Tom grudgingly paid for the bottle and gave the tavern maid a bit extra for her trouble. This time she smiled and winked at him. In years past, he would have talked with her, but no woman came close to Catherine.

"That'll be all."

She left with a pout.

Once Boyce had taken a gulp from his cup, Tom pressed the point. "Where upriver?"

Boyce shrugged. "How'd I know?"

"You've been on it, haven't you?"

Boyce's gaze darted toward the door and then around the

room. DeMornay wasn't here, naturally, but that glance coupled with the perspiration on Boyce's brow meant he feared someone. The captain or a crew member, no doubt. DeMornay was no sailor, not from what Pa had told him. The man needed the expertise of a skilled navigator and crew.

Tom leaned close and whispered, "No one will hear you."

Boyce wiped his mouth with the back of his hand. "Can't say."

"Can't say?" Agitated, Tom spat out the words in a harsh whisper. "It's my father's ship. DeMornay stole it, and I aim to get it back."

Boyce jerked backward and nearly fell off the tavern bench. "Run. Get away while ye can."

The startling resemblance to the Negro woman's plea caught Tom's attention. "Why?"

"The devil be in that man." Boyce crossed himself, though Tom suspected the man hadn't seen the inside of a church in decades.

"Why do you say that?"

Boyce leaned close, his fetid breath assaulting Tom's nostrils and leaving no question as to why the man had lost at least one tooth. "That ship hauls bad cargo. Don't look fer it. No, sir. Take my advice and get yourself outta here while ye can."

"Bad cargo?"

Boyce would say no more.

Tom prodded, "It's my father's ship."

"Ain't no more."

"It will be. The law will uphold a man's ownership. I have the bill of sale and enrollment certificate."

Boyce scoffed, "You think papers mean anything to a man like that?"

"They'll mean something to a judge."

Boyce shook his head slowly. "Why d'ya think that man gets away wid what he's doing?"

Tom didn't know exactly what DeMornay was doing, except that apparently it was illegal.

Boyce leaned close again. "Ain't no lawman or judge gonna take the word o' an outsider over one o' their own."

Fear skittered down his spine as he thought of Catherine. He should never have left her.

"Would he harm an innocent woman?"

"Woman? Thought ye wanted a ship."

"There's a woman involved."

Boyce shook his head again. "That's a bad business, there. Ye love her?"

The bold question gave Tom a start. Did he love her? The thought had never quite crossed his mind. "I'm very fond of her."

"Ye love her." Boyce whistled again. "Poor lad. All the worse for you."

"And her?" He couldn't shake the feeling that Catherine was in harm's way.

"She met 'im?"

"Yes."

Boyce grunted. "Too late, then. They always believe. Ain't never met one that didn't. He done swoop in, and afore ye know it they're his."

"Not Catherine. She's independent minded."

"Don't matter. They always fall."

Tom couldn't match Boyce's assertions with fact. DeMornay had no wife or even a mistress that Tom could detect. "There weren't any women with him."

"Oh, he don't keep 'em. He don't keep any of 'em long. One day they appear. Another day they disappear."

"Where do they go?"

Boyce again glanced toward the door. "Only one man knows, an' only a fool would ask 'im."

"DeMornay."

Boyce flinched. "All I'm sayin' is ye best steer clear, or you'll disappear like the rest of 'em."

"You're saying men vanish too?"

"Haven't ye listened to a thing I told ye?"

Tom's skin crawled. "You're saying men and women vanish from Black Oak?"

Boyce cringed. "Don't say that name."

"Why?"

"Ye don't understand, but ye will." Boyce scooped up the half-empty bottle. "Don't come asking anything more from me. I won't answer." He stood on somewhat wobbly legs.

Tom couldn't let Boyce go. This was the closest he'd come to finding his pa's ship. It could not slip from his fingers now.

He rose. "The ship is at Black Oak, isn't it?"

Boyce glared at him. "Dint I tell ye not ta say the name o' that place?"

"I must know. Lives depend on it."

Boyce hesitated and glanced again at the door. No one was there, and no one in the tavern gave them more than a cursory glance. Boyce stepped close enough to whisper and poked a finger into Tom's chest.

"If ye're fool enough ta risk yer head . . . heard say it's due back within the week."

"And then?"

"Gots ta pick up fresh cargo."

"Sugar?"

Boyce snorted. "Sugar." He cackled and moved away, waving a hand at him.

Tom desperately followed. "They do haul from the plantation, don't they?"

Boyce ignored him and plunged into a group of compatriots
who clapped him on the back and promised to relieve him of
the bottle he was carrying.

Tom stood rooted to the spot. Boyce had intended to frighten
him, but no rumor or superstition could scare Tom Worthington. The sailor's fears were doubtless enhanced by the rum.
Though questions remained, Tom had learned enough. The
Rachael Deare still sailed. Though Boyce had refused to divulge
the exact location that Pa's ship would be moored, he'd revealed
enough to determine Tom's next steps.

A week. The black ship, as Boyce referred to it, was due to
return within the week. By then Tom would be in place, ready to
greet it. Between now and then, he would meet with Catherine's
cousin and do all in his power to extract Catherine from De-
Mornay's grip so he could bring her back to Key West with him.

He clenched his fists as Boyce and his sailor friends roared
with laughter, possibly at Tom's expense. One thing was left
to settle, and it could prove most difficult of all. As skilled as
Tom was, he couldn't sail a schooner by himself. He needed a
crew. Given the undercurrent of fear that ran through Boyce,
hiring a crew would be no easy or inexpensive task. He fingered
the few coins in his pocket.

"Worthington!"

The familiar voice snapped Tom out of his thoughts. He
turned to the doorway, filled with the imposing figure of the
man he'd let down back in Key West.

"Captain." He swallowed. "What are you doing here?"

15

I be here ta dress you, miss."

Catherine blinked as Aurelia pulled back the curtains to allow the bright sunlight to stream into the room. Considering the heat and angle of the sun, it must be quite late.

"I've overslept again."

"Dat's what happens when ya creep around half de night day after day."

"You saw me?"

Instead of answering, the housekeeper hummed softly as she tugged open the doors of the large armoire. She selected a white muslin gown dotted with green and gold flowers and laid it on the bed. "This be better in de heat. A lady like you ain't used to it."

"Like me? An Englishwoman, do you mean?" Catherine wondered what sort of ideas about England filtered down to a slave on a Louisiana plantation. "What do you know about England?"

"I heard Massa Henry's papa—God rest his soul—talk 'bout

it bein' colder 'n ice. Didn't never understand why yo' mama din't come back."

"I heard they had a funeral for Maman and declared her dead."

Aurelia continued humming.

Catherine couldn't let this go. "She's not buried in the tomb here. Now you're saying Uncle Henri knew it too. Then who pretended to bury her, and why?"

"Wouldn't know. Come before my time."

"Then you didn't know Maman?"

Aurelia shook her head slowly. "She gone long 'fore I come here."

Of course. Aurelia had said she'd been here only a decade or so. But perhaps she knew some of Maman's beloved servants. Rufus, Winnie, and one she'd simply called Nurse still hung in the recesses of Catherine's memory. They were likely all gone, but she had to ask.

Aurelia selected a pair of slippers and shook her head when Catherine finished listing the names Maman had mentioned. "None of dem here now."

Catherine breathed out in disappointment. Perhaps she shouldn't have hoped so much for a link to the past. According to DeMornay, servants moved around more than she'd imagined. Maman had made it sound like the servants were so intertwined with the plantation and the family that they would always be there, like the sugarhouse and the pigeonniers.

"Where were you before you came here?"

The housekeeper clucked her tongue. "One plantation pretty much like 'nother, 'cepting de massa and de missus."

Catherine supposed that was true, though she'd hoped for the impossible, that this woman might be Elizabeth's nurse. "Then you've never been to Key West."

"How'd I git way off dere?" Aurelia snorted. "I cain't jess up and leave."

The reality of Aurelia's situation sank in. She'd come to Black Oak because she'd been bought. If she left, it would be because she'd been sold.

Aurelia hefted the petticoats onto the bed. "Let me git ya dressed."

Silence ensued while Aurelia performed her duties and Catherine stood where she was directed. The servant had deft fingers, and soon the underpinnings were complete.

"Did anyone from Key West ever come here?" Catherine prodded. "Or have you ever met another . . . servant . . . who came from there?"

Another pause. "Why'd ya think dat?"

"A friend, Elizabeth, misses her nurse, who was sold to a planter here."

"Wouldn't know 'bout dat."

The housekeeper's answer came too quickly. Catherine glanced at the woman, whose expression had gone blank. She would learn nothing more from her this morning.

Aurelia lifted the gown over Catherine's head and tugged it into place. Then her fingers hastened from button to button, securing the bodice. "Dere. Dat's de last of 'em. Sit now and I'll brush out yo' hair."

Catherine glanced at herself in the mirror before taking a seat. She looked fresh, though she felt anything but.

Aurelia deftly undid the plait that held Catherine's hair in place when she slept and began to brush. Knots came undone in her skilled hands without a single pinch.

"You've been a lady's maid," Catherine remarked.

"No, miss. I'm de housekeeper. Ain't been a missus here fo' years."

In the mirror's reflection, Catherine saw Aurelia's gaze dart to the door and back. Fear hung in the air, thick as the mosquitoes at dusk. Had the housekeeper heard DeMornay outside the room?

With a few quick twists, Aurelia worked Catherine's hair into a pretty knot, which she secured with pins. A few graceful tendrils framed her face.

"Would you be wantin' a cap?" Aurelia asked.

"No." Catherine despised them as a relic of a bygone age, best worn by elderly matrons. In this heat they would be intolerable. "This will do. Thank you."

"Very well, miss." Aurelia began to move away.

Catherine caught her arm. "One moment."

The whites of the housekeeper's eyes shone from her dark face as her every muscle tensed. "What you be needin'?"

Catherine loosened her grip and lowered her voice. "It's not what I need. I just want you to know that if you ever need to talk . . ." She let the rest go unsaid. Given Aurelia's warning upon their arrival, she would know what Catherine meant.

The woman's gaze dropped to the floor. "I best be gettin' back ta de cookhouse."

Aurelia slipped from the room, her steps hastened by fear. Catherine wondered what horrors had driven fear deep into the woman's soul. If only she could find a way to help.

⌀

Tom couldn't find any words as Captain Rourke O'Malley steered him out of the tavern.

"Well?" Rourke demanded. "The last place I expected to find one of my crew is in a New Orleans drinking house."

"What are you doing here?" Tom asked again. "I thought you were wrecking the *Allerton*."

"John has charge of the *Redemption*, and Rander is running

the crew on the *Windsprite*." Rourke glared at him and didn't release his grip on Tom's upper arm. "But that's not the point. You left my employment without notice."

"I asked—"

"And I denied."

"I left a letter with your wife."

"Letters are for cowards. A man gives notice face-to-face."

Tom felt awful. He hadn't done this the right way. Moreover, he'd just contributed to another man's sins by providing the temptation. Rourke must think the worst of him. "I'm sorry, sir. I'm not proud of the way I handled it, but I had to go. I couldn't let Catherine—uh, Miss Haynes—travel unprotected."

"Are you saying she is in that grogshop?"

"No! Never! She's at the plantation."

"Good. Then you did your part." Rourke's expression softened slightly, revealing he wasn't as angry as he'd first appeared. "But it doesn't explain why I found you frequenting a black hole of iniquity. You know where that path leads."

"I didn't drink one drop. But a tavern is the best place to get information from sailors and dockworkers."

Rourke released him. "What sort of information is so important that you left us shorthanded?"

"You could have easily replaced me."

"I could fill your spot, Tom, but I couldn't replace you."

That only made Tom feel worse. "I shouldn't have left when you needed me."

"No, you shouldn't have." Rourke's expression eased. "Thankfully, they don't need all three of our vessels on-site anymore."

Tom breathed out with relief. He hadn't cost his captain as much as he'd feared.

Rourke didn't relent. "I still expect you to tell me why you really left."

Tom rubbed his arm and swallowed. He hadn't told Rourke about his quest. He'd told no one until revealing it to Catherine. There was no sense keeping it secret now, especially from a man with the integrity of Rourke.

"I think I've found my father's stolen ship."

Rourke digested that a moment. "Explain. You told me your father is dead."

"He is, and the man who stole his ship and set him adrift in the ship's boat is to blame."

"Go on."

"This man told my father he was a Spanish nobleman. Don Luis Mornez. He's here."

"In New Orleans." Rourke sounded justifiably skeptical.

"At Catherine's family plantation. Except he now goes by the name Louis DeMornay. I'm certain it's him. He has the exact scar that Pa described, just below his left eye. Moreover, Catherine told me that a man fitting DeMornay's description arrived at her father's estate a couple months before this thief approached my father. She said he left in haste, and she later found an entry in the accounts referring to a man by the name DeMornay."

Rourke followed the train of thought faster than Tom could get it out. "And this man is at Catherine's family plantation."

"He's the manager."

Rourke looked around. "At the plantation where you left Miss Haynes."

Tom squirmed. "Leaving her was a mistake. I'm going back at once."

"I trust her family is there to protect her."

"That's another peculiar thing. There's not one family member on the plantation, just DeMornay and the slaves."

"Yet you left her there."

"She insisted. I couldn't convince her to leave. She's trying to figure out what's going on there. The place is dilapidated, and there aren't many slaves, at least not that I could see. DeMornay says they're harvesting the farthest sugarcane fields. They didn't show up at the main house the day I was there."

Rourke pondered that for a moment. "All very believable, yet you think he's lying?"

"I do."

"What reason would he have to lie?"

Tom didn't mention the uneasy feeling he had about the man, especially after speaking with the seamen ashore. "DeMornay pretended he'd never heard of my father or his ship. Yet that's not what I learned here on the wharves. DeMornay has a ship, and it could well be Pa's."

"You would recognize it?"

"I know every plank and seam, every place where she leaked, every gouge and mark. I'd know her in an instant, and the moment she comes back to port, I'll be able to identify her for the authorities."

"You have a bill of sale or enrollment certificate?"

"I have both, as well as the disposition of the legal proceedings when Pa returned. I have all the proof I need, but there are some who think the judges here have a local bias."

Rourke nodded. "We'll cross that bridge when we get to it. First, we need to find the ship. When is she due in?"

"Within the week. Time enough for me to check on Catherine."

"We can pay a call on Miss Haynes and perhaps search the shore on our way there."

"We?" Tom finally caught what Rourke was saying. "Who all is here?"

"Enough crew to sail the *James Patrick*. Perhaps my presence will convince this plantation manager to divulge what he knows."

Tom doubted any single person could sway DeMornay. The man made deception an art. But Tom did relish his mentor's strength and integrity. Perhaps Rourke could sort fact from fiction.

"Who knows what we'll find," he murmured.

"Answers, I hope. We'll leave at once. The *James Patrick* is moored nearby."

Tom began to follow, but his business wasn't finished here. "First I need to pay a call on Catherine's cousin Henry Lafreniere. I promised her I would tell him of her arrival."

"Good. We'll meet later aboard ship, unless you want me to go with you."

"No." Tom was certain of that much. He must handle this meeting with great care. Henry Lafreniere might not even know of Catherine's existence.

༄

To Catherine's surprise, DeMornay joined her for a late breakfast. She had taken the light meal on the gallery, which enjoyed the breezes off the river. Catherine had pulled aside the curtains so that she might see the vast lawn extending from the house to the road paralleling the river. Just five days ago she and Tom had walked up that road, uncertain of what they would find. Today she was no more certain.

"Good morning." DeMornay slipped into the chair opposite her. "You are lovely as springtime this morning."

His eyes drank her in a little too familiarly.

She looked away. "Surely you have work to attend to. Harvest, for instance."

His chuckle carried no mirth. "I can see you are a woman who never tarries. You will soon learn that life beside the river moves at a much slower pace than in your native land, where a season's harvest might be ruined with an early frost."

"You have no bad weather here, then."

"Touché, my dear, but the sky is clear and the winds cool from the northwest. No storms will ruin the harvest this day."

The endearment made her cringe. "Tomorrow is another day, with challenges of its own."

"Then why worry about it today?"

"I simply see no purpose in procrastination."

"An admirable view, but we can at least agree to enjoy each other's company for the moment." DeMornay reached across the table and caught her hand before she realized what he was doing. "You are too lovely to ignore."

Catherine withdrew her hand and clenched the napkin on her lap. His civility was overdone, as if he was trying too hard to direct her attention away from something. Since they'd been discussing the harvest, she assumed that was it.

"You are expecting additional workers to arrive for the harvest?"

She watched his reaction. He gave away nothing.

"Is it always business with you? I have never met so single-minded a woman."

"This is now my home." The word caught in her mouth, but she got it out. "As a Lafreniere descendant, I am naturally concerned with everything that relates to the family's livelihood."

"As I've already told you, your cousin Henry has given me complete authority to manage the plantation. If he is pleased with my management, then surely you can be."

She couldn't. "Speaking of my cousin, have you received any response to your letter telling him of my arrival?"

"Not yet." His expression was taut.

"Then I ought to pay him a visit. I saw a carriage parked under the house. Might it take me into the city?" At the same time, she might locate Tom, whose absence had made the days pass slowly.

DeMornay sat back ever so slightly, but it was enough for her to realize that she'd surprised him. He'd expected her earlier refusal to visit Henry Lafreniere to mark the end of the subject. That made her all the more determined to see her cousin. Perhaps his relationship with his manager wasn't as well understood as DeMornay claimed it was.

"Now, now, my dear Catherine. Why the hurry? I'm certain your cousin will arrive the moment he is free from business matters. There's no reason for you to endure the grueling carriage ride into the city."

"How long could it be? Surely no more than a few hours."

His gaze narrowed. "The road is poor, the way treacherous in places."

"Then I shall take the ferry."

"Equally treacherous. Moreover, the city is no place for a beautiful woman like yourself without the protection of a strong man."

"Such as yourself."

He nodded slightly. "I would be glad to escort you after the harvest. That is your primary concern, is it not?"

"Yes, but how long will the harvest take?"

"Two weeks for the bulk of it. Perhaps sooner, depending on circumstances."

"Such as the arrival of labor."

His smile grated on her nerves. "You are astute, Miss Catherine. Your father taught you well."

"Papa also taught me to stand my ground. I wish for a carriage to take me into the city this afternoon."

"But did you not hear my concerns?"

"I heard and took them under advisement, but as a Lafreniere by blood, I insist on the use of a carriage. I will accept no excuses." To emphasize the point, she stared straight into his black eyes.

This time he paused a little longer, though his smile never wavered.

"That will be most difficult, Miss Haynes." He reached into an inner pocket of his coat and withdrew an ivory envelope, which he handed to her.

In a glance she saw it had been sent by Judge Graham. She turned it over to break the seal only to discover it was already broken. "You opened this?"

He flicked a hand, as if it was of no consequence. "I didn't realize it was addressed to you. How would I know you had already made acquaintance with a neighbor?"

She gritted her teeth. The damage was done. Hopefully the judge hadn't written anything personal. She slipped the single piece of paper from the envelope and scanned the brief message.

"I've been invited to a dance. In Titchwood." Her pulse accelerated at the thought of leaving the plantation for even a short while. "It would be good to meet our neighbors. In fact, I should welcome such society."

"It is merely a country dance in celebration of the harvest. Simple, perhaps, compared to what you are accustomed to experiencing."

"It will be delightful."

"It is tonight."

"Tonight!" Catherine had missed that detail. "Why did the invitation arrive only now?" Unless it hadn't. Unless DeMornay had withheld it. Judge Graham said no one visited Black Oak. Perhaps it was also the case that no one from Black Oak attended social gatherings at nearby plantations and towns.

DeMornay gave her nothing. "One can only assume it was delayed somewhere along the route."

"From Titchwood to here? It is not a long distance."

DeMornay's taut smile never wavered. "Some darkies are indolent. Regardless of the delay, the dance is tonight."

She rose to her feet. "In that case, there is much to do to prepare. You will ensure I have use of the carriage."

"Of course, my dear." He leaned back, content as a cat stretching after a nap. "We shall leave at seven o'clock."

"We?" She choked on the word.

"The mistress of Black Oak must have an escort." He swept forth his hand. "It will be my pleasure."

The brief glimpse of freedom vanished.

16

P lease sit." Henry Lafreniere motioned to a ponderous leather-cushioned chair, appropriate in an attorney's office.

Tom stifled his aversion to the occupation. Attorneys had claimed they would help Pa but ended up taking everything. They'd fought over the spoils like the Roman soldiers had with Jesus's clothing.

Henry Lafreniere bore little resemblance to Catherine. From the high widow's peak carved from thinning brown hair to the bland gray eyes, he revealed none of the spirit that infused Catherine's every movement. Lafreniere removed his spectacles and leaned back in his chair, the gray silk waistcoat clean and unrumpled.

"My clerk informed me that you are here about some long-lost cousin."

"Catherine Haynes."

"That is a married name?" Lafreniere twirled the bow of the spectacles between his fingers, sending the lenses side to side. "I'm not familiar with anyone named Haynes."

"No, she is not married. She's from England."

"England? We have no connection to that country. My family has lived here for generations. Before that, we came from France."

Was it possible Lafreniere didn't know about Catherine? Had he believed the tale that Lisette Lafreniere had died after her grand tour and was buried in the family crypt? Tom judged Lafreniere to be in his mid- to late thirties. He would have been a child when Catherine's mother supposedly died. He might never have heard the truth.

"Her mother, Lisette Lafreniere, married an Englishman."

Lafreniere smirked. "Lisette Lafreniere is interred in the family crypt."

"A casket might be there, but Catherine assures me that her mother is buried in England."

"I see, though perhaps you do not. Miss Haynes must be a fortune seeker. We see them from time to time." He brushed at the air. "They are soon sent their way."

"She's no fortune seeker." Yet a worm of doubt wiggled into his mind. What proof did he have beyond her comely face and assertions? "She has her baptismal record."

"False. They always are. Would you care for a cigar?"

"No, thank you."

Lafreniere opened a box and extracted a single fat cigar. "I can take a look at her so-called document." He cut off the end of the cigar and lit it. "I'll soon find errors proving it a fake and put an end to her ambitions."

A cloud of foul-smelling smoke made Tom's eyes burn. "It isn't false." Catherine had shown nothing to indicate she was posing as an heiress to claim an inheritance. Given the state of the plantation, there wasn't much worth inheriting. "I don't see her seeking to inherit. She wants to make the plantation profitable."

Lafreniere's gaze narrowed. "What does she know about Black Oak, or any other plantation, for that matter? Nothing. As a woman, she couldn't possibly know what is or isn't profitable."

"She can see. The plantation certainly doesn't look prosperous."

Lafreniere tapped lightly on his cigar. "Is that her assessment or yours?"

"Both."

"You are familiar with the operation of a sugarcane plantation?"

Tom felt the blood creep up his neck. "No, but the buildings ought to look tended. Whitewashed at the very least. And there should be more help around." He could name a dozen things, but that was sufficient to alert an absentee landowner. "Maybe you haven't been out there recently and don't know its current condition."

Lafreniere blew out a plume of smoke. "Your speech marks you as a northerner. You know nothing of our ways." He leaned forward. "Since you are Miss Haynes's advocate, I suspect she too lacks any knowledge. If this supposed heiress has something to say to me, she can do so in person without an intermediary. Please ask her to call on me. Alone. Meanwhile, I suggest you return home, Mr. Worthington."

That was the third time Tom had been warned to leave, all by different people. He ought to head back to Key West with Rourke and leave well enough alone. Catherine's future was not his business. She had given him no reason to think they had a future except for the way she'd clung to him in the pigeonnier. Even though he'd fought the urge to kiss her, he'd felt her desperate passion.

She was afraid.

That was reason enough to stay. But there was also the matter of his father's ship. The black ship, as Boyce had called it. Perhaps Lafreniere knew of it.

The attorney blew out another cloud of smoke. "If that's all, I am a busy man." After drumming his fingers on the desktop, he stood and began to make his way around the desk.

Tom did not rise. "Does the plantation have its own ship?"

Lafreniere halted. The pause was tiny but enough to tell Tom that this question had caught the wily solicitor by surprise. "Why would it?"

"To ship out the sugar?"

Lafreniere smirked. "There are plenty of barges and steam tugs willing to haul sugar."

"For a fee."

"Less than the cost of maintaining a ship and hiring a crew."

Lafreniere had a point. Yet the earlier hesitation told Tom he'd hit upon something that Lafreniere didn't want to discuss. Further questions would only make the man more wary. Something peculiar was going on at Black Oak, something that neither DeMornay nor Lafreniere wanted him to discover. Something that could very well put Catherine in danger.

Tom slowly rose. "You make a good point."

Lafreniere's expression stayed taut, his gaze still narrowed. "Why do you ask, Mr. Worthington?"

"I am a sea captain."

"Ah." At last Lafreniere relaxed. "Seeking employment? Or a fortune, like Miss Haynes? I assure you that neither is to be found here."

"So I see."

Disappointed, Tom bid Lafreniere farewell and stepped out into the sultry air. The bustling streets filled with pedestrians, hawkers, peddlers, carriages, and horses did nothing to ease his discomfort. Something was very wrong at Black Oak, and Catherine was stuck in the midst of it.

⁓✦⁓

"Are many dances held here at Black Oak?" Catherine asked Aurelia as the maid arranged her curls for the evening.

"Ain't never been none since I got here." Aurelia glanced toward the door even though DeMornay had not returned from the fields yet.

During yet another long afternoon of unsuccessfully looking for items on Tom's list, Catherine had come to the conclusion that none of them were on the premises. Tom must be wrong about DeMornay stealing his father's ship. That made her feel a tiny bit better about tonight's arrangements.

"Of course you will come with me to Titchwood." Often Catherine had brought a maid when no family member was available to escort her. This evening she needed someone as a buffer between her and DeMornay.

Aurelia's nimble fingers stilled. "No, miss."

Catherine fought a wave of panic. "Then who? Surely not just Mr. DeMornay and myself."

"Walker see after you and drive de carriage."

"No footman?" Catherine had scraped to save every shilling at Deerford, but she always had both driver and footman when taking the carriage.

"Don't know. Ain't never seen Massa take out de carriage for a ball."

"It's not a ball. It's a simple country dance. I insist you join me."

"Massa won't like it."

"Master?" Aurelia's wording perplexed her. "Don't you mean 'the manager'? Mr. Lafreniere is your master, not Mr. DeMornay."

201

Aurelia finished Catherine's hair and adjusted the ruffles on her regal blue gown. "Don't never see Massa Henry."

"Never? Surely he visits the plantation at least once a year."

"No, miss."

"Wasn't he raised here?"

"Don't know. I weren't here den."

Catherine was getting nowhere with this. Clearly the family had become deeply estranged if the son never visited his father, even at his deathbed. Deep sorrow welled as she recalled her papa's gradual decline.

"Then there truly is no family," she whispered. The deepest hope of her heart was crushed.

Aurelia set down the curling tongs. "Dey go off here and dere, like boys is wont to do."

"I have no experience with that, never having had a brother." Catherine shifted her perspective to another point that had troubled her since she arrived. "What is it like living here? How are the servants treated?"

Aurelia fiddled with Catherine's already completed hair. "Don't know about dat, but if I was you, I'd be gettin' gone right soon."

Catherine ignored the repeated warning and returned to the subject Aurelia was avoiding. "You know how your family is treated."

Aurelia busied herself tidying Catherine's bottles and jars of creams and liniments.

"If I'm to be mistress of Black Oak," Catherine continued, "I want to do everything possible to ensure contentment, even happiness."

"Happiness ain't for dis life." Each word was coated with bitterness.

Again Catherine wondered about Aurelia's past. "How did you come to be here? Who brought you?"

The housekeeper's face hardened. "Done come by ship."

Could it have been Tom's father's ship?

"How long ago?"

"Ten, twelve years. Cain't say exactly. We don't count da passin' days like white folk do. We count days ta glory."

Aurelia's words tugged at Catherine's heart. With no hope here on earth, those like Aurelia must cling to God's promises of a mansion prepared for those who love Jesus. "One day you could be free. Great Britain freed the slaves."

"What man can free someone's soul?"

"A courageous man can write laws—"

Aurelia's derisive snort cut her off. "Laws don't mean nothin'."

"They do. It can take time, but the enslaved peoples are now free throughout the British empire. One day that will be true for you too. America will see reason."

"Change come wid great cost."

Catherine couldn't deny that. The upheavals, the poverty, the repercussions were serious. "But right must prevail."

Aurelia didn't respond, and Catherine began to wonder if such drastic change could ever happen in this woman's remaining years. The streaks of gray meant she was not a young woman. Her worn frame, once tall and strong, bespoke a life of hardship. Lives without hope wore down quickly.

This place seemed caught outside time. Would tonight's dance be the same? Catherine's nerves fluttered as Aurelia put away her day dress.

"What should I expect tonight? Will there be many people there? What sort of dancing? Are ladies expected to accept every invitation? What is considered proper?" She knew nothing of this society. What was considered mannerly in Staffordshire might be offensive in Louisiana. Why had she agreed to attend?

Aurelia closed the armoire doors. "If dat be all, miss." Her gaze remained rooted to the floor.

Catherine could expect no help from her. Aurelia likely had no experience with Louisiana society. Catherine must muddle through and hope the neighbors would grant her leniency.

She sighed. "I suppose so."

Aurelia turned to go but paused at the door. "You oughta wear jewels."

What a peculiar statement. "I have no jewels. All Maman's jewelry is gone." Except the pearl earrings.

"He has some."

"He?"

The housekeeper didn't answer. She simply slipped from the room.

An answer wasn't needed. The only person Aurelia could have meant was DeMornay. But why would a plantation manager have jewels? He received only wages. Unless he skimmed profits from the plantation. She recalled the "corrected" accounts.

There was another possibility. The strongbox. What if the lost inheritance was Maman's jewels? What if DeMornay had stolen them? Was that what Papa regretted losing?

The plantation manager had not yet returned.

She slipped onto the veranda. Bumping on the shutters the other night had opened them. She could get into the office before DeMornay returned and learn once and for all what was in that strongbox.

DeMornay lifted her gloved hand to his lips and pressed a kiss to it. Catherine fought a wave of revulsion. She had failed to get into the study before DeMornay returned from the fields. The shutters had not sprung open this time, and before she could find something to pry at the latch, he had ridden up on horseback.

Gibson had run into the yard and taken the horse. DeMornay didn't even acknowledge the boy. Catherine had slipped behind the veil of a curtain and watched Gibson walk the horse to the stables. The young boy, perhaps nine or ten years of age, had a proud, erect carriage. His coloring was lighter than that of Aurelia. The younger boy, Hunt, tagged along after Gibson like a puppy. No one had called them brothers, but the resemblance was too great to think otherwise.

Tonight the children were nowhere in sight. Neither had Tom returned or sent word in the four days he'd been gone. Had he returned to Key West? Had he fallen into danger? Why no word? She'd expected something, even a note thrown through her open bedroom window. Nothing. She was alone.

Except for DeMornay, who at last released her hand.

"You are more beautiful than any woman I have ever seen," he said. "Your hair the color of a fine stallion, your eyes like emeralds."

The last caught her attention. Aurelia had hinted that he had jewels. "You have seen emeralds?"

She'd hoped to catch him in a falsehood, but DeMornay was too quick.

"An expression, my dear, though I have seen an emerald's fire. I go often to the city and have entered jewelers' shops on business for my employer."

"My cousin buys emeralds for his wife?" The plantation must be more profitable than it appeared.

"No, but the jeweler had one on display."

"Oh." Somehow DeMornay always managed to find a plausible explanation. "I have never owned an emerald." But Maman had. The sudden memory flashed through her mind. Maman had held the pendant up to the light so Catherine could look through it.

"Do you see the mark on one corner?" Maman had prompted.

Catherine nodded while her mother explained that it was a flaw. "My mother, your grandmère, gave it to me when I was a little older than you are now. She showed me the flaw and told me to always remember that only God is perfect. Nothing and no one who will ever live on this earth can claim perfection except Jesus. From the first, your papa admitted his flaws, and that is how I knew he was the man destined to be my husband."

Catherine had measured every suitor by the same standard. If he interested her in any way, did he admit his failings? Thus far, none had. Even Tom, who made her pulse race, did not see his flaws. Not that he had many.

Her thoughts fled at DeMornay's next words. "Perhaps you soon will have your emerald, my dear."

The endearment made her shiver. How she wished Tom were here. She cast a prayer into the heavens. *Bring him to me, Lord.*

"You are chilled," he exclaimed. "Aurelia, fetch a shawl for Miss Haynes. The finest one."

Catherine doubted Aurelia would dare return with anything that did not match the finery of Catherine's blue silk ball gown.

DeMornay stepped into the unused chamber located directly off the entrance and returned with a glass of dark liquid. Spirits, no doubt. She had smelled them on him before, though he never drank enough to lose his head.

Aurelia brought Catherine's fine white shawl shot through with gold threads. It sparkled in the lamplight.

"Thank you, Aurelia," Catherine said after the housekeeper helped her put it on. Though DeMornay frowned on kindness toward the servants, she would continue, even before him.

Tonight he did not reprimand her.

206

"Shall we go, then?" DeMornay held out his arm.

Though she hesitated to take it, she had no other choice. There was only DeMornay. Tom had not bounded to the door in answer to her prayer. She must accept that she would arrive on the arm of hired help. That was certainly not a proper escort, even if he did assume greater authority than most plantation managers. What would people think? If Titchwood was anything like home, the rumors would soon fly.

She did not under any circumstances want to be linked romantically to DeMornay. How she longed for Tom's presence. An ache settled over her heart and refused to leave. What would he tell her to do? Refuse to go. Lock herself in her room if necessary. But that would solve nothing. As possible heir, she must behave like the mistress of Black Oak. That sent a fleeting smile across her lips. Very well. That's what she would do.

Once they'd settled in the carriage and the wheels began to roll, she took command. "Naturally, you cannot escort me into the dance."

His black eyes stared at her, and nothing issued from his lips.

"It is not proper when we are not in any way attached." She spoke more forcefully than she felt. "Our stations cannot ever be considered equal, since I am of Lafreniere blood. I must uphold the standards of my upbringing."

His lips twisted ever so slightly. "Do you wish me to follow at a safe distance?"

His comment made her wishes sound callous. Yet propriety was essential when one was first introduced to new neighbors. This was her chance to learn what they really thought of Black Oak and DeMornay. She did not need him hanging on every conversation.

So she lifted her chin, determined to have this her way. "I appreciate your understanding. This is how it must be."

"I will not allow any harm to come to you."

"That would be your duty."

"But you wish not to be seen with me."

She steeled herself not to flinch. "I do not want anyone to misconstrue our relationship. I am a Lafreniere. You are the plantation manager."

"If you are concerned about others' opinions, I can inform you of them now, before we arrive."

"I wish to determine that for myself. You will learn that I seldom take the word or opinion of others as fact."

DeMornay chuckled. "I have already learned that, but this time perhaps it will be to my advantage. Of course I will heed your wishes, but do not expect me to leave you to the vultures. Should anything untoward occur, I will sweep you off to safety."

Apparently DeMornay intended to extend the cage well past Black Oak borders.

"I am no fragile dove, Mr. DeMornay. I have undergone my Season in London and am well acquainted with the wiles of men." She paused, letting that thought sink into his mind. "Nothing escapes me. Nothing."

Hopefully he understood that arrow was meant for him.

17

Tom was glad to leave the city. The light winds made their journey upriver a slow one. Though the *James Patrick* was a swift sloop with copious sail and a shallow draft, they battled current and wind direction that forced them to tack from side to side. The relatively short distance would take until well past nightfall.

The slow progress also gave them ample time to view the ragged shoreline buttressed by levees. The springtime river clearly flooded over the lands where the levees were low or had failed, and planters kept the houses far from the riverbanks. All manner of vessels dotted the shores. Many were steam powered and paddle wheels. They weren't subject to the vagaries of the wind, like sailing craft.

"Keep a lookout for a black clipper ship," Tom told Rourke. He itched to pull out his spyglass, but he was manning the wheel.

"Black hull?"

"She might even have black sails."

"Do you know its name?"

Tom shook his head. "Boyce never told me that. I doubt they'd keep it the *Rachael Deare*. But I'll recognize its lines."

Though Rourke looked skeptical, he shouted the order up to Jules, who was perched in the lookout. "But most of all watch out for snags and logs."

They'd already come close to hitting one of those.

"Shoal!" Jules called down almost at once. He pointed to larboard, and Tom steered in the opposite direction.

Rounding this shoal took them close to the starboard bank. As they drew near, Tom realized that the shoreline wasn't as unbroken as it had appeared. A small cut led off the main waterway, creating a miniature harbor. The perfect place to hide a ship. The trees were tall there and would conceal even the mast of a sizable sailing vessel.

He turned toward the mouth of the cut.

"Where are you going?" Rourke demanded.

"To that little cove. It would be perfect for hiding a ship."

Rourke lifted his spyglass, peered at the shore, and then collapsed it with a snap. "You think it's there?"

"We haven't seen it yet, and you heard what the stevedores said, that it had come upriver earlier today. Probably while I was sitting in Lafreniere's office."

"Perhaps they were wrong. Boyce did say it wouldn't arrive for a week."

"He said it was due within the week. That's entirely different. Besides, it won't hurt to look."

"Unless we run aground. It'll take a lot of work to kedge us off a sandbar."

Tom had helped in his share of kedging operations, usually for a stranded vessel that they'd hoped to salvage. If the master insisted on being hauled off the reef, they would use anchors and line to ever so slowly winch the ship free. On the ocean, the rise and fall of the tide had to be taken into account. If the ship had grounded at low tide, high tide might bring relief or at least an easier procedure. Here, there was no chance of rising water except due to rain. It hadn't rained more than a smattering here and there since he and Catherine had arrived.

Catherine. The thought of her almost made him forget his father's ship.

She was stuck in the house with DeMornay. Every moment delayed meant one more minute in the man's clutches. On the other hand, Tom had waited ten long years to avenge his father. It was finally within reach. He must chance looking in the cove.

It would take only a few minutes longer. Surely she could hold out.

⁓

In spite of Catherine's wishes, DeMornay stuck to her like a scratchy burr. Oh, he allowed her to enter the hall first and greet her neighbors, but he followed on her heels and made the introductions. Anyone could easily assume he was courting her. His overly solicitous manner only made things worse. Soon the glances her way had clouded or become suspicious.

She could think of no way out.

At first, the younger gentlemen begged a dance, but once the quartet began playing, none of them approached her. Apparently their interest had been corrected by concerned relations.

"Would you care to dance, Miss Haynes?" DeMornay bowed ever so slightly and extended his hand.

At least he hadn't used any familiarities when addressing her, but she feared it was only a matter of time. Dancing together would both encourage the suit that he was apparently making and the rumors that were doubtless forming.

"No, thank you. I don't care to dance."

He retracted his hand. "I'm amazed you insisted on attending if you do not dance."

"It's an opportunity to meet my neighbors."

If only she could speak to them without DeMornay listening to every word. She fiddled with the clasp on her bag. How could she get away from him long enough to speak to someone—anyone—in peace?

"Shall I take you home?" he asked.

She shook her head. That would not help her purpose. If no one would come to her, she must go to them—once she'd freed herself from her jailer. "I would like some punch, however. It is quite hot in here."

Since they were standing on the opposite side of the room from the punch bowl, he would have to step out of earshot.

He must have realized that at the same moment, for his expression tightened. He held out his arm. "Of course. Allow me to escort you."

She gritted her teeth. Would he never give her a moment alone? She fanned her face. "I believe I shall sit."

An elderly gentleman drew near. "Then allow me to lead you to an open chair that my wife is saving." It was Judge Graham.

Catherine beamed at him. "I would be much obliged." She took his arm. "Perhaps Mrs. Graham would like punch also. Would you fetch two glasses, Mr. DeMornay?"

Even his stoic expression couldn't hide his annoyance.

Without waiting for a response, she and the judge moved to a small grouping of chairs. Thankfully, DeMornay did not follow.

The judge, however, guided her slightly to the left. "Would you care to take a turn on the veranda? The night air is cooler."

"Thank you. I would like that very much." She glanced back to see DeMornay navigating through the dancers. His back was to her.

"Perhaps we might escape while your shadow is occupied," the judge suggested.

"Lead the way."

He whisked her through a hallway just a few steps away and out of view of DeMornay. Moments later, they exited the building onto a broad veranda populated by a few couples who hung in the shadows. A single lamp lit the doorway. None illuminated the grounds, where the carriages waited. The drivers gathered on the far side of the conveyances, laughing and jesting and sharing tales.

"The far corner is unoccupied," the judge noted, "if it doesn't trouble you to spend a moment or two in the company of an older man."

Catherine laughed. "An older and happily married man, if my observations are correct."

"They are." He directed her toward the corner of the veranda. "From here we have a view of both the rear door and anyone approaching from the front."

Though he named no one, she knew who he meant.

Once they settled in the corner, she asked, "Might I ask how a manager can gain control of a plantation? Is it common?"

"It's not uncommon for an owner to place confidence in his manager. However, most planters live on-site."

"Not my cousin Henry Lafreniere."

"Ah, your cousin, is he?"

She nodded. "My mother and Uncle Henri were siblings, though he was older than her by a decade."

"I see. Then they were not close."

Catherine thought back. "Maman said he was selfish and ambitious. She wanted nothing to do with him."

The judge nodded. "Men—and women—can change over time."

"I hope so, but can they change their true nature?"

Judge Graham chuckled. "A good question that many have

asked." He sobered. "Miss Haynes, I believe I have something that belongs to you."

"To me? Did I leave something behind on the ferry?"

"No, no. Nothing like that. Your uncle left a document in my care, to be given to you if you ever arrived at Black Oak."

Her jaw dropped. "Then he knew of me."

"Apparently your mother sent letters to her mother."

"Maman," Catherine whispered. "Then they knew. All that charade about a tomb, and they knew she was alive."

"I suspect so, but the charade, as you call it, had already taken place."

Catherine sighed and closed her eyes against the foolishness of the situation. If only Grandmama or even Uncle Henri had acknowledged the truth, this schism in the family might never have occurred. The family would still control the plantation and would not have given authority to a man who did not merit it.

"That's why you invited me to the dance."

"It is," the judge responded.

"You have the document with you?"

"It is too large for you to hide on your person—and from your shadow." The judge glanced toward the rear entrance. "Perhaps you could come to my office."

"Not without DeMornay. He follows me everywhere."

"Then there is no time when you're alone?"

It took only a moment for her to answer. "In the late morning. By then he has ridden out to the sugarhouse and far fields to check on the workers."

"Then I will meet you at Black Oak during that time. Tomorrow?"

She nodded. "Can you tell me now if I have any claim to part of Black Oak?"

He shook his head. "Later. In the daylight."

Catherine looked into the inky blackness that surrounded them. Anyone might be listening, especially DeMornay.

The judge stepped deeper into the darkness. "Good evening, Miss Haynes. You would do well not to mention our conversation to anyone."

The moment he left, DeMornay arrived. "It's not wise to go outdoors alone."

Though it might have been caution from a caring relation, from DeMornay it only tightened the chains binding her.

❧

"This is it." Tom perched on the gunwale, ready to jump from the *James Patrick* to the deck of the black ship. "It's my father's ship. I'm sure of it."

"It's growing dark, and you haven't seen the ship in ten years. You were much younger then." Rourke had expressed skepticism from the moment Tom insisted they explore the cove.

"I'd know the *Rachael Deare* anywhere. It's her."

The *James Patrick* drew near. Another couple feet and Tom could make the leap.

"Ahoy!" Rourke called out.

Tom whipped around. "Why did you do that?"

"What if someone's aboard?"

"There isn't anyone, or they would have come on deck the moment we approached." The crew of the *James Patrick* had been as noisy as a New Orleans street. Rourke's shout sealed that the ship was unoccupied.

Tom sprang off the gunwale and landed on the black ship's deck.

No one came racing above decks to challenge him. Nonetheless, Tom kept one hand on his dagger.

"She's moored to the trees ashore," he reported. "Probably anchored as well."

"What do you intend to do?" Rourke called across the narrow gap.

Soon the crew of the *James Patrick* would have the two ships lashed together, as if undergoing a salvage operation.

"Sail her out of here." That response came to mind first, though Tom had no idea what he would do then.

"And leave Miss Haynes to her own defenses?" Rourke pointed out.

Tom swallowed his disappointment. He mustn't act rashly. He needed to take everything into account.

"The owner might take offense," Rourke added, "and send the law after you."

"Then he will put his own thievery on display. I have the documents proving Pa owned this ship."

Rourke crossed to join Tom aboard the black ship. "Suppose the thief is no longer the owner?"

That possibility had never dawned on Tom. Mornez—or DeMornay, if that was his true name—might have sold the vessel. Except . . .

"Boyce all but said that DeMornay is the owner." He stared at the huge tree just inland from the riverbank. It looked familiar. At last he recognized it as the blackened oak that gave the Lafreniere plantation its name. "Moreover, we're practically on Black Oak plantation. If I'm not mistaken, that's the tree marking the boundary. This is Pa's ship."

"Then why hide it now, all these years later? The landing is a short distance away."

"Because DeMornay knows I'm here and will look for it."

"Or this cove offers better protection than the landing," Rourke mused.

Tom bristled at Rourke continuing to offer alternatives. "I can show you proof, a mark I made when a lad."

"You think it would still be there?"

"Even Pa never found it." Tom moved to the quarterdeck. Railings would be sanded top and bottom. Not the underside of the bottom step. He dropped to the deck and lay down to examine it. "Can I use your lantern?"

Rourke handed it over.

Tom had to hold the light close to make out the initials he had carved into the wood as a boy. *TW*, with the *W* upside down atop the *T* like a crown.

He scooted aside. "It's there. My initials."

He explained the configuration to Rourke, who took a look.

The man groaned as he rolled to a sitting position. "Then it is your father's ship, but you can't stoop to stealing it."

"Stealing from a thief isn't stealing."

Rourke got to his feet. "Is that what the Good Book says?"

Tom knew better. Theft was theft in God's eyes. No conditions.

"There's nothing you can do tonight anyway," Rourke pointed out. "We don't know these waters well enough to take an unknown vessel downriver in the dark."

"You expect me to leave Pa's ship when I've just found it?" The very idea galled Tom. "It's been ten years. I can't just leave."

"Can't you? What is more important? Doing what's right or ensuring justice on your terms?"

Something pricked Tom's conscience. He shook it off. "Justice has gone unserved for too long. From what I've heard, folks around here will welcome real justice."

"They will appreciate it even more when they can see that justice carried out before their eyes, not in the dead of night."

Sometimes Rourke could be too overbearing.

"I have to do this," Tom insisted.

Rourke clapped a hand on his shoulder. "I understand, but you can't sail this ship by yourself, and I won't lend you any of my crew. We will take this to the proper authority."

"By then it could be too late. Even now DeMornay might be planning to move the ship."

"Then we will find it, but we must not stoop to thievery."

"He destroyed my father."

"Will taking this ship bring your father back?"

"No, but—"

Rourke cut him off with a single uplifted finger. "To whom is your allegiance, Tom? No man can serve two masters. You know that well."

"I'm not after money." But Tom knew what Rourke meant. Though the Scripture referred to the love of money, it could apply to anything that took precedence over God. Such as revenge. "It's not a sin to seek justice."

"How do you plan to find it?"

Tom ran a hand along the well-polished rail. He'd looked for Pa's ship for so long. Now that he'd found it, Rourke was asking him to give it up.

"You know the right course," Rourke urged, "and where the wrong one leads."

He would not demand that Tom abandon his vengeful plans. Instead, he laid out the consequences.

Tom's resolve began to crumble. "Prison, pain, death."

"Seek life, son." Rourke added the final blow. "Miss Haynes needs you."

18

Catherine paced before the windows of her darkened bedroom. The evening's events had left her too curious to sleep. What document could the judge possibly have for her? Did it have to do with inheritance or something else entirely?

DeMornay had answered her questions with unusual frankness on the carriage ride home. Henry was an attorney by trade. He needed to do business in the city and thus had left the plantation to DeMornay's care. His younger brother, Emile, commanded a regiment in Tennessee. He too had no interest in the plantation. There were no other cousins.

Catherine recalled Maman's regret. She had missed her mother, Catherine's grandmère. She was lonely. She had chosen to live in a foreign land and lost her family as a consequence. Catherine had come to a foreign land hoping to regain that family.

Memories swirled with the exotic scents and sounds of the dance. Though DeMornay had called it a country dance, it bore no resemblance to the pastime she had enjoyed on occasion.

The dances were different and the ladies a swirl of bright colors. Gaudy even. Other than the initial greetings, only the judge spoke to her. The rest talked *of* her—she was sure of that—but none extended a hand of friendship.

So different from Key West, where the citizens opened their homes to her and the other passengers on the *Justinian*. Just thinking of Elizabeth brought a smile to her lips.

"What would you do?" she whispered into the darkness.

The night air could not answer. Even Aurelia, if she lurked in the shadows, did not betray that she'd heard. No, the night carried no comfort of human voice.

Restlessness had plagued her days and tormented her nights. How she longed to speak to Tom or Elizabeth. One day in Key West surpassed a week at Black Oak, and that troubled her. Though DeMornay had softened toward her, even insisting Maman's portrait hang above the salon fireplace, she could not shake the sense of foreboding.

How long must she wait? Days had passed with the slowness of a snail. Much needed to be done to restore the plantation, but she could do nothing without her cousin's approval.

Tonight she leaned out the window and breathed in the sultry night air. A broad halo surrounded the full moon. Did that moon look also on Tom and Elizabeth and Rourke? Would anyone have the answers she needed?

Clunk.

Something struck the veranda beside her window.

Catherine looked around and saw nothing. Perhaps it was her imagination. Though no trees overhung the veranda, perhaps some nut or twig had found its way to the porch.

Clunk.

The second occurrence was not imaginary. "Who's there?" she hissed.

No answer, naturally.

"Goodness. Get control of your imagination." She walked to a different window.

This time the moonlight revealed movement near the pigeonnier.

Tom! He'd promised to return with news. Was he back? If so, he would meet her there. Unless this was a trap. Her skin prickled. What if DeMornay had overheard their plans and even now was leading her into a trap where she would have no means of escape? More and more that man frightened her. What had happened to the housekeeper before Aurelia? Where were all the servants? His explanations didn't soothe her. She could not see beneath his polished surface, and experience had taught her that trouble lurked in darkness.

Even so, she donned her slippers and made her way out of the house and across the yard. The door to the pigeonnier was ajar.

"Tom," she whispered into the black interior.

A hand clapped over her mouth at the same time another pulled her against a tall, masculine form.

A scream shot up her throat, but it was stifled by the man's hand.

"Be quiet," Tom whispered into her ear. "It's me."

She relaxed, and one second later she wanted to punch him for frightening her so.

"Why?" she whispered.

He pulled her into the pigeonnier. "We're being watched."

Again her skin prickled. "Who?"

"I'm not certain, but whoever it is, they'll know I'm back."

"Aurelia wouldn't tell DeMornay." But even as she said it, she knew she couldn't be certain. The housekeeper confided nothing and was wary of everything. Catherine's hope lay in one certainty. "She fears him. That's why she told us to leave."

"Under duress, a person will reveal anything, especially to someone who holds the power of life and death over her."

Catherine sucked in her breath. "He could do that?"

"From what I've seen and heard, yes."

"Surely my cousin wouldn't approve of such a thing."

"Your cousin has no interest in the plantation beyond its profitability."

Catherine eagerly clawed for more. "You did meet with him, then. You told him about me. Is he coming here?"

"I'm sorry, but he acted like he's never heard of you. He thinks you're a fortune seeker."

The words crushed the last hope she'd harbored. No one wanted her here.

"A fortune seeker." She shook her head. "What fortune? I can't see much of value here."

"That's not what he believes. He is confident the plantation makes a handsome profit."

"How can that be?" She twirled a strand of hair around her finger. "If only I could look through the accounts."

"You haven't had a chance to look?"

Catherine had to admit she had not. "DeMornay keeps the study locked. Even the windows are latched from the inside. I did look for the items on your list, but I couldn't find any of them."

"That's disappointing. But I found my father's ship. It's moored just inside Black Oak boundaries."

"It is?" Catherine's heart sank. She'd hoped there wouldn't be a connection between the theft of the ship and her family plantation, but more and more it appeared there was. "Maybe my cousin doesn't know about it."

"He might not." Tom paused. "I asked if the plantation had a ship, and he acted incredulous that I would even think such a thing."

"At least he's not involved." She didn't want to think ill of her cousin.

"He doubts you even exist."

As much as she didn't want to admit it, cousin Henry, who must have been very young at the time Maman left, would have believed whatever his elders told him.

"The family not only claimed Maman died but erased her from the record." That put Catherine in a very tenuous position. "They will never accept me." The realization hurt.

"You can prove it with the records you brought."

"But what good will the baptismal record do when Maman is listed as Lisette Haynes? It comes down to my word."

"I believe you."

"Oh, Tom." She leaned against him as her heart swelled. Who had ever trusted her that much, even endangering his life for her sake? "What have I gotten you into?"

He lifted her face with a finger beneath her chin. "You have gotten me farther than I could ever have gotten on my own."

Though he surely meant that her desire to rejoin Maman's family had led to the discovery of his father's ship, she lingered a moment in the tenderness of his embrace. If only it were that simple. If only their lives weren't so different. If only her future wasn't tied to liars and thieves.

"What do we do?"

His lips swept close to hers. So close that his words tickled her cheeks. "We press on."

"How?"

"The judge. I will speak to him in the morning, tell him about my father's ship and where it's hidden."

"He is coming here late tomorrow morning. You can speak to him then."

Tom leaned back to look at her. "The judge is coming here?"

"He has some sort of document for me, something my uncle entrusted to him."

"I can fetch that for you, but you need to get out of here. Tonight. It's too dangerous to stay."

A large part of her wanted to do just that. She could run away from everything with Tom at her side.

But she twisted from his arms. "I can't. I have to see the document myself. The judge wouldn't entrust it to anyone else. I won't leave until I see it."

"We could stop by his house on the way to the ship."

"Titchwood is more than a mile inland. It isn't on the way to any ship."

Tom held her. She could feel and hear his desperation. "We will take the time to get it. You're the most important thing in my life. Leave with me now, while you still have the chance."

She almost agreed. Almost. Then she remembered Maman's portrait and the love her mother had for this plantation. Too many questions remained unanswered. "I can't. Not yet."

⁂

How could Tom make her see that this place would destroy her? She had lost her home in England and was clinging to this as the only possibility for a new home. Yet it wasn't. Based on how Lafreniere acted, Black Oak would never be hers.

"Your family doesn't even recognize you."

She turned away.

Tom tried another tactic. "I'm afraid something illicit might be going on here. Smuggling, using my father's ship. No doubt DeMornay is in charge. You are in danger here. Leave with me."

"And go where?"

"To the *James Patrick*." Tom grasped her by the shoulders. "Rourke is here. He has a full crew. We can leave this place."

Even in the dark he could feel her shaking her head. "I can't. This is my home now."

"Home isn't a place. It's the people who love you."

He heard a sob escape her lips. She felt alone. The realization crashed on him like a severed mast.

"I love you." The words escaped his lips without thought, though the moment they were out, he knew their truth.

She gasped. "But you know so little about me."

"I know enough." He grasped her by the shoulders and pulled her close. No woman had ever felt as perfect as Catherine. "I know you are strong and determined and witty and spirited. I know you're the most beautiful woman I've ever seen. From the moment I first saw you looking me in the eye through the windows of the *Justinian*, I could not get you from my mind."

"But you don't know *me*."

He cupped her chin and gazed into eyes that reflected the pale moonlight that sifted through the open door. "I want to learn everything about you, to spend a lifetime exploring every tiny thing. Why one corner of your mouth tilts up a little higher when you're amused. When your eyes are dark as a forest and when they're bright as an emerald. What makes you laugh and how to take away the tears." He swiped a thumb across her cheek.

She shivered. "You're simply saying that so I will leave with you."

"No, I mean every word," he whispered, so close to her face that he could feel her breath against his cheeks.

Her lips were so close, so tempting, so perfect.

"I thought of you throughout each day," he whispered, letting her melt against him. "I couldn't bear being separated, wondering what had happened to you, if he had harmed you."

"He didn't."

That eased his conscience a little, but not the desperate urge to claim her. He cradled her chin between his hands and lowered his lips. The first brush sent a thrill through every nerve. She did not object, so he lingered longer, claiming her as his own. Then she responded, and he lost his head.

Fortunately, she broke the kiss and stepped away.

His heart raced as if he'd run from the Key West harbor to the far side of the island. He swiped at his lips. "I'm sorry."

"Don't be." Her voice was soft and languid as slack tide. "I missed you too."

"Then come away with me." He caught her hand. "Leave while you still can."

"I can't. Not until I know what Judge Graham has for me."

"I told you. We'll stop there first."

She shook her head and backed away. Before he could react, she'd slipped through the pigeonnier door.

He stumbled after her and grabbed at her hand but missed. She hurried across the lawn. He followed only a few steps before halting.

DeMornay stood on the staircase, a lantern in his hand. "Catherine! I've looked everywhere for you."

Had DeMornay seen Tom?

Catherine's heart pounded. She could not turn back, lest she betray Tom's presence. She must walk forward as if glad to see DeMornay when that was the last thing she felt.

Tom's kiss still lingered on her lips. She should have left with him.

"Miss Cate." DeMornay glided down the steps. "I feared something had happened to you when Aurelia said you were not in the house."

The unfamiliar nickname grated on her nerves, but she brushed it off for Tom's sake. She must draw DeMornay into the house so Tom could escape.

"I came out to look at the moon." It was a flimsy excuse, since she had come from the direction of the pigeonnier, whose interior afforded no view of the night sky. "Then I decided to walk about the yard since I was restless."

DeMornay lifted the lantern to peer at her, likely to ascertain the truth of her statements. "You could have come to me. I was working in the study."

"I did not want to disturb you. Moreover, you could not sort out my jumbled thoughts."

He cupped her jaw and ran his thumb along her cheek.

She pulled away, unable to bear the man's touch.

"You are chilled." DeMornay slipped out of his smoking jacket and placed it on her shoulders.

She wanted to throw it back at him but had to play along with her stated purpose for being out of doors at this hour. "I was deep in thought and didn't pay attention to the temperature."

"A beautiful woman should not trouble herself with deep thought."

"No. I should sleep." She extended her hand. "Will you assist me back into the house?"

"Of course." DeMornay's covetous grin turned her stomach, but he did lead her up the steps and into the house, giving Tom time to escape. "Aurelia will draw a hot bath for you. That will ward off the chill and relax you for slumber." He halted as the housekeeper approached.

"De bath is ready, Massa," Aurelia said, her gaze cast down.

"Very well. Miss Haynes will follow you to her room in a moment."

Aurelia hurried off, and Catherine slipped out of the jacket.

"No, no." He stopped her. "Keep it for now. Aurelia will bring it back to me." His hand grazed her cheek. "I want only the best for you. Do you believe that?"

His black gaze could mesmerize if she let it. But she was no longer a child. She fought off his attempts to woo her. "Good night, then."

"Beautiful dreams, my sweet."

She hurried across the salon but stopped to look back. De-Mornay was gone. She tiptoed back to the veranda. The man was rushing toward the pigeonnier. For a moment she feared he would discover Tom. The thought caught in her throat, and she moved forward to warn Tom.

"He be gone."

The whisper came from behind her.

"Aurelia."

The housekeeper motioned for her to return to the shadows. "Your friend gone."

The fear dissipated. "You saw him leave?"

Aurelia nodded.

Catherine heaved a sigh. "Thank goodness."

"Massa suspects."

A new fear welled. Aurelia had seen Tom. Would she tell DeMornay? "Don't say a word." But Aurelia did not take orders from her. "Please."

Aurelia's eyes glittered in the moonlight. "Leave dis place while you can."

Catherine did not miss the ominous tone. Everyone warned her. Why? What was happening at Black Oak that no one wanted her to discover?

"This is my home. Why should I leave?"

Aurelia looked left and right as if someone was listening to their conversation. "You don't know de truth." The whispered words barely reached Catherine.

She stepped closer. "Tell me."

Instead of explaining, Aurelia turned without a word and retreated to Catherine's room.

Catherine followed and closed the door behind them. "Explain."

Aurelia moved behind her to unbutton her gown. Her whisper was very soft. "Gibson, Hunt, and Angel be mine."

The words shivered down Catherine's spine along with Aurelia's icy fingers. "They are lovely children."

"Dey all got de same papa."

"I didn't know you were married." Catherine hadn't seen a man on this plantation the right age to be Aurelia's husband. Maybe he was one of the workers that DeMornay said were out in the farthest fields.

"Ain't no slave be married de way white folks is."

"What do you mean? They deny you marriage?"

Aurelia didn't speak for some time. When she did, it was with icy hatred. "Dis man take what he want."

Surely the woman did not mean what Catherine suspected. The father of Aurelia's children had forced himself on her. She could not speak the word. *Rape.* "Was it . . . that is, is their father my cousin?"

Aurelia shook her head. "He here now."

Catherine breathed out in relief. Not one of her cousins or even her late uncle. But this could not continue. "Does he still . . . harm you?"

Again Aurelia was silent for a long moment while she undid the corset and petticoats. When she spoke, each word was spat out with fierce desperation. "Gibson be 'most ten. Dey go away when dey old enough."

"Go away?"

Aurelia began to hum, leaving Catherine to ponder. It didn't take her long.

"Sold?" she asked the housekeeper.

"Dat de way. But it better den bein' a woman an' catchin' Massa's eye."

DeMornay's attentions had increased daily. Was Aurelia jealous or warning her? "What happens to the women?"

"Dey disappear."

"Sold?"

"No one know."

Catherine felt ill. "None of this will happen when I'm in charge here."

Aurelia's laugh was bitter. "You never be mistress of Chêne Noir. He never let you."

Catherine's mouth was dry, though steam filled the room from the hot bath. "Who?"

"De devil."

19

S leep came fitfully that night, interrupted by terrible dreams of DeMornay locking her in a room from which there was no escape. She awoke with a start and dropped to her knees beside the bed to ask for God's protection. Though her heart beat wildly, in time it calmed, and she slipped into that half-awake state where she could fight off the dreams.

The following morning, Catherine stood on the veranda and watched Aurelia's children move around the yard. All had the same father, a fairer-skinned man. Thankfully the father was not her uncle or cousins. Then who?

The girl, Angel, played in the mud near the pigeonnier. Her rough, flour-sack dress was stained, but like most children her age, she didn't care. Waves of curls fell below her shoulders. Something about her looked familiar, but Catherine couldn't place it. She was drawn to the girl's innocence and beauty. After DeMornay rode off to instruct the field workers, she crossed the yard and squatted beside Angel. The girl ignored her presence, humming to herself like her mother did.

Catherine hazarded the first words. "What are you making?"

"Pie." The girl, perhaps five or six at most, did not look up. "Mud pie."

Catherine had watched the tenants' children do the very same thing. As a child, she'd begged Maman to let her join them, but Maman always refused, saying that wasn't the sort of thing the future mistress of the house ought to do. At the time, Catherine had thought her mother quite unfair. Now she wondered what Maman meant. She must have known the terms of settlement placed on Papa's estate. Most likely she meant that Catherine would be mistress of a house once she married, but what if she believed Catherine would inherit Chêne Noir? Marrying Papa had cost Maman dearly, unless she believed she had protected that inheritance for Catherine.

"Miss Haynes."

The familiar voice made her rise. "Judge Graham."

"I trust you are well."

She gave a nod.

"I am here on the business I mentioned." He withdrew an envelope from the leather portfolio he was carrying. "Is there somewhere we might speak in private?"

Her heart pounded. Not the house. She never knew who might be listening. She led him to the far side of the pigeonnier, out of sight of anyone inside the main house.

He nodded toward the house. "Is anyone home?"

"Mr. DeMornay rode out to the fields not half an hour ago."

The judge's tension eased. "Good. This is not something you should reveal to Mr. DeMornay or even to your cousins. I suggest you hire a good attorney. I can recommend an honest one who will not be swayed."

"Swayed by whom?"

"By those who will lose what they thought they'd gained."

She sucked in her breath. "Do I inherit a portion of Black Oak?"

"Perhaps."

"I don't understand."

He handed her the envelope. "Read, and then I will explain."

She turned over the bulky envelope. The seal was intact. "Do you know its contents?"

He nodded. "Your uncle had me draft it a year ago. I was to give it to you if you ever set foot on Lafreniere land."

The judge's actions when they first met now made sense. "That's why you questioned me."

"I had to be certain you were indeed Lisette's daughter."

"I have my baptismal record."

"Good. You may need it. Please, read." He nodded toward the envelope.

She broke the seal and pulled out a lengthy document written more like a letter. Though she'd read a few legal documents while caring for Deerford, this one soon confounded her.

"I'm sorry. I don't understand." She held out the papers to the judge.

"These things can be difficult to decipher." He indicated she should keep the papers. "Your uncle Henri approached me, wanting to right a wrong."

Catherine gave him her full attention.

"Given the forced portion allocated by the law and adding in the disposition by your grandparents, your mother stood to inherit the bulk of the plantation upon your grandfather's death."

"Forced portion?"

"The law stipulates an equal division of an estate between all heirs. However, a certain additional percentage may be granted to one or several heirs."

Catherine still wasn't certain she understood. "Wouldn't Uncle Henri have inherited the bulk of the estate?"

"Only if your grandparents granted him an additional percentage. Instead, they gave that to your mother."

"But they were upset by Maman's decision to stay in England."

"Perhaps they hoped an inheritance would change her mind."

"It didn't. Why wouldn't they change it?"

The judge shook his head. "We will never know."

"Uncle Henri must have been angry, and yet Maman did not inherit."

"Actually, she did. As her only child, you would then have inherited her portion upon her death, providing your mother made the proper agreements before her marriage."

"Proper agreements?" Was this what Papa had meant in his final regrets?

"It's my understanding that in England, without prior agreement, a woman's holdings become the property of her husband upon marriage."

"Papa would never have taken that away from me." Or had he? Was that what he had lost?

"Let's set that aside for a moment and return to this document. Your uncle would have been left with only a quarter ownership of Black Oak. If your mother died before having offspring, however, he could claim it all."

She gasped. "The funeral and burial in the family crypt. It was orchestrated so my uncle could own all of Black Oak."

Judge Graham nodded. "In later years, he regretted his role in that sham and in his subsequent actions to ensure you received no inheritance."

Her skin prickled.

"Your uncle sent Mr. DeMornay to England with an offer to purchase Lisette's portion of the plantation. He offered a generous sum, far more than the land was worth. Your father accepted, and the transaction was done."

"Papa." The gasp came from deep within. That's what he'd considered lost. "He must have assumed I would never go to Louisiana since the family was estranged. He must have wanted to set aside the money for me so I would have a fine dowry. That's what Papa would have done." Except Deerford was always in debt. Failed crops, unpaid leases, high taxes. Many things had taken a toll. He must have borrowed from her dowry, intending to pay it back in better times. "But there never were better times."

"Pardon?"

She shook her head. "My poor father. He did what he thought was best and regretted it on his deathbed."

The judge nodded sympathetically.

"Then I have no claim on any part of Black Oak," she summarized.

"Perhaps you do. Your uncle wanted to return a share to you, an eighth."

"Not exactly generous."

"It is not much but more than you would have had, with one possible exception."

He had her attention again.

"I can't find any record that the purchase and transfer of ownership was ever recorded. Further investigation is needed, but you might still have claim to the bulk of the estate."

"Not recorded? I can't imagine Uncle Henri would have paid handsomely to purchase the land and then not follow through."

"My thoughts exactly. He must have assumed it was filed properly, or he would never have had this document drafted."

"Then what happened?"

"I intend to find out," the judge said. "I will search the records to see if the purchase was misfiled or entered incorrectly. You should check here to see if it is still on the premises."

That would not be easy. DeMornay would never let her near

the study. Perspiration broke out on her brow. As it stood, she was part owner of the plantation. For now.

"Maman lost her right to the property when she married. What would happen if I marry?"

"It would depend on the terms of any agreement you make with your prospective husband."

Cousin Henry would not be pleased to discover he owned very little of Black Oak. The profits he'd been enjoying would vanish. She would need an attorney to guard her interests and ensure she claimed her role as mistress. How she wished Tom and Rourke were here now. But they were on a sailing ship moored out of sight somewhere.

"I have no funds for an attorney."

"My friend will wait for payment until you have received your inheritance."

Catherine feared even a moment's delay. "Couldn't you represent me?"

He smiled indulgently. "No, my dear. I would be the justice before whom you would bring the case."

She took a deep breath, and her head finally cleared. "Then I must act."

"I suggest you leave, Miss Haynes. Take a room in the city and secure my friend's services. His address is noted inside the envelope."

She nodded, but how could she escape without DeMornay following? And what of the missing document? No doubt DeMornay had it hidden somewhere. He'd probably carried it from Deerford in the strongbox. Somehow she must find it.

Her gaze drifted to Angel, who was carrying the mud pie in her hands, heading for the slave quarters. Her back was erect, her head held high. The sun highlighted her loose curls, which were tucked behind an ear with almost no lobe.

Catherine drew in her breath sharply. That was it! The resemblance she'd spotted earlier but hadn't been able to place. The wave in the hair was far looser than Aurelia's tightly kinked hair. But it was the ear that cinched it. Only one other person on this plantation had an ear with virtually no lobe.

Louis DeMornay.

❧

Tom's palms sweated as he and Rourke walked up the road to Black Oak plantation.

"Are you sure this is the right thing to do?" Tom had second-guessed their decision to present themselves to DeMornay dozens of times during the sleepless night. Birds chirped overhead, oblivious to the tension about to erupt. "I'd rather meet Catherine again at night and convince her to leave with me. Pushing DeMornay might make him tighten his grip."

"Perhaps," Rourke mused, "but he already knows you're back. The housekeeper saw you."

Tom regretted that mistake. The kiss had dismantled every bit of restraint. He'd wandered from the pigeonnier with a jumbled mind and didn't see danger until it was too late.

"But he doesn't know about you," Tom pointed out.

"Nor does he care. I am no threat. You, on the other hand, are the enemy. If you're certain he recognized the Worthington name—"

"I am."

"Then there's nowhere to hide. He will be on the lookout for you."

Tom blew out his breath in frustration. "What will happen to Catherine? He won't just let her walk out the door."

"Why not?"

"She believes she inherited a share of the plantation." When

Rourke stared at him blankly, Tom added, "That could threaten whatever her cousin and DeMornay are doing here."

"You still think there's something illegal going on?"

"Based on what I heard and the fact that Pa's ship is painted black and hidden, yes."

"Do you think either man would harm her?"

Tom thought back to Lafreniere's response to Catherine's arrival. "I believe her cousin would find a way to discredit her claim and force her from the land. As for DeMornay, it depends how much she pushes."

Rourke nodded as they drew to the head of the carriage drive leading toward the main house. "Then we must convince her to join us. We can take her to New Orleans or wherever she needs to go."

They began the walk up the long drive.

"I'm not sure DeMornay will let her go." Tom knew his fears sounded irrational.

Rourke halted. "How can he stop her? She is a free woman."

"I don't know." Tom stared at the bleak house. "I only know that he is very persuasive in a dark and deceptive way. Everything he says sounds good on the surface, but it's all lies underneath. She's faced him alone these last few days." He thought of how she'd run from him after the kiss. "It's my fault. I never should have left."

"Catherine is a strong woman. Elizabeth tells me her faith is solid. She will not believe lies."

Tom wasn't as certain, but he would soon find out.

Aurelia drew in her breath sharply. "What he be doin' here?"

Catherine crossed the salon to the open gallery, rag in hand after dusting the frame of Maman's portrait. Thus far she hadn't been able to get into the study, and no amount of cajoling would persuade Aurelia to unlock the door. The housekeeper insisted only DeMornay had the key. Catherine had resorted to examining every nook and cranny of the house on the pretense she was helping remove the dust that reappeared each day. The moment she looked across the lawn, all thoughts of the missing document disappeared.

"Tom!" Her spirits leapt. "He's returned."

He walked toward the house in broad daylight with Captain O'Malley at his side. The sight of that upright man gladdened her. He would help her find the missing document. He would bring her to New Orleans. He would help her sort out what she must do.

She turned back to the housekeeper. "Quick!" She shoved the rag at Aurelia. "To my bedroom. You must make certain my hair and gown are presentable."

Aurelia tucked the dust rag in her apron pocket and led the way. Within moments, her deft fingers captured any stray locks of hair. A quick brushing of Catherine's skirts removed all trace of dust. She was ready to greet her guests.

"If you won't be needin' me, miss." Aurelia drifted out of the room.

"Please receive our guests and tell them I will be there shortly."

A knock sounded through the house.

"Gibson'll answer it. I oughta see ta dinner. Massa'll return hungry."

Catherine thought quickly. "Bring tea service. It's early, but I must serve something."

"Yes, miss." Aurelia nodded and scurried away.

A second knock rang out. She flew through the butlery and pantry, crossed the main salon, and found the men on the front veranda.

"Tom! Captain O'Malley!" She had never been so pleased to see a familiar face. Rourke would know what to do. "Please join me on the gallery. Aurelia will bring tea."

"Thank you, and may I say you look well," Rourke said as she led them to the table.

"A bit tired, I'm afraid, but generally well."

She glanced at Tom, who had been silently observing her. After helping her into her usual chair, he took the seat across the table from her. Rourke then claimed the head of the table.

"I did not expect to see you here, Captain O'Malley," she began, knowing it was her duty to start the conversation. As eager as she was to ask for help locating the document, she could not begin the visit with a request.

"I told you that the captain was here," Tom interjected. "The *James Patrick* is nearby."

"Yes, of course." She felt her cheeks heat. "You did tell me that, as well as finding your father's ship. Is it in good condition?"

Tom sat on the edge of his chair, clearly anxious. "It's much the same as the last time I saw it. It is painted black, though, doubtless so it can sail at night unseen."

Catherine glanced toward the salon doors. No sign of De-Mornay yet, but he could arrive at any moment. "The *James Patrick* has a black hull too. Is that so it can sail unseen?"

Rourke roared with laughter. "She got you on that one," he said. "But we are not here to discuss ships. We want to know how you are faring."

Catherine gave Rourke a grateful smile. "Well, thank you. I'm honored that you paid me a call. How were Elizabeth and the children when you left them?"

"Quite well, though Jamie is a bit too much like his father. He already wants to sail and put up a fuss when I would not bring him along."

"At such a tender age," she exclaimed. "He will be five soon, won't he?"

"December second."

They exchanged further details of life in Key West, and a strange longing tugged at her heart. Though she had spent but one month in that tropical port, it had become home for her. Would Black Oak ever fill that void?

"DeMornay isn't here?" Tom interjected, pulling her from much more pleasant thoughts.

"He rode out this morning to instruct the field workers." Was this the time to ask for help?

"I understand it's harvesttime." Rourke's calm contrasted with Tom's obvious impatience.

"Yes. He says they are cutting the farthest fields and will work their way toward the river."

"That doesn't make sense," Tom said, that scowl still in place. "Why not cut the cane closest to the road so wagons can haul it to market?"

Rourke looked like he was trying to stifle a grin. "The sugarhouse is likely located centrally or at the farthest reaches of the plantation. I assume they boil the cane there."

Catherine realized how little she knew of the plantation's workings. "I believe so. Mr. DeMornay did mention that they were cutting near the sugarhouse."

"The midday meal isn't far away. You must expect him soon." Tom looked left and right.

"True." She wiped her damp palms on her napkin.

Rourke glanced at Tom. "We shouldn't stay long. I have a ship and crew waiting for orders. Tom wanted to bring you news—and an offer."

A crash just inside the house brought Catherine to her feet. "The tea service!" She hurried through the doors to the salon to find Angel sobbing and picking at the pieces of broken china.

"No, no. Don't cut yourself." Catherine guided the girl away from the mess.

Angel recoiled, her hands up to shield her face. "Don't hit me!"

Shocked, Catherine stepped back. "I would never strike you. It was an accident, that's all. This tray is too heavy for someone your age to carry. Where's your mother?"

"Mama! Mama!" the little girl wailed.

Aurelia ran into the room and picked up her daughter. "Hush now. Hush, less yo' papa hear."

Angel's father. DeMornay. "He's here?"

"Ride up jess now."

Catherine felt ill. She looked back and saw that Tom and Rourke had followed her into the salon. DeMornay did not like Tom and certainly did not trust him. What would he do if he saw Rourke and Tom here with her? She couldn't forget the way he'd gone after Tom at the pigeonnier last night.

"You must go," she urged the men. "Now." She tugged on Tom's arm and motioned to the front steps, hoping Rourke would take the hint.

Instead, both men stood rooted to the spot, staring past Catherine.

20

DeMornay stood in the doorway between the butlery and the salon.

Aurelia had frozen at her daughter's side, her expression hard as stone. Catherine tried to take it all in even while panic knotted her stomach. DeMornay had returned, and he was not pleased.

The plantation manager's boots clattered across the salon. "What happened here?"

Catherine secretly motioned for Tom to leave.

He did not move.

Angel began to sob again, and Aurelia buried her daughter's face against her shoulder. She backed away, still holding Angel. "Gots to get de food on de table."

Fear clearly gripped Aurelia just as it did her daughter.

"Who broke my teapot?" DeMornay demanded.

"*Your* teapot?" The arrogance set off Catherine's temper. Her response also gave Aurelia time to hurry her daughter from the room. "It is more mine than yours. I am a Lafreniere. You are not."

She saw the corner of Tom's mouth inch upward, and confidence rushed in. She was much more an owner than DeMornay ever would be. He was only a servant.

DeMornay scowled briefly before recovering that calm facade. "A matter of semantics. I am looking out for your best interests, *dear* Catherine."

The emphasis infuriated her. "I can look out for my own interests. This was an accident." She waved at the broken tea service.

DeMornay tugged off his leather gloves. "Are you going to introduce me to your other friend?"

The smile might lead a stranger to believe he was genuinely interested in meeting Rourke, but Catherine could sense an undercurrent of anger beneath the placid surface. DeMornay did not welcome uninvited guests.

She took a deep breath, hoping to still her racing heart. "This is Captain Rourke O'Malley from Key West."

"A pleasure to meet you." The handshake appeared firm. "You are here to bring Mr. Worthington home."

Not a question. A statement.

"If he wishes to leave," Rourke replied without the slightest indication he was ill at ease.

Catherine glanced at Tom's rigid expression. Her heart leapt. He was here for her. They both were. Tom had asked her to go with him last night. She had refused at the time, but now she would gladly accept transport to the city. Then she could settle the matter of inheritance once and for all.

"Tom is in my employ," Rourke was saying, "but he will make his own decisions."

Tom glared at DeMornay, as if by doing so he could force the man to admit he had stolen Tom's father's ship. He must have known how impossible that was. DeMornay was as closed as a secure safe.

"You may leave now," DeMornay said in a low voice.

"No." Catherine addressed all of them at once. "Rourke and Tom are my guests. We will dine on the gallery." She cast a triumphant smirk at DeMornay. "Let no visitor say Black Oak plantation treated them without the utmost courtesy. Gentlemen, you may join me while Mr. DeMornay changes into something fresher."

She saw Tom's eyebrows lift in surprise and a flash of admiration cross his face. So, she had impressed him. Catherine smiled to herself as she led Rourke and Tom back to the gallery. She had not commanded such a presence except during her father's illness. It felt good to be in control again. When DeMornay reluctantly retreated to his quarters, she wanted to shout for joy.

Instead, she directed the men to the table. This time she placed Rourke and Tom on the same side. DeMornay always sat at the head of the table. Today she selected that seat.

"Do you think Aurelia is Elizabeth's mammy?" Tom whispered to Rourke after they sat.

"No. I knew the woman well. Though ten years can change a person, this woman could not be her. The stature and coloring don't fit."

That settled the question niggling Catherine since Key West.

Rourke leaned closer to her. "We don't have much time. If you want to return to Key West with us, let us know now."

"Return to Key West?" Though her heart longed for just that, she couldn't leave until she knew if she owned part of Black Oak.

"But you must," Tom hissed. "Can't you see what that man is doing?"

"Of course, but I can't leave Louisiana yet. I would be grateful if you would take me to the city, though." She would have to give up on finding the sale document for now.

Rourke looked into her eyes. "When?"

"At your earliest convenience."

"Then after that you will go home with us." The hope in Tom's voice almost broke her heart.

She shook her head. "Not yet. Not until I know if Black Oak is mine." She lowered her voice as a thought occurred. "But Aurelia and her children . . . perhaps they could go to Key West with you."

Concern etched deep lines in Rourke's face. "For an enslaved Negro to set foot on Key West soil, the owner must show proper papers."

"I could free them."

"You have that authority?" Tom asked.

"I do." She hoped.

Rourke shook his head. "No free colored people are allowed ashore."

Catherine didn't understand. "Even Anabelle's husband?"

"He established residence before that law was enforced." Rourke's expression betrayed his dismay with the regulation. "Even if that were not the case, we couldn't get out of New Orleans without the owner and papers aboard. Otherwise we would be accused of slave trading."

Catherine knew nothing of American laws. "That is not allowed, then?"

"It is not. If caught, the ship would be seized, and we would all face prison."

Catherine squeezed her eyes shut. Was there no way to help Aurelia and her children? She took a deep breath. It was the only way. "Will you stay until I have those papers?"

Rourke did not answer at once. "I have a business, a wife, and children."

"I ask too much. Forgive me. There will be another way."

246

"I will stay," Tom said.

Catherine knew where that would lead, yet she had no other choice. "And bring me back here when they have been delivered?"

Tom's expression grew black. "Back here? Why? Because of him?" He waved toward the back of the house. "Can't you see who he is?"

"Who am I?" DeMornay glided onto the gallery with clean trousers and frock coat, his hair neatly combed.

Catherine quaked. How much had he overheard?

No one spoke.

DeMornay stared at Catherine just long enough to send a shiver of fear up her spine. *Leave while you can*, Aurelia had begged her. Everyone echoed that sentiment, yet she could not let go of the hope of resurrecting Maman's beloved home.

She extended an arm toward the empty side of the table. "Please join us, Mr. DeMornay."

If menace could be delivered in the scrape of a chair's legs, every person at that table heard it.

Tom could barely focus on the conversation during the meal. That portrait above the fireplace must be the one Catherine had lugged across the Atlantic. Her mother. It hadn't been there the last time he was in the parlor. She was settling in. How would he ever convince her to leave?

DeMornay fawned over Catherine and seized control of the conversation as if he owned the plantation. She held her tongue, but he could see the temper building in her fiery eyes. Catherine Haynes now believed that she was the mistress of the house and DeMornay was merely an employee.

In truth she had little real power. She did not understand

DeMornay's capacity for deception. Pa had considered himself a fine judge of character, but he didn't spot the man's duplicity. DeMornay had left Pa for dead far out to sea without food or water. Only the grace of God had sent the ship's boat ashore before Pa perished. What would DeMornay do to Catherine?

Tom fisted his hands beneath the table.

Even if she succeeded in claiming Black Oak and sent De-Mornay away, Tom faced an intolerable separation. He could not stay. She would not leave. That fact clawed at his heart.

"We are making fine progress in the harvest," DeMornay said, his gaze fixed on Catherine. "If the weather holds, we should finish in two weeks' time."

Though DeMornay spoke calmly, his eyes betrayed the storm within. He was angry, furious, and someone would pay. For a second Tom feared for Catherine, but DeMornay wouldn't risk alienating her. Not until he was absolutely secure. No, someone else would pay. A servant, most likely.

A boy of perhaps ten brought the meal to the table. Aurelia never appeared.

While the others exchanged polite conversation about the harvest and the weather, Tom considered his dilemma. Could he stand to be a river pilot? Would anyone hire him?

Finally the inevitable question was posed.

"To what do we owe the honor of your visit, Mr. Worthington?" DeMornay reclined in his seat, running his finger around the rim of his bloodred wineglass. "I thought you left for Key West, yet here you are."

Catherine looked stricken.

Tom stuck to the bare facts. "I saw Captain O'Malley in New Orleans before I secured passage. Since he is heading back that way, there was no reason to seek passage elsewhere."

DeMornay knew he wasn't telling him everything.

"Then, Captain, you sail soon for Key West?" DeMornay shifted his focus to Rourke.

"As soon as my business here is finished," Rourke said smoothly, his expression so calm and confident that it appeared to shake DeMornay. "My wife would never forgive me if I didn't pay a call on Miss Haynes."

"Of course." DeMornay took a deep draft of his wine. He then lifted the bottle. "Are you certain you wouldn't care for some?"

"I don't drink spirits any longer," Rourke stated.

Tom echoed his words when DeMornay gave him the same offer.

DeMornay didn't ask Catherine. He simply filled a glass and set it before her. She ignored it in favor of tea. By the end of the meal, her glass remained untouched.

"A pleasant repast, gentlemen." DeMornay rose, signaling the end of the visit. "I have the accounts to manage. Catherine asked to learn, so I am planning to instruct her." He cast a proprietary look her way.

Her smile seemed forced and fluttered away the moment he wasn't looking. Something was very wrong.

Tom could not bear to leave her, yet he must. If she'd wanted to go with them, she could have done so. He and Rourke would have protected her with their lives. Instead, she gave a weak smile and waved farewell as they left.

Tom held his tongue until he and Rourke reached the river road. "Do you see what I mean?"

Rourke was frowning. "Something is wrong there. I could feel it."

"Evil."

Rourke nodded. "Perhaps. Certainly the man is hiding something."

"Did you see the way the housekeeper acted? The child's fear? The way everyone tiptoed around DeMornay? I must get Catherine away from him."

Rourke gave him a long look. "Even if you have to give up your father's ship?"

Tom choked on that thought. "Why should I have to give up the ship? Once I prove ownership, it's mine, and I'll sail it out of here."

"If this DeMornay is the one who stole it, do you think he will sit idly by?"

Tom knew he wouldn't.

"And if he was willing to cut your father adrift without food or water, wouldn't he use whatever or whoever is at his disposal to defeat your claim?"

"Catherine." The certainty sank into his soul. "That's why he clings to her, why he's trying to gain her trust."

Rourke sighed. "Never underestimate the enemy."

Tom had. But he couldn't give up justice for his father.

"I will get both. There has to be a way."

Catherine could feel DeMornay's calm mask dissolve the moment Tom and Captain O'Malley disappeared down the long carriage drive.

"How dare you."

The cold edge to his voice made her step away.

He grabbed her arm. "You aren't going anywhere." He yanked her into the house.

She pulled against him, but his grip only tightened until she cried out. "You're hurting me."

He didn't loosen his grip. "You hurt *me* by assuming my place."

"Your place?" She feigned ignorance, though she knew full well that taking the seat at the head of the table had offended him. "I am family."

He pulled her close. "You claim to be a blood relation. It could all be a lie."

This was the first time he had questioned her story. Considering everyone else's doubts, DeMornay's initial belief could only be explained if he'd known of her arrival and expected it.

"You did receive my letter. That's why you weren't surprised by my arrival."

"Irrelevant. Anyone could write a letter claiming to be someone she isn't."

She could not draw a breath. His eyes, black as tar, sucked her into a pit. She clawed to get out. "My mother—"

"Lisette Lafreniere lies dead in the family crypt."

"Her grave is in England."

"Lies that no one will believe."

"Her portrait—"

"It could be any woman. It certainly bears no resemblance to Henry Lafreniere, who, by the way, has never heard of you." His grip on her arm tightened, and she cried out again. "Calling out will do you no good. No one will come to your aid." He yanked her through the house.

"I don't need to learn the accounts," she managed to say through the throbbing pain.

He halted and shoved her against a wall. "From the start you've been trying to see the accounts. Why? So you know how much there is to steal?"

"No!"

"You are a thief and an interloper."

"You're wrong." Ironically, those were exactly the accusations Tom had leveled against DeMornay. "I speak only the truth."

His laughter rang cruel, and the pain shook her resolve. She stood alone against a man who was physically stronger than her. If only she had left with Tom. If only she'd listened to him. Instead, she had let him and Rourke walk away.

"Why are you doing this?" she cried.

"Understand one thing. You are a woman, and as such, you will never command Black Oak." The ice in DeMornay's voice chilled her to her toes.

She could not give up. She must stand strong for Maman and Aurelia and Angel and the others.

He shook her. "Understand?"

"Yes." The weak word at least spared her from further abuse, for he let go of her arm. She cradled the throbbing limb, rubbing where he'd clenched her.

"That's better." His eyes glittered. "But it is not enough."

"What?" she gasped.

"You must learn this lesson thoroughly. Someone must pay for your crimes." He stepped to the back door and shouted across the yard, "Aurelia! Bring Angel."

"The girl?" Catherine ran to him and clutched his arm, pleading. "She's just a child."

He shook her off.

Aurelia hurried across the yard, gaze cast down, dragging Angel behind her.

Catherine couldn't breathe. Whatever happened, she could not let harm come to the girl. "Please, take out whatever punishment you must exact on me."

Aurelia stopped at the base of the steps, Angel at her side. Both clasped their hands before them and did not look up.

"Oh, you will suffer." DeMornay took Catherine by the hand this time, as if they were master and mistress of the household, and headed down the stairs.

At the bottom, he kissed her hand and then let go. It was all a charade. Everything he did was for his own purposes. Nothing was true. She backed out of his reach, conscious that Aurelia watched her every move.

DeMornay stood with his hands gripped behind his back, legs spread wide. "Rules were broken today. You know what happens when someone does not follow the rules."

Catherine's heart nearly pounded out of her chest.

DeMornay reached up to where a thick leather strap hung on the supporting column of the veranda. Below a handle, it was cut into long strips, terminated by metal rivets. He gripped the handle.

"Someone must pay." His ominous words echoed through her head.

Those bits of metal would tear apart flesh. Catherine's thoughts flashed to Jesus, who had endured terrible flogging and pain to bear the punishment that belonged to us. Belonged to her. Catherine had sinned, had let pride and covetousness govern her actions. *Forgive me, Father.* Though her limbs trembled in anticipation of pain, what was this in comparison to all Jesus had suffered?

Angel let out a sob before her mother silenced the little girl by pressing her against her hip.

"Don't coddle her," DeMornay growled. "It's time the child learned discipline."

Surely he would not harm a child.

Yet he stepped toward mother and child.

"No!" Catherine rushed forward, placing herself in front of Angel. "The fault is mine. I should never have asked for tea service at that hour."

DeMornay tossed her aside like a stalk of sugarcane. "The fault may be yours, but the punishment will be borne by others. You choose. The mother or the child."

21

Though Catherine covered her ears with her hands and squeezed her eyes shut, she could not block out Aurelia's groans as the whip struck her back. Blood soaked her gown. Angel sobbed. Catherine had tried to take the child away, but DeMornay forbade it.

She despised him.

Pleas to stop only increased the punishment. It went on past Catherine's endurance.

All she could do was hold on to Angel and sing refrains from the hymns that had comforted her as a child. Even so, anger seethed within. Jesus said to turn the other cheek, but how could anyone turn away from such undeserved punishment? Not her. Not on Maman's beloved plantation.

If only it was hers. She must find the papers that Papa had signed. If she had them in hand, if she destroyed them, then Chêne Noir would be hers. A day ago, she might have said that was wrong. Papa had sold her portion and received the funds. That large credit on the accounts confirmed it. By all rights, the plantation did not belong to her, but she could not stand by in the face of injustice when she possessed the means to correct those ills.

When DeMornay was finished, he hung up the whip as casually as hanging a hat. He then brushed off his hands and demanded Catherine go back into the house.

"I will not." She was the only protection Aurelia and her children had. She led Angel to her mother, who remained crouched on the ground until DeMornay left. She then helped Aurelia to her quarters and the straw pallet covered with ticking that served as a bed.

"Rest here while I fetch medicine, soap, and warm water."

Aurelia's wide eyes were filled with pain. "Don't come back. You jess bring trouble."

Catherine felt a pinch of guilt. She should have realized DeMornay would grow angry when she sat at the head of the table. "I didn't think he was capable of such a thing." Especially since Angel was his daughter.

She retrieved soap, water, and bandages. When she returned, she found Angel dabbing at her mother's wounds with a dirty cloth.

"Here. Use this one." Catherine dipped a clean cloth in the pail of water and squeezed it out. She then gave it to Angel.

Aurelia glared at her from the pallet. "Shouldn't've come back."

"I had to."

"He won't like it."

Catherine dipped the bloody cloth in the bucket and squeezed it out again. "Apply pressure anywhere it's bleeding."

Angel nodded solemnly.

"I couldn't find anyone in the cookhouse. Where is Walker?"

"In the overseer's house." That was said with bitterness. "The rest are in the fields. Except my boys, Gibson and Hunter."

Her boys. And DeMornay's.

Catherine looked up to see two sets of eyes watching her from the other room. The boys.

"Who will take care of you?" Catherine asked.

"My Angel."

Catherine was still trying to wrap her mind around the scarcity of servants. "Were there ever more household servants?"

Aurelia didn't answer for so long that Catherine figured she didn't know. Then she whispered, "When old massa Henri alive, dere be more, but dey go. One by one."

"What happened to them?"

Aurelia shook her head.

"Mammy. Her last name was Benjamin. Was she one of them? Is that how you learned of Key West?" Catherine held her breath.

This time Aurelia didn't clamp her mouth shut. "He wanted her. She die rather'n let 'im have her."

Catherine tried to control her trembling hands. Was this the horror under the surface of Black Oak? "Where did she go? Did he sell her?"

Aurelia stared at her. "He beat her 'til she dead."

A cry threatened to burst from Catherine's throat, but she could not break down in front of the children, lest they fear DeMornay would do the same to their mother. Instead, she took the cloth from Angel, cleansed it in the basin of water, and took over caring for Aurelia's wounds.

The children silently watched. Catherine's insides knotted at the terrible thoughts crowding into her mind. Would DeMornay go too far the next time he took out his anger on an innocent? Would he lash out at her? She'd assumed he wouldn't dare touch her, but she was no longer certain. Crossing DeMornay brought terrible repercussions.

Once the bleeding subsided, Catherine applied liniment and bandaged the wounds. "I will come back in the morning to change these."

"Don't," Aurelia warned. "He jess git mad. Make things worse fo' us."

Catherine swallowed the truth that this was her fault. "I'm sorry. I will do what I can when Mr. DeMornay is not here."

Aurelia looked away. "Don't be doin' me no favors."

"I must. This is no life, not one worth living. I will bring you—all of you—to freedom."

Her impulsive declaration drew a sharp look. "Don't be talkin' foolish. He'll hear."

"How?"

"He hear everything."

Fear shivered down Catherine's spine.

Again, silence stretched between them.

When Aurelia next spoke, it was in such a whisper that Catherine had to lean close. "You ask where de others go. After Massa Henri pass, dey disappear. Some die. Most jess go. One night dey here. Next mornin' dey gone."

"Where?"

"Only de devil knows."

Catherine drew in a breath, trying to shake off the fear that had her on edge. "He said he hires workers for the harvest."

"Don't believe nothin' he say." Aurelia glanced at the doorway to the other room and scolded the boys until they slunk outdoors. "You think you strong, like yo' mama. He break you."

Catherine drew on her reserves of strength to give the woman hope. "I'm not easily broken."

"Leave. Find dat captain, go, and don't come back."

"But I can't." In that moment Catherine knew it wasn't just because of the plantation and the terrible hold that DeMornay had on it. She must find a way to take Aurelia and her children from this misery.

Only after Catherine returned to her room did the force of what had happened hit her. She collapsed onto the bed in tears. She was too shaken to take supper. Aurelia was in no condition to cook or move about, but DeMornay would probably force her to cook. Thankfully, he did not demand that Catherine appear.

That evening she paced from window to window in her bedroom. The bright moon held no joy. The stars twinkled unknowingly over this evil place. Her heart was ripped to shreds. She must seek Judge Graham's help to free Aurelia and her children. Captain O'Malley insisted she needed to travel to Key West with ownership papers in order to then emancipate them. Perhaps she could do it here. If she was indeed the owner of Black Oak. The judge would know what must be done.

The door to her room creaked open, and Catherine spun around. "Who's there?"

DeMornay entered. "You did not join me for supper."

She should have latched the door. "I was not hungry."

"I will have Aurelia bring you something." He lifted a hand to ring the bell.

"No, don't!"

He lowered his hand. "If you hope to be mistress of Black Oak, you need to learn the ways of life here."

Bile rose in her throat. "If that's normal life, I don't care to learn it."

He stepped farther into her room. "England is very different."

She crossed to the window farthest from him. From here she could flee onto the veranda. A bitter laugh escaped her lips. What good would it do? DeMornay could outrun her. His physical strength was far superior. No one was here to help.

The only household servants present were a groom devoted to his master, an injured older woman, and three small children.

She should have left with Tom and Rourke. They would have ensured her safety. Where was Tom now? On a ship moored along the river or sailing downstream for New Orleans? Had she thrown away her only chance?

DeMornay moved close. She felt it in the prickling of her skin.

"I'm sorry for that harsh lesson," he said softly. "Perhaps I should have warned you. Life here is hard. To maintain control over a labor force that far outnumbers you requires a firm hand."

"And fear."

"And fear." He touched her arm, and it took all in her power not to jerk away. "That is a difficult lesson for someone as kind-hearted as you. That's why it's best to leave the management of the plantation to those who can bear it."

"Such as the manager."

Had he flinched?

She drove home the point. "That's why my cousin gave you control, isn't it? So he would not have to deal with the *labor force*."

"I'm glad you understand."

"It's not the way I was raised. At Deerford, we treated the tenants with dignity and respect. They were our friends as well as our tenants."

"And your estate fared well?" Even his voice seemed to smirk.

She would never acknowledge that his cruel ways were right, not when the Bible laid out the relationship between masters and servants so concisely in Paul's letter to the Ephesians. "'Masters, do the same things unto them, forbearing threatening: knowing that your Master also is in heaven,'" she quoted.

He recoiled a step. "A noble if impractical sentiment. What do you want, Catherine?"

She did not answer.

He did for her. "Black Oak. It's in your blood, and you can have it—with the right alliance."

He meant himself. She felt it as certainly as it was night. "Please go. I am tired."

"Clearly you are still distressed. I will send Aurelia to prepare you for bed. A good night's sleep will restore you. In the morning you will see everything much differently."

She would not. Ever.

⌘

"It's gone!" From the deck of the *James Patrick*, Tom stared at the empty cove where his father's ship had been moored. "You saw it. Everyone saw it."

Rourke nodded. "Did you expect DeMornay to keep it here now that he knows you've returned?"

Tom raked a hand through his hair. "I should never have shown myself."

"You were worried about Catherine."

Tom blew out his breath. "But my ship!"

"Your *father's* ship at best," Rourke corrected. "Even with the proper documents, it would take time and persuasion to convince a court."

"Where would DeMornay take it?" He scanned the river. "It can't be far away. He must be hiding it somewhere."

"Or they set sail and are on their way to the Gulf."

"Why would they sail? They only just returned. The ship hasn't been here long enough to load anything, and there was no crew aboard."

"They might have taken it to the city."

"That makes no sense. Why would they come up here only to turn around?"

"Perhaps there was something they needed to load or unload here. Regardless, it is gone. If it sailed downriver, it has the advantage of speed and time. We would never catch it."

Tom squeezed his hand into a fist. "To have it this close after all these years only to see it vanish. I can't accept that." He slammed his fist onto the rail.

"What do you plan to do? Hunt for it in New Orleans?"

That was the problem. DeMornay wouldn't keep it in broad daylight in the city. He'd send the ship to another hiding spot.

"We'll scour the area," Tom insisted, "search for another place it might be moored."

"We can do that for a couple days, but then we need to make a decision. As much as I care about you and your concerns, I can't hold my crew here indefinitely. What do you plan to do?"

Tom had no idea. Not once during the night had it occurred to him that DeMornay would set sail. No, Tom had fretted over Catherine and what that man might do to her. Never the ship. He'd been dwelling on the wrong problem. DeMornay would never harm Catherine. She was a Lafreniere. Her family might not want to admit kinship now, but they would in time. DeMornay had everything to gain from an alliance with her.

"We should have anchored outside this cove last night."

"'Should haves' won't solve anything," Rourke said calmly. "The question still remains. What do you intend to do now?"

"I don't know." Tom hated to admit that, but he was at a loss. "You're leaving, and I won't have a way back to Key West."

"Except the way you came."

Tom groaned. "I can't leave without her, but she refuses to leave. She seems to think she will one day become mistress of Black Oak."

"Perhaps she will."

"DeMornay would never allow it."

Rourke nodded. "I asked you this before, but a decision is now urgent. If you can have only one, which is more important to you? Catherine or your father's ship?"

Tom squirmed. "I thought we weren't going to discuss hypothetical situations."

Rourke laughed and clapped him on the shoulder. "I admire that stubborn determination in you. Catherine has it too. Perhaps that's why you're drawn to each other."

"Perhaps that's why we'll succeed."

"Or fail. I won't ask you to answer that question now, but you need to ask yourself which one you're prepared to lose. Seldom in life can you have it all. Pray on it, Tom. Ask God for guidance. His way is always the right way."

Tom knew that in his head, and it made sense with the bigger things like life or death. But a ship? Did God care if he got Pa's ship back? Yet that quest had ruled Tom's life for ten years. He would never forget how broken Pa had been when he returned, only to suffer pitying looks. Thomas Worthington Sr. had gone from proud shipowner and master to defeated deckhand who couldn't even provide for his family—a family that was now in the care of Pa's rival.

Tom flexed the fingers he'd been clenching so tightly. "I can't forget."

"No one ever can. Not completely. I can't forget the arrogance I showed my father. He died before I asked his forgiveness. Though my mother told me he'd forgiven me, it was hard to forgive myself and impossible to forget what I'd done. Yet God says He not only forgives but forgets, as far as the east is from the west."

"I've heard that before."

"Elizabeth says it helps to say the words over and over."

Tom stared at Rourke. "You expect me to say that I forgive DeMornay? Never."

Rourke looked at him a long time before heading to the captain's cabin. Tom was left alone on deck with the bitter taste of hatred and a quest cut short.

⚬⚬⚬

Catherine had to get away from the plantation and especially DeMornay. The man disgusted her. Moreover, he clearly had designs on her that she could not and would not fulfill. On the other hand, she could not leave Aurelia and her children in that man's grasp. She needed help, and Judge Graham was most likely to be able to give it. He could find a way for her to get Aurelia and the children away from DeMornay. Since there was no transfer of ownership on record, she might have sufficient control. The judge could give her answers.

A trip to the stables revealed three horses and Walker, the groom who'd driven the carriage the night of the dance.

"Can you take me to town?"

In spite of her clear question, the groom's eyes widened. "No, miss. Need four horse fer de carriage."

"I don't need a full carriage. A small buggy would do." But no matter how many times she asked, she got the same response.

He wouldn't hitch a horse and buggy for her. That left walking.

"How far is it to Titchwood?"

He shook his head slowly. "Two mile each way, maybe more."

She had walked that far many a time, for the village lay a good two miles from Deerford. It had never been this hot, though. By the time she reached the junction where the judge had let her and Tom from his conveyance, she was wilted from the heat.

The oak, part of its trunk scarred black, offered cooling shade. No carriages had passed her on the road thus far, but now that she was heading toward the village and off Black Oak lands, surely someone would pass. A respectable couple might offer to let her ride with them, sparing her the heat of midday. In the meantime, she would rest a spell beneath the oak.

She set down her small bag containing the documents the judge had given her and laid her head on it. Soon the sound of the river's coursing coupled with the heat drove her eyelids downward. No matter how much she fought, they grew heavier and heavier until she lapsed into a fitful sleep populated with terrible images of a woman getting beaten. Except this time it wasn't Aurelia. It was her!

She awoke with a start.

"I had a mind to let you sleep. You looked so peaceful."

The familiar voice drove sleep away. She squinted to make out Tom standing with the sun behind him. "You could offer to assist a lady to her feet."

"I could. If she would give me the slightest indication that she wished to get to her feet. A hand, perhaps?"

Though her heart had leapt at the sight of him, his teasing annoyed her already bruised emotions. Nevertheless, she stuck out her hand and he pulled her to her feet. She brushed off her skirts.

"You are the last person I expected to see here." The bits of dried grass and leaves clung fiercely to her gown.

"Who did you expect to meet? DeMornay?"

She glared at him. "Someone respectable who might offer me a ride to Titchwood."

Tom laughed. "I gather that I am not respectable enough for your tastes."

"You do not have a carriage," she pointed out.

"Ah, then you would abandon the demand for respectability if a scoundrel had a proper carriage."

"You are the singularly most frustrating man I have ever met. Do you intend to stand there mocking me, or will you assist me?"

His grin faded. "As you see, I don't have a carriage. So how can I assist you?"

"I need to get papers drawn up for Aurelia and her children. I can do that in Titchwood." A thought crossed her mind. "Or New Orleans. Is Captain O'Malley still here? He would take me to the city."

He looked around her. "You haven't any baggage."

"It's a short trip."

He didn't look pleased by that answer. "Then you don't plan to leave?"

"Not without Aurelia and the children."

That brought a smile to his lips. "I can take you to the *James Patrick* in the ship's boat. It's pulled ashore between the landing and here."

He held out his arm, and she gratefully took it. Tom had always been a gentleman—well, except perhaps when he'd stolen that kiss from her in the pigeonnier. She smiled at the memory.

"Let's hurry," she urged.

DeMornay would soon return from the cane fields and find her missing. It wouldn't take long for him to figure out where she went. Walker would not keep a secret. Only when she reached Captain O'Malley's ship would she feel free.

Tom led her around a fallen log. "Nervous?"

"No. Why do you ask?"

Tom smiled. "Because you're gripping my arm like you're afraid I'll leave you."

"I'm sorry."

"I wouldn't, you know. Leave you, that is."

The words swirled through her consciousness with a delightfully calming effect. He would never leave her. "Even in difficult times?"

"Especially then."

"Even if it gets so hot that I can't walk any farther?"

He grinned. "I would carry you."

She laughed at the image of him struggling to carry her. "Shall we put that to the test?"

He looked stricken. "It might not be the best time."

She laughed again but then sobered as a far more important possibility crossed her mind. What if she did end up the owner of Black Oak? "Even if I ask you to stay here with me?"

He hesitated long enough to give her the answer.

"You wouldn't stay," she said for him.

"I'm a sailor."

"There are ships here. We could get one for the plantation, to haul sugar to market."

He looked even more uncomfortable. "That is a big endeavor."

But his manner gave her the answer to the niggling question of a future with Tom Worthington. It wasn't possible. Not on her terms, anyway.

"You might go to Key West with me," he said a bit too eagerly.

As much as that island tugged on her heart, she could not leave matters here unaddressed. People suffered. She could not step away when she had the ability to help.

"We need to go through the bushes here." Tom indicated a seeming wall of vegetation. "I will lead. Hold on."

She grasped his hand, and he plunged into the foliage. Branches swatted her face, and twigs tore at her skirts. They climbed a sweltering levee and plunged back down the other side and into the foliage again, even denser here. The uneven ground made her stumble, but Tom caught her.

He drew her so close that she could feel the beating of his heart and his breath upon her cheek. She hazarded a look up and lost herself in those brown eyes, dotted with flecks of gold revealed by the sunlight.

"Catherine." Her name sat ragged upon his tongue. His finger traced the curve of her jaw.

She trembled beneath his touch, losing the will to resist him. Her eyelids drifted shut, and her breaths came quickly. Her lips tingled in anticipation.

He did not disappoint. The first brush of his lips was light as a butterfly's wing. The next deep as the chasms of the ocean. She fell into it, forgetting the world around her. The river, the plantation, everything retreated into the sanctity of that kiss.

"Oh, Catherine," he groaned softly when their lips parted. His forehead dropped to hers.

She drew in a ragged breath. What had she done? He would expect her to join him, would expect her to leave with him, but how could she? She needed Rourke to take Aurelia and her children to Key West. Even if she had to travel with them in order to convince authorities that the slaves belonged to her, she must still return to Louisiana until ownership of the plantation was resolved.

"We should go," he whispered, but he did not move.

"Yes." She must be the stronger one, the practical one. She pulled from his grasp and attempted to navigate the sloping ground. Her feet kept slipping.

"Here we go." He lifted her into his arms and carried her down the slope.

She held tight, drinking in this moment.

Then he halted.

She adjusted her bonnet to see what had caused him to stop. She gasped at the sight.

"Miss Haynes. Mr. Worthington. Going somewhere?" De-Mornay stood on the riverbank beside his horse, holding on to a line leading to the rowboat that Tom had tied to the bank.

Tom set her feet on the ground but did not let go of her. "We are if you will step out of the way."

"I think not." DeMornay tossed the line into the boat and kicked the skiff out into the river.

The current caught it and sent it spinning away.

22

Catherine hung on to Tom. If DeMornay could whip a woman who bore his children, what would he do to a man trying to reveal him as a criminal?

Tom's jaw was set, his gaze narrowed. He did not tremble like she did. Then again, he did not know about Aurelia's flogging or any of what had happened. She had wasted precious time with verbal sparring.

The ship's boat, their last tie to Rourke's vessel, drifted away.

DeMornay took an oar from a bush, where Tom had apparently stowed it, and cast it into the river. The other oar soon followed. "What a pity to lose a life so young."

The hair stood up on the back of her neck. Surely he would not kill them.

Tom squeezed her shoulder. He must have sensed her fear and was holding her tight. He would protect her with his life. Tears rose unbidden. He had proven faithful every step of the way, yet she'd hesitated to trust. Altogether too much like her walk with the Lord. Rather than trusting His plan, she rushed into her own, never stopping to listen. Even so, God remained faithful, waiting for her.

So too Tom. Her feelings for him had deepened beyond friendship. When had attraction and affection turned to love? Perhaps in that very moment, for she would rather face death than see Tom perish.

The answer came clearly to mind. It would work but would come at a great cost.

To save his life, she must give up all hope of a future with him.

She stepped from Tom's grasp. "I will return home with you, Mr. DeMornay. Tom was just saying farewell before rejoining Captain O'Malley aboard the *James Patrick*." Hopefully that was enough to allay DeMornay's suspicions.

Tom caught her shoulder again. "I will not leave without Catherine."

DeMornay grinned. "I believe the lady has made her wishes clear. However, midday is no time for a drowning." He pulled a revolver from his saddle. "You will return with us, Mr. Worthington."

Catherine gasped. Tom's reaction was ruining her plan. She must make another attempt.

She wrenched out of Tom's grasp. "I want nothing to do with you." How difficult to feign anger with him. She prayed DeMornay didn't recognize the tale she was attempting to spin. "After the undignified way you treated me, I cannot tolerate even having you on my plantation. Leave him, Mr. DeMornay. He is not worth our trouble."

How her heart pounded in the seconds of silence when all hung in the balance. Tom could not help her as a captive—or dead. A free Tom could meet her by night and arrange for the escape she now knew was necessary.

For added measure, she threw out, "I don't care if you have

to swim to the *James Patrick*. Leave this place and return to Key West."

Tom blinked. "But I thought—"

"You thought incorrectly. Key West is a provincial town. Here I have everything I've ever wanted: family, land, and a vibrant city. Key West can offer none of that."

Tom hesitated a moment before a mask cloaked his expression. "As you wish." He bowed stiffly.

"Lovely performance," DeMornay smirked, "but not believable after the kiss you two shared a moment ago."

Catherine felt her cheeks heat. DeMornay had seen that? Then they were indeed ruined. She would never get Aurelia from the plantation. She couldn't even get Tom away.

"Hand over your blade." DeMornay waved the gun at Tom until he slipped the dagger from his belt. DeMornay took it from him and threw it into the river. "You will walk alongside my mount. Miss Haynes will ride with me."

He then mounted, grabbed Catherine's arm, and yanked her up onto the horse with him.

❧

Tom walked ahead of DeMornay's horse. No doubt the Colt revolver was aimed at his back. It didn't take much imagination to see what DeMornay intended to do with him. After nightfall, the man intended to murder him—or have someone else accomplish the evil deed. Tom hadn't seen the man's murderous side until now. Though DeMornay had stolen Pa's ship, he had spared his life and presumably the lives of the crew.

That was not going to be the case tonight.

The heat made the dust rise, even from this lowland where the water was so close to the surface. It parched his throat and scratched his eyes.

271

This day had begun so well. He'd planned to find and rescue Catherine. DeMornay would be a man of habit. That meant Tom could reach Catherine unhindered before the midday meal. He'd left the *James Patrick* at an early hour, but it took much longer to row across the wide river than he'd planned, and then he'd ended up farther downriver than he'd intended.

When he saw Catherine at the black oak, he'd counted it a blessing. But the blessing soon turned to a curse. Now he and Catherine were in DeMornay's hands.

He kicked at a stone. It skittered ahead and elicited a growl from DeMornay.

"Walk!"

The barked order only irritated Tom. He had to find a way to get Catherine away from DeMornay. Punching an armed man would only get him killed. He had to find another way.

He wasn't about to play along with her solution. At first he'd been perplexed by her cool words and the way she'd acted annoyed with him. The taste of her kiss, sweet as honey, still lingered on his lips. That had not been the kiss of a woman who despised him. Oh no, it had given him hope.

Then he realized what she was trying to do. If she thought DeMornay could be so easily fooled, she was mistaken. The man was too cunning to fall for such a transparent ruse.

Tom preferred to act boldly and decisively.

What if it led to the ultimate confrontation? Could he kill a man?

A whip slashed down on his shoulder. "Walk faster. We don't have all day."

The leather bit through his shirt and drew blood.

Catherine gasped. "Don't!"

DeMornay ignored her. "Faster, Worthington, or you'll feel the whip again."

Tom could endure far more pain than DeMornay thought, but a whipping would not save Catherine. At this moment, Tom couldn't see how to save her, but then Rourke would say that God has answers we can't even imagine . . . if we place our trust in Him.

"'The Lord is my strength and my shield; my heart trusted in him, and I am helped.'" That verse from Psalms had fortified him many a time. Whether facing an irate drunken man or a sea that threatened to tear the ship apart, Tom could turn to this Scripture.

"Is that so?" DeMornay sneered. "Then where is this god of yours? I don't see him. All I see is a man acting with his heart. Don't you know the heart is irrational and not to be trusted? Call on this invisible god of yours all you want, but I assure you that real power will prevail."

Tom heard Catherine gasp again and could imagine her shudder. He had to get her away from this place. But how?

Show me, Lord.

Rourke said that God always answers prayer. Not always on our timeline or in the way we expect, but He does answer. Tom had to rely on that, because he was fresh out of ideas. DeMornay would not allow him to roam the estate freely. But he wouldn't kill Tom in front of Catherine. He would lock him away somewhere until he could accomplish the feat undetected. Worse, he might lock up Catherine too.

What was the man's purpose?

DeMornay's actions today exposed him for who he really was. There would be no more pretending that he was the benevolent administrator of the plantation. That lie was dead and buried.

No, DeMornay must want something very badly, something that only Catherine could give him. But what? To gain any inheritance through her, he must get past Henry Lafreniere and his brother. Surely he would not kill two men to get a decrepit plantation. It made no sense. Unless there was something beneath the surface that he hadn't seen yet.

Think. Think.

But Tom's head was fogged from heat and thirst.

DeMornay already had full control of the plantation, yet he did not do much with it. Lafreniere had claimed it was highly profitable, yet the fields looked overgrown and the plantation lacked slaves.

That was it! Somehow the answer was tied to this peculiar situation. Even if a full crew was far off in the fields, the house and grounds should look better. When added to the fear and dread that everyone expressed about the place, it meant something illicit was going on, quite possibly with Pa's ship.

Black hull. Black sails. It would blend into the night unseen.

The only reason for that was smuggling. But what? Whatever it was, it brought such a hefty profit that Lafreniere didn't question DeMornay's management and DeMornay was willing to kill to protect his secret.

❧

Catherine watched helplessly as DeMornay handed Tom to a large and impressively muscular Negro, who pressed a knife to Tom's neck and led him away. Tom was quick and strong but no match for this armed man whom DeMornay addressed in another language. Not French. Perhaps Spanish.

Tom cast her a defiant look that promised he would attempt to escape, but Catherine could not leave this to his skill, not with such a jailer. For all she knew, the man would shackle Tom or lock him in a windowless room. For how long? DeMornay had threatened to drown Tom. Something had held him back from doing so at once. From what Aurelia had told her, Tom would soon vanish—either dead or sent away. She must convince DeMornay to let him go.

"This is not necessary."

DeMornay's gaze was inscrutable. "We have much to discuss."

He took her hand and placed it on his arm. Though every fiber of her being revolted at his touch, she did not resist. Better he think her agreeable.

"He is mistaken about my affections," she added, spinning a new tale. "Poor, deluded man. I could never love someone of his class."

That caught DeMornay's attention, judging by the glint in his eye. "Do you make no exceptions?"

Catherine sensed he was no longer talking about Tom, but she would not stray from the subject until she extracted a promise to release him.

"Not in Mr. Worthington's case." She forced a sigh. "Though I long to rise to the standards set in the Bible, society dictates a certain amount of separation between the classes. Mr. Worthington is in the worker class"—how it hurt to say that—"and thus never capable of rising to marry a gentlewoman."

"Is a plantation manager also considered part of the worker class?"

Catherine had to carefully navigate this answer. "It is possible for a steward, or manager as you call it, to rise." She searched her memory for any instances but could find none in her acquaintance, so she turned to fiction. "A steward's son might capture the heart of the master's daughter."

DeMornay walked her up the front steps. "And that is accepted?"

She truly was in trouble. "These days, with love taking

precedence over arranged marriages, such a thing would be accepted." But not with him. Never with him.

He led her into the house, which still retained a bit of last night's coolness. "We will go to the study."

She instinctively tightened her grip. The last time he had brought her there, he'd locked her inside. She struggled to hide her discomfort.

He noticed. "Are you nervous? I would never harm you, Catherine. My plans for you are for your well-being."

She could not miss the echo of Scripture in his words, though he had twisted them to his own purpose. What did the Bible say about men who did such things? Aurelia had called him the devil.

She managed to choke out, "What is in the study?"

He opened the door and motioned for her to precede him.

By now her legs felt like jelly and her heart was in her throat. He clearly had something planned. The loss of control was unsettling. She must seize the advantage.

After a deep breath and prayer for strength, she strode across the room and threw open the shutters. "It's stuffy in here."

To her surprise, he made no move to close them.

She next went to the strongbox and lifted it from the shelf. "I recall a box like this from my childhood. Papa sent it away with a dark stranger, a man much like you."

"It was me."

The confirmation shook her to the bones. "But you said—"

"I saw no reason to explain the past when I was not yet certain of your claims."

"But you seemed to accept my story." Only his slip in referring to Staffordshire had betrayed his prior knowledge of her.

He waved that away as inconsequential. "I wanted to learn your purpose before passing judgment."

"Then you are certain now that I am who I say I am."

"Of course." He settled behind the desk.

"You received my letter from England."

Some men appeared small behind a desk, as if using it as a shield. Not DeMornay. If anything, he appeared larger and more menacing.

"We have been through this before." He gazed out the window as if unconcerned about anything. "Soon we will be rid of all distractions."

Tom. That's what DeMornay considered a distraction. But he was much more. If only she'd acknowledged her feelings for Tom sooner, if only she'd listened to his pleas to leave, neither of them would be in this situation.

"Bring the box here," the man said. "There's something inside that I want to show you."

Perspiration dotted her forehead. Her fingers slipped against the metal bands binding the strongbox.

"It is light." That surprised her. For years she'd wondered if Maman's jewels were inside. "No jewelry?"

"Jewelry? What use would that be to me? Ah no, my dear, this is something much more precious."

Her hands trembled as she carried the box to the desk. DeMornay sat tall, as arrogant as cousin Roger. She set the box before him.

"It is locked?"

"Not at all." He turned the box toward her. "Unlatch it."

All these years she had wondered what was in this strongbox. Today she would find out—assuming he had not removed the contents or replaced them with something else.

"Papa would have locked it."

"I am not your father, but if you wish to lock it afterward, I will give you the key." He pulled it from a desk drawer and dangled it before her.

The key looked like any other. She didn't know what she'd expected. She unlatched the box and grasped the lid. All these years of wondering.

She caught her breath and lifted the lid.

The box was empty. No, not empty. A single piece of paper lined the bottom.

"That's all?" She stared at DeMornay, incredulous. "The contents are missing. What did it once hold? Maman's jewels?"

His expression gave nothing away. "Many years have passed. The paper will explain."

The paper. A single sheet of paper would answer all her questions? She pulled it out.

To every appearance, it was a legal document, signed by her father.

"Read it," DeMornay urged.

She took the piece of paper to the window, where the light was better. Though the stiff legal language was difficult to read, the document's intent could be easily deciphered. In exchange for a large infusion of Lafreniere money, Papa had signed away her portion of Black Oak. This was the document she and the judge had sought. It would take the plantation and everything belonging to it away from her. Including Aurelia and the children.

"Oh, Papa." Her heart broke, though she understood her father's reasoning. He hadn't wasted the money. He'd used it to keep Deerford running long enough for her to marry well. Her father must have believed it the only possible solution. Still, when she did not settle on a suitor and begged off the marriage mart, he had yielded. He'd done it all for her. Yet on his deathbed he'd regretted signing this paper. He had indeed lost her inheritance.

"The document has not been recorded." DeMornay had drawn close while she was lost in memories.

She had to feign surprise. "What?"

He turned her gently from the window so she faced him. "It has not been recorded. You can still be mistress of Black Oak."

"But cousin Henry—"

"Does not know that it was never recorded. He believes he is the full owner."

She pressed a hand to her midsection. "Why wasn't it recorded?"

"Your uncle left the matter to me. I told him it was done."

"But you didn't record it. Why? What possible reason could you have?"

"You, dearest Catherine." He lifted her hand and kissed it. "You remember me. You told me as much. I will never forget the moment I first saw you in your father's house. I knew then that I loved you."

"I was just a girl of thirteen."

"Girls grow up. I am a patient man. I waited, and you came to me, just as I predicted you would."

"I don't believe it." The idea that he'd planned this ten years ago was preposterous. It also made her ill. "A grown man can't possibly fall in love with a child."

His lips curved into a covetous smile. "Was Juliet merely a child to Romeo? She was just thirteen, the same as you at our first meeting."

"But Romeo was nearer her age, and that love ended tragically."

"It needn't have. I've been waiting for you, Catherine, waiting and hoping."

Lies. All lies. No man in his right mind would believe a girl halfway around the world would mysteriously arrive on his doorstep ten years later. She might easily have married or inherited Deerford. DeMornay couldn't possibly know the calamity that had befallen her beloved home or her sudden decision to return to her mother's family. No, his purpose in not recording the document was not to reinstate her inheritance. He intended Black Oak for himself. This story he was now weaving had another purpose—to weaken her defenses.

She edged away slightly. "How could you know I would come here? There was no communication between the families." She shook the paper. "The terms of this document ensured it. Moreover, I never knew about this."

He took the paper from her hand. "Curiosity, dear Catherine. I could see it in your eyes that day ten years ago. You wanted to know about me, and your father forbade any questions." His grin chilled her. "I knew you would come to me."

She shivered and rubbed her arms. "I came to Chêne Noir, not to you."

"It is one and the same, don't you see? I am Chêne Noir now."

"My cousins own it."

"You can own the vast majority."

"I don't. That paper ensures it."

His voice curled around her like black tar smoke. "All it would take is for this document to disappear." He carried the paper to the fireplace and lifted a burning candle from its holder.

"You would do this? Why?" A sick feeling settled in the pit of her stomach as his plan became perfectly clear. On his own, he could only drain Black Oak dry. With her, he might rule it.

He replaced the candle. "For us. For what you've wanted all these years. We will reign over Chêne Noir, restore it to glory, and begin a new dynasty together."

"Together?" Exactly what she'd feared.

"Our children will inherit for generations to come. The De-Mornay name will loom large in Louisiana. You will have the finest winter house in the city, every entertainment and diversion, and a husband utterly devoted to you. Marry me, and I will destroy this document."

Every limb shook. "But I do not love you."

His gaze grew black. "You will grow to love me."

"No, I won't." She edged to the side, but he blocked her. "I love another."

"Worthington?" He spat the name with such vehemence that she knew she'd erred. "That distraction will be removed."

She'd just sealed Tom's death unless she could convince De-Mornay she loved another. But who? He could not be in England. A woman would not travel halfway around the world when in love with someone at home. She had met no one here. Rourke was married, and DeMornay knew it. That left Tom.

There was only one way to save Tom. It made her stomach heave, but DeMornay would never let him go under any other circumstances.

"I-I-I made that up." The words stuck in her throat. She instinctively moved away from DeMornay.

He gripped her arm and pulled her close. "Did you?"

"I'm not ready to marry." The words came easier, for they were closer to the truth. Still, if Tom had asked for her hand, she might well have agreed.

His grip tightened. "You are no longer a child."

"I-I might be persuaded." She must word this right. It was her only chance. "For a price."

He looked into her eyes, delving deep for the truth in her words. "What price?"

"Ownership of Aurelia and her children must be given to Tom Worthington."

"A woman and three children? Do you know what you ask?"

"It is costly, but we have others. You said they are in the field."

"Male slaves do not produce babies." He ran a finger down

her jaw. "Fertile women are worth a fortune. Their offspring can be sold."

The way he said that made horrible ideas crowd into her mind. The contents of her stomach threatened to come up. She swallowed. For their sake she must remain calm. "Then we shall buy another. Aurelia is getting up in years anyway."

His grip loosened. "That is true. Another can be gotten."

While his temper had eased, she broached the last part of her request. "You will ensure Tom, Aurelia, and the children reach Captain O'Malley's ship. They will then be allowed to leave. No one will pursue them or attempt to stop them. I must learn that they have safely reached Key West before I will speak the vows."

"Four lives in exchange for one. A steep price."

"Five," she corrected him. "You've forgotten Tom."

"His only value to me is how much someone would pay for him."

Pay? Her skin crawled. DeMornay would sell a man? He had sold slaves. Aurelia's assertion that servants had disappeared made sense. "But he is a free man."

DeMornay gave her a pitying look. "Any man can fall into indenture and need to work off his debt."

"Surely no one would agree to that. Not here." Yet she was certain of nothing. She did not know this land, knew nothing about it except that coming here had been a terrible mistake.

His lips curved into a cruel grin. "There are places hungry for workers, places not that far from here. He is strong and would bring a good price."

Her heart pounded. He was holding Tom's future over her as bait. If Black Oak was not enough incentive, Tom's freedom might force her to give in.

He ran a finger across her cheek, setting each nerve on edge.

She tried to steel herself but trembled ever so slightly. She bit the inside of her lip. Better to suffer pain than give DeMornay the impression that she liked him in the slightest.

"Dear, innocent Catherine. There is no need to trouble yourself with such things. I will take care of everything. Your only concern is my pleasure."

This time she could not quell the heaving of her stomach. She ran out of the room and fell to her knees on the veranda.

23

Tom shook the door to the pigeonnier, but the Spanish-speaking servant had bolted it. When his eyes adjusted to the dim light, he surveyed the interior. He stood on bare ground, packed hard over time and coated with guano. Above, small slits gave access to the pigeons who had largely abandoned the dovecote. He heard very little cooing from nesting birds. A ladder led to the nest boxes and could be moved from side to side by leaning it against crossbeams a few feet over his head. The lower level had some bins and nothing else. Certainly not the comforts he'd enjoyed in the garçonnière during his first visit.

Aside from the bolted door, the only other opening larger than pigeon-sized was a small shuttered window on the upper level. He shifted the ladder and climbed up to it. One of the residents objected, and he had to ward off the flapping wings with one arm while testing the shutters with the other. They didn't budge. There must be a latch somewhere.

Now that he was still, the pigeon had stopped flying around. He ran his hand over the rough boards, picking up plenty of splinters. Where was it?

He found the hinges and the gap between the shutters, but no latch on the inside.

Tom groaned. It must be latched on the outside or nailed shut since this pigeonnier wasn't tended. He was trapped.

He pounded a fist on the ladder with frustration. DeMornay had divested him of his dagger. He couldn't even hack his way out.

Think.

Escape from the upper level was not possible. He descended the ladder and looked again at the ground level. Servants would have shoveled out the guano here, taking it out the only door. Did they feed the pigeons? Was that the purpose of the bins? If so, then the grain would be stored in the bins. Food brought mice and rats, both adept at gnawing through wood. Perhaps the wood inside one of the bins had been compromised enough that he could push out the boards.

The sun must be lowering, for the light was diminishing. Within an hour or so, darkness would fall. If he found rotten boards, he could escape this prison tonight. He hoped the servant who'd thrown him in here wasn't posted outside.

Breaking out boards would make a racket. Any fool would hear it. Tom must risk waiting until everyone fell asleep. Catherine would not sleep tonight. When upset in the past, she paced back and forth in front of the window. Today's events couldn't be more upsetting.

What was DeMornay doing? Clearly he wanted Catherine. It made Tom sick to think of her in that criminal's arms. The man must see her as the means to become master of Black Oak. Tom could not let that happen, even if it cost him his life. But first he had to get out of this prison.

The light had gotten so low that he had to feel along the walls to locate the bins. Shadows cloaked much of the room.

He edged along until he bumped into something solid. There it was. Rectangular. Deep enough to contain a great deal of grain. It had a lid. No clasp or lock. He lifted.

Squee!

The squeal of a rodent sent Tom flying back a step. He hated rats. They boarded the ship using the mooring lines and gangway. They came aboard in cargo. They ate precious stores. They wormed into and behind anything.

He shuddered.

Investigating the bin meant sticking his hands—or feet—into an unlit, rat-infested place. He opted for a foot. His leather shoes covered him to the ankle.

He stuck one foot in the bin.

Nothing squealed.

He kicked the sides. Only wood met the toe of his shoe. Solid wood.

Yet the rat must have gotten in and out somewhere.

He kicked again, this time moving his toe just a fraction to the right with each kick. At last he found the weakness. His toe went through the small opening and pushed aside a bit of the wood. When he pulled back his foot, light filtered through the small opening.

Success! But was the wood rotten enough to break away a hole large enough for a man to fit through? He leaned over the edge and pushed around the opening with his hands. At first, small bits crumbled away, but that was all. The rest of the wood was solid. He'd managed to clear a hole big enough for a large rat.

A knock on the door sent Tom to his feet. He quickly and quietly lowered the lid on the bin and retreated to the center of the room.

"Come in." It seemed a foolish thing to say when whoever was outside must unbolt the door in order to enter.

Whoever it was, he or she did not answer.

The latch scraped open.

Tom tensed his muscles, prepared to fight.

It could be DeMornay, come to finish him off. How had the man known he'd landed the ship's boat at the corner of plantation property? Tom had hauled the boat ashore no more than thirty minutes before DeMornay arrived.

DeMornay must have seen it, perhaps from atop the levee. Or from the veranda of the house he might have spotted Tom leaving the *James Patrick*. Or he had lookouts. DeMornay must have been on alert. He knew Tom and Rourke were in the vicinity. He might have discovered Rourke's ship by sailing his own. The black ship. Pa's ship.

The door slowly swung open, and Tom braced himself for more rough handling by his jailer.

Instead, Aurelia entered, carrying a tray. "Supper."

Behind her, the jailer blocked the door, arms crossed as if taunting Tom to attempt escape.

Aurelia turned and snapped, "I don't need no fool watchin' me." She then said the same thing in Spanish.

The jailer retreated, though Tom suspected not far from the door.

Aurelia handed Tom the tray.

"Thank you." Tom hadn't expected food. A condemned man's final meal? He set the tray on top of the bin. Before the housekeeper could leave, he asked, "How is Catherine?"

"I no see de mistress." Aurelia lifted her head, her eyes flashing, completely unlike the woman he'd seen in his previous visits. She stepped closer and lowered her voice to a whisper. "Get help. Soon as you can." Retreating, she cast a final word over her shoulder. "Knock on de door after yer done an' Santiago'll take dem dishes, but don't wait too long or he be off eatin' by hisself."

Santiago must be the jailer's name. So he was Spanish. Or Cuban. Like DeMornay.

A shiver raced over Tom. Aurelia would never have told him that Santiago would soon be leaving to eat unless she wanted him to recognize a window of opportunity. Moreover, the tray was covered with a napkin. She must have left something for him on that tray. A weapon? Or a note?

He carried the tray to the base of the ladder, where faint light from above filtered down. This was the best light he would get.

He braced the tray on a rung and carefully removed the linen napkin covering it. A plate of stewed fish—catfish by the look of it—and rice. He'd eaten worse. A spoon and a cup of tepid water. No weapon. Nothing he could use to chisel his way out. No help at all. He lifted the plate. Nothing under it. He looked under the cup. Nothing there either.

Tom raked a hand through his hair. What was Aurelia trying to tell him? Surely she knew that he couldn't get help unless he could get out. He couldn't believe it was as simple as asking Santiago to let him go. Tom had picked up some Spanish while sailing. It was enough to understand most of what he heard but not enough to carry on a conversation.

Frustrated, he settled down atop the bin and ate the stew. He would need fortification to maintain concentration and face what lay ahead.

His spoon hit something hard. A bone? No decent cook would leave the fish's spine in the stew.

He dug away the stew and uncovered a small kitchen knife, slender and long. It wasn't big enough to kill a man or even do much injury, but it might eventually dig through the wood behind the bin. Tom's pulse increased. Aurelia had brought him a way out.

DeMornay pulled Catherine to her feet. "Come, my dear. This is no time for an unsightly display. We must prepare for Friday's soiree, where I will announce our engagement."

Hasty words could send Tom to the bottom of the river. She must continue her plea without making DeMornay think she would refuse him. "But you did not agree to my conditions."

He laughed. "How charming you are when you think you have the upper hand. Yet how mistaken." The stroke of his finger across her cheek turned to an aching grip of her jaw. "I am in charge." His eyes flashed. "Never forget that."

Before she could react, he pressed his lips to hers, hard, unforgiving, demanding.

She squirmed, trying to get away, but he was too strong, and her strength was flagging. She managed to get one hand to his face and pushed.

He grabbed her wrist.

In the instant that he let go of her waist, she jumped backward.

He reacted just as quickly, pushing her back into the study. He then slammed the shutters closed.

She stumbled and caught herself on the edge of the desk. After a steadying breath, she lunged for the door. He grabbed her arm in his viselike grip and struck her—not on the face where a bruise might show, but on the chest, which doubled her over to catch her breath.

He then yanked her up by the hair. "I am in charge, and you will marry me, or every person you tried to set free will drown. Everyone, including your precious Worthington. Even the girl."

She could not breathe, could not think, could not believe her beautiful dream of Chêne Noir had come to this hellish end. A lifetime of anguish awaited unless she could think of a way out. What choice had she? DeMornay was cruel enough to drown his own children. He would not hesitate to get rid of Tom. For now, she must play along.

"All right," she gasped.

His lips curved into that sardonic smile. "That's better. I'm sorry you had to learn this lesson the hard way, but now that we understand each other, things will proceed much better for you." Again he ran a finger along her cheek.

She fought the urge to recoil.

"I have invited guests for our grand announcement." His black gaze bored into her. "Tomorrow, you and I will direct the servants to turn this house into the exquisite mansion your mother remembered. I will be by your side, dear Catherine, every step of the way, so don't even contemplate trying something underhanded. Friday evening you will dress in your finest gown—the gold silk would be perfect—and greet each guest with all the excitement of a woman just betrothed and soon to wed."

"How soon?" she managed to choke out.

"I have convinced the minister that we must wed in haste. We will go to chapel Saturday."

Saturday. She could not draw a breath. That was only three days away. Three days to save Tom. Three days to save Aurelia and the children. Three days to save herself.

Time was running out. Her only chance was to get to Tom when DeMornay wasn't watching.

Tom waited until dark and then knocked on the door. When it didn't open, he called out Santiago's name.

Again, no answer.

This was his chance.

He opened the top of the bin and began hacking at the

wood. The knife made little progress. By the time Santiago returned for the tray, he'd managed a hole big enough for his fist. At this rate it would take a week or more. By then, someone would spot the hole, and his means of escape would be gone.

Still, he had no choice but to try. All night he worked, managing a large enough hole to discover a bush just beyond the pigeonnier wall. It would shield his efforts from view. While he sawed, his thoughts drifted. Ma would have married and moved into Tinker's house by now. His younger brothers and sisters would have taken the Tinker name. Two months ago, anger over the situation had consumed him. Now he had located Pa's ship, the culmination of his quest, and he felt no better. The anger was gone, but in its place came emptiness instead of the satisfaction he'd expected. Weary, he put the situation at home from his mind and concentrated on hacking a way out of this prison.

For the next day and a half he continued to enlarge the hole in the wood, but it still wasn't big enough when Aurelia brought supper on what must be Friday.

Every other time she'd remained silent. Tonight, her eyes bored into him. "Bolt," she whispered harshly. "Too late after tonight."

Then she left.

Her words sent his thoughts swirling. Something was happening tonight. He had to get out or lose everything.

What did she mean by saying to bolt? Usually she told him to leave. By using that word, she meant something else—such as the dead bolt.

He stared at the knife. What if she hadn't intended him to use it to dig his way out? What if he was to use it to open the bolt? The knife might be long enough to lift the metal bolt.

After Santiago wandered off for supper, he slid the knife between the door and the frame. The bolt would be above the handle. By wiggling the knife upward from the handle, he was able to locate the bolt. Now, would it lift, or did he need to slide it?

Please, God, he prayed, *let it open quickly*.

The Lord must have a fine sense of humor, for no matter how much he wiggled and tugged, it did not come free.

That meant he had to somehow slide it. Tom visualized a typical bolt. It would have a knob that allowed a person to grab hold and slide it. That knob was pointed away from Tom. How could he reach it? He would need something with an angle to it, not the knife.

The spoon! The one Aurelia brought today was very old with a straight, thin handle and a nearly flat bowl. He got the bowl of the spoon through the space at the top of the door and slid the spoon downward. He then bent the handle and wiggled until the bowl of the spoon caught on the bolt's knob. Pulling proved another challenge. The handle acted as a lever.

Tom wedged and pushed and wiggled until he felt something give. The door creaked, and he pushed slightly. If Santiago was waiting, he would pound Tom senseless. Perhaps this was the time for the knife.

He pulled the kitchen knife from his belt, ready to attack. A quick jab to the face would stagger the jailer long enough for Tom to run. He pushed the door slowly open.

Every muscle tensed, waiting for ambush.

Nothing.

He pushed the door a little farther. Now he could slip out. A quick glance revealed no one guarding the pigeonnier. Lamps blazed in the kitchen. The house was lit brightly, the curtains pulled behind the columns. Lanterns lined the steps and carriage drive. If Tom hadn't known better, it looked like guests were expected. Impossible. No one visited Black Oak.

A laugh sounded from the direction of the kitchen.

Tom spotted a large, dark form stepping out. Santiago.

Time was running out. He stepped outside, pushed the door closed, and slid the bolt in place. If he could escape unseen, no one would know he'd left for hours.

Someone called out to the lumbering jailer, and he turned back to answer.

Tom took the opportunity to slip as quietly as possible through the shadows until he was on the far side of the pigeonnier. Then he ran. Not on the carriage drive, where he would be seen, but through the long grasses and weeds until he was beyond the light of the lanterns.

He must get help tonight. Aurelia had made that clear. But he couldn't get to the *James Patrick* without a boat. Looking for an untended rowboat would take time. Then he had to row to the last spot that Rourke had moored the ship. He might have moved it in the two days since Tom saw him. He might even be looking for him. He glanced back at the plantation house. Rourke could even be there tonight. If so, Tom must get help from other quarters.

He could think of only one person. Judge Graham. The judge had shown sympathy toward them when no others would. But it was a long hike to the town where he lived. Then he had to find the man. Where had he told them he lived? Tom wracked his memory until it came to mind. The judge lived in the white house next to the courthouse.

He should hurry, but he took one last look at the plantation house. Though every fiber of his being wanted to leap to Catherine's defense right now, he had no weapon except a paring knife. If he hoped to succeed, he needed help. Lots of it.

Lord, he prayed, *bring me to the right person before it's too late.*

Tom had never put all his trust in God, least of all for something so important. Tonight he had no choice. Like King David cornered in a cave, he had to trust that God would come to his aid.

24

A bruise marred the pale skin on Catherine's chest Friday evening, but the gold taffeta gown almost covered it. She patted some powder over the spot. Only the most discerning would notice.

Aurelia pulled up Catherine's hair and used tortoiseshell combs to secure it. The housekeeper began to enhance Catherine's natural curl with curling tongs, making ringlets that cascaded on either side of her face.

"It's good enough," Catherine said when Aurelia began another.

"Massa want you pretty."

Naturally. Catherine must look perfect on the outside even though her insides were a jumbled mess.

"I'm afraid," she whispered.

Aurelia's hand stilled. "He only hit when he don't git his way."

Catherine could not imagine a lifetime of bending to his will. "Surely someone would object. My cousin Henry."

"He love only money. Massa make money."

"How? The plantation does not look profitable."

"De black ship, it sail back an' forth. Some go. Some come."

The black ship. Tom's father's ship. But Catherine couldn't make sense of the rest. Not tonight. Her thoughts rambled elsewhere. She needed to escape. Somehow. And free Tom. And bring Aurelia and her three children with them. Since DeMornay's unwelcome announcement of their pending marriage, Catherine had considered a dozen times how to free Aurelia. It all came back to getting ownership papers. She needed to see the judge. Perhaps he would come to the soiree tonight. She could speak to him when DeMornay was occupied elsewhere. But the papers must be written tonight. Once wedding vows were spoken, DeMornay would take ownership.

She struggled to breathe. Vows would not be spoken. Could not. There must be a way out of this.

"Santiago from Havana," Aurelia said, "jess like Massa."

Catherine pulled her attention back to the present. "Santiago? Who is that?"

"He watch Missa Tom."

A cool breeze fluttered the curtains. Tom was the answer. He would know how to escape—if she could free him. She glanced at the closed door. DeMornay might even now be listening. She could not ask directly what she needed to know. "How is Tom?"

"He have all he need."

That didn't answer Catherine's question, but she would learn nothing more, for DeMornay knocked on the door.

"Is she ready?" He pushed the door open, and his gaze drifted to Catherine's face and then downward.

Her skin crawled, and she wished she could do anything but go through with this tonight. DeMornay had everything exactly where he wanted it. She had only a promise. He must release Aurelia, Tom, and the children before she took the next step.

She stood and forced a smile. "How handsome you are."

He returned the smile, though it was cold and possessive. "And you are lovely, my dear." He entered her room without asking permission.

This was how it would be. She would have no escape from him. But he would not harm her if she did everything he wanted. Her stomach churned. She could not bear it.

"Leave us," he said to Aurelia.

The housekeeper slipped from the room without a word. That's how Catherine must become. Quietly obedient, submissive. Yet subtly defiant. Would DeMornay flog her also?

She swayed and held on to the edge of the dressing table to steady herself.

He caught her shoulder. "Did you eat the light dinner I had Aurelia bring up for you?"

"Some." Her stomach had revolted at the thought of food, but Aurelia had urged her to force it down because she would need the strength.

"Good." He released her shoulder and touched the edge of the bruise. "That won't do."

She tugged at the gown's neckline until it was covered. "There. Taken care of."

"And if someone should remark on it?"

"A careless step. I am still getting accustomed to the house and grounds."

The viper's smile returned. "Very well put." He reached into the inner pocket of his evening coat. "I have something for you tonight that will distract from anything else. Close your eyes."

That was the last thing she wanted to do in DeMornay's presence, but she must pretend to trust him. He would do nothing to hurt her now, when guests would soon arrive.

His lips pressed against hers, tasting of strong spirits. She fought the revulsion and waited for him to pull away. Then she felt something cool around her neck.

"Perfect," he proclaimed. "You may open your eyes now."

She touched the heavy necklace, which felt more like a neck iron than a thing of splendor.

"You may look in the mirror," he prompted.

She glanced in the glass and froze. "This belonged to Maman."

"Your father sent it here with me for safekeeping."

Safekeeping? Had DeMornay not told her there was no jewelry in the strongbox? She wanted to spit out the words that rose to her tongue. He had stolen it. No doubt this was not the only piece. "Where is the rest?"

DeMornay clucked his tongue and ran a finger down the nape of her neck. "Now, that is no way to show gratitude for a gift." His fingers reached around her throat.

Father in heaven, help me.

She drew a shaky breath. "Of course not. Forgive me. I lost my head in the excitement. I am so relieved that you preserved it for me. Shall we greet our guests?"

He withdrew his hand and offered his arm. "You are learning quickly. Continue in this manner, and your life will be filled with every delight."

Lies. All his promises were lies.

Yet she placed her hand on his arm and fixed a smile on her face as they swept from the room. No one must know the truth. Not until she could find a way out. Not until she got Tom and Aurelia and the children to safety.

The first buggy passed while Tom was still on the lawn. Its lanterns bobbed as it navigated the ruts on the river road and carriage drive.

So, guests were expected. Even more astonishing, at least one invitee had accepted in spite of the general fear of Black Oak plantation. Tom could think of only one explanation. DeMornay held something against them. Blackmail, perhaps. It might have to do with Pa's ship and the illicit cargo smuggled into or out of the area. Perhaps others profited from it, and those others must leap when DeMornay called or face exposure to the authorities.

If that was the case, the judge most likely was not invited, making Tom's trek that much longer.

A second carriage followed the first. The open box and lanterns revealed husband and wife in resplendent finery. Two more followed at an interval, but none of the carriages belonged to the judge.

Tom walked along the edge of the road and hopped into the shadows whenever another carriage lamp appeared ahead of him. The next had twin lanterns that illuminated the occupants. Tom's heart quickened as the carriage drew near.

"Judge Graham!" He waved down the carriage and then ran to meet it.

"Who is it?" Mrs. Graham asked with trepidation. "A robber?"

"Why, it's Mr. Worthington." The judge peered at him. "What are you doing out on the road in the dark?"

"Hoping to find you," Tom said, panting. As much as he wondered why the judge had accepted an invitation to Black Oak, time was short. "Can you spare a moment?"

"Of course." He said something to the driver, who pulled the carriage to the side of the road. Judge Graham exited. "Good to see you again, Tom. I thought you might be gone by now." He sniffed at the air, and Tom realized he must smell dreadful after days cooped up in the pigeonnier.

"Forgive my appearance, but I've been held captive." That sounded fantastical, but Tom had to trust the judge would believe him. "I fear Catherine is in danger."

"I see." The elderly judge stroked his long sideburns. "Give me a moment, and then we'll take a little walk."

Tom waited impatiently while the judge issued instructions to his wife and the driver. The former did not look pleased at all. She did not understand that lives could hang in the balance.

At last Judge Graham left the carriage and strolled toward him. "Now, let's head back a pace, and you can tell me what's going on."

Where to begin? "I believe DeMornay has designs on Catherine." When the judge didn't express surprise, Tom continued, "He threatened to drown me but instead locked me in the pigeonnier. I don't know what he's planning for Catherine."

"Hmm. That explains a great deal." The judge steered him in the other direction. "Walk."

Tom did as requested.

"I gather Miss Haynes did not go to New Orleans then." The judge strolled at an easy pace.

"No." Tom regretted that he hadn't insisted more forcefully that she follow Rourke and him back to the *James Patrick* the first time he proposed the idea. By the time she had warmed to the idea, it was too late. "We were waylaid en route by DeMornay."

"I see, and that's why you suspect he has designs on her."

"That and the way he looks at her, as if he owns her."

"That explains the invitation. If she does not object, there is nothing to be done. Not in a legal sense."

"But she couldn't possibly agree." Tom didn't believe one word of the charade she'd given DeMornay. "What if he's forcing her or holding her captive?"

"He would not invite guests if he has her locked up some-where."

Tom had to admit that made sense. "And if he's forcing her to agree to a liaison?"

"She can refuse."

The judge didn't understand. DeMornay was ruthless. Some-how Tom had to convince him. Perhaps telling of DeMornay's dealings with his father would sway the judge.

"Ten years ago, Louis DeMornay stole my father's ship and set him adrift in the ship's boat." Tom told the entire story, not leaving out a single detail. "I came here to seek justice. DeMornay knows that."

"If this happened ten years ago, how do you know this ship you've found was the one stolen from your father?"

"I can prove it, if I can find the ship. But he's painted it black and moored it out of sight."

"Black, you say?" The judge halted. "The hull?"

"The entire ship, even the sails."

The judge shook his head. "Then the rumors might be true."

"What rumors?"

"I've never cared to pass on rumors when they can't be proven."

Tom took a shot. "He's smuggling, isn't he?"

The judge drew in his breath, telling Tom that his shot had hit true.

"Like I said," the judge said slowly, "I haven't wanted to speculate. Since you already suspect, I will allow that the rumors center on trafficking slaves from Cuba."

"Everything now makes sense. The lack of servants, the fear in their eyes." His imagination ran wild. "What if Cath-erine refuses him? What would he do? He nearly murdered my father."

"Murder is a grave accusation."

"We must get Catherine away from him. I think he's using her to get Black Oak for himself."

"Of course." The judge shook his head. "I should have seen it. It's as obvious as the nose on my face, especially if he knows the terms of inheritance. It would also explain the missing transfer of deed."

"What deed? What terms?" Tom couldn't forget her insistence that she owned part of the plantation.

"She is the rightful heir."

"To a portion."

"To nearly all of it."

A shiver ran down Tom's back. "Not her cousins?"

"An eighth each to Henry and Emile. Her uncle was only entitled to a quarter, but he sent DeMornay to England to purchase the three-quarter share that had belonged to Miss Haynes's mother. Apparently that sale took place but was never recorded. In effect, Miss Haynes still owns three-quarters of Black Oak plantation."

Tom thought back to his visit to Henry Lafreniere. "Does her cousin know this?"

"I don't think so. His father didn't appear to know, even though he had me make a bequest to Miss Haynes shortly before his death. Only after speaking with her did I think to check. That's when I discovered it wasn't recorded. Henri believed he was awarding Miss Haynes an eighth share of the plantation."

"An eighth! That's nothing."

"Remember, Henri Lafreniere believed he was sole owner of the plantation after legally purchasing his sister's share. That's what he would have told his sons."

"The sale. When did it happen?"

"About ten years ago."

"The same time my father's ship was stolen. DeMornay must have returned from England by way of Boston." Tom pieced together the puzzle. "It does explain why Catherine's uncle went to great lengths to convince everyone that Lisette Lafreniere was buried in the churchyard long before she actually died. Until he got legal ownership, he could make everyone believe he owned all of Black Oak."

"But he did not know of Miss Haynes at that time."

"DeMornay must have told him about her when he returned."

The judge shook his head. "Are you suggesting that he's been planning all along to seize control of Black Oak?"

"Exactly." The last pieces fit together. "But to do that, De-Mornay would have to . . ." The rest was too unpalatable to speak.

"Marry her."

"But she would never agree to that." Catherine loved him, not DeMornay. Her kisses told that truth.

"Then you have nothing to fear."

"DeMornay is a master of manipulation." In that instant, Tom realized Rourke was right. He needed to make a choice between avenging the theft of his father's ship and saving Catherine. The choice was clear. "I need to get Catherine out of there at once, but I need your help."

"I'm no help in a fight."

"Not combat." Tom had considered this while inside the pigeonnier. "Legal help."

"In what way? I won't destroy proper legal documents."

"I understand, but the only way I can get her to leave is if she can bring Aurelia and her children with us to Key West." Tom explained the situation. "She will need written proof she owns them in order to bring them into Key West. You can do that for us."

The judge nodded thoughtfully. "Very well, I'll get the documents to you in the morning."

"We might not have that long. Tonight."

The judge pondered that for several moments. "Perhaps we can take care of a great many questions tonight. Let's return to the carriage. We'll need to go back to Titchwood so I can draw up the papers for Miss Haynes. I'll also speak to the sheriff. We might have enough information to issue a warrant to search Black Oak."

A thrill ran through Tom. At last justice might be served. DeMornay might suffer for the pain he'd caused Pa and others. A thought popped into his head. "How long will it take? DeMornay might get suspicious if you don't show."

The judge chuckled. "Perhaps, but my wife will be delighted by this turn of events. If not for Miss Haynes, we would never have come tonight." He raised his hand, and the carriage turned slowly.

Before long, they were headed back to Titchwood. Tom hoped the delay wasn't too long. What could DeMornay do in one evening? Surely not marry her.

⁂

The salon had been turned into a gleaming display. A candelabra highlighted Maman's portrait over the fireplace. Chairs had been pulled to the perimeter and were occupied by a dozen and more people, none of whom Catherine knew. She searched for the judge and his wife. They had not yet arrived.

A tall, slender Negro youth, dressed in the black of a servant, carried a tray of drinks that were offered to the guests. Through the open doorway, she noted the dining table set in fine china and silver that she had never seen.

Tonight this house looked like the one Maman had described

to her. If Catherine did not look too closely in the corners or at the molding, she might imagine it in its heyday, instead of the tattered reflection of what used to be.

DeMornay hung at her side and smiled imperiously at each person who came forward to greet them.

The guests' nerves were readily apparent. No one was at ease.

Catherine complimented each one on something—style of hair, cut of cloth, jewelry, even eye color. Anything to break the tension in the room.

But they approached cautiously and backed away with relief.

Maman, what has become of your grand plantation? Nothing here was how she'd portrayed it. Had the schism over her elopement caused this decline?

"Good evening, honored guests." DeMornay's voice boomed across the room.

All conversation, whispered though it was, stopped.

"News travels fast in these parts, especially when it is good news. You no doubt have heard of Miss Haynes's arrival." He smiled at her, and her skin crawled.

She forced a smile. "Welcome to Black Oak." Though Maman had always used its French name, she'd learned that most now preferred the English. "My mother would be pleased."

"Yes." DeMornay lifted his glass of port, which had been refilled several times while they greeted guests. "To Lisette Lafreniere, who has risen from the grave."

Catherine shivered.

DeMornay took another deep draft of the spirits. "She would welcome this day heralding her daughter's future." He handed the glass to a servant and grasped her arm.

Catherine gasped softly and smiled to cover her distress.

"Though Catherine and I have known each other a very short time, we soon recognized a similarity of purpose and an affection for each other that could not be denied. I am pleased to announce that she has agreed to become my wife."

A couple soft gasps issued from the ladies, and as one the guests turned to look at her. On their faces she saw pity, sympathy, and something else. Fear. Not for themselves but for her.

Catherine's legs trembled. Her hands shook. Only by pressing her lips into a tight smile could she prevent them from quivering.

This was not how it should be.

She must pretend for this moment and find a way out the next. If only Judge Graham had been here tonight, she might have sought him out for help. He might have had a suggestion. But she was alone.

"Come now, dearest." DeMornay pulled her close and planted his lips on hers. Though she was able to move her face slightly to the side, he pressed hard and then held his mouth close to her ear to whisper, "No errors, or Worthington dies."

Tears rose. She blinked them back.

"To Catherine!" DeMornay lifted his glass in a toast. "To my bride."

Polite applause and muted congratulations filled the room. DeMornay left her side to accept handshakes from the other gentlemen. The women surrounded Catherine. One by one they embraced her. No one said a word, but each embrace carried a note of sorrow.

They knew.

25

Catherine walked through the remainder of the evening in a daze. The meal was sumptuous, but she couldn't recall one item. She managed only a few bites of food and declined the wine. She must keep her head tonight.

Judge Graham never appeared. Perhaps he had not been invited. The guests left immediately after supper, there being no musicians or inclination to dance. DeMornay had achieved his goal at the very beginning. Though he acted the perfect host the entire evening, danger lurked beneath the surface. Everyone felt it. Catherine could barely get a simple response out. Conversation lagged. She smiled when necessary but could not summon joy.

"I expected better," DeMornay said when he returned to the salon after seeing off the last of the guests. "The mistress of Black Oak must be the perfect hostess. I expect you to treat each guest's remarks, no matter how mundane, with avid interest."

He poured a glass of port and downed it in a single gulp.

Then he directed the servants to leave the house for the night and return to their quarters. Each silently obeyed. That left Catherine alone with him.

"We are resurrecting Chêne Noir." He turned to face her. "Together we will make it great again."

"It was once great. Maman spoke of it thus. What happened?"

"Neglect." He poured another glass. "Your uncle cared only for profit."

"Did he not live here?"

"Part of the year, but he preferred the city, like your cousins. The plantation house was too old, too far removed from society. Once he died, none of the family visited. If they had, they would have found the house as unpalatable as they'd long claimed. But they never came, content to simply take in the profits." His lips curled into a sneer. "They never suspected what I was doing. A small profit for them, more for me. And the source? None of them wanted to know. Fools! So easily misled."

The discourse had taken a boastful turn, one that she could use to her advantage.

"Then you always wanted control of Chêne Noir."

"I have control," he scoffed before draining his glass. "I wanted it to be mine. Ours."

The possessive, hungry way he looked at her sent chills down her spine.

"I am tired after such an eventful day." She stepped back, toward her room. "You will forgive me."

He caught her wrist. "Not so quickly. Our night is not done."

He pulled her close, and she wilted under the strength of his grip. His breath reeked with the overpowering smell of spirits. Surely he would not force her into anything else. Already this day had soured beyond imagination.

"My head aches," she said.

"Ah no, dear Catherine. There will be no excuses, not after all I have done for you. I have made you an heiress."

"Grandmama and Grandpapa made me an heiress."

His grip tightened. "Your uncle would have taken it away if not for me. I paid the recording clerk to tell him that the papers were properly filed. You owe me everything, dear Catherine. Everything."

Lust burned in his eyes. Her stomach turned. Surely he would not . . . Yet he did not release her. She could barely breathe, couldn't possibly escape him.

"Come, my beauty, we have much to discover of each other tonight." He ran his thumb down her jaw.

She trembled. No force of will could stop it.

"Don't be afraid." He gripped her jaw, still holding her wrist with his other hand. "Tonight will be the beginning of a new dynasty. You will be remembered forever."

She drew a shuddering breath, attempting to stall until she could figure some way out of this. "Immortality?"

"Precisely."

"There is no such thing except through God."

He slapped her across the face. "You will never mention religion again."

Truly he was the devil that Aurelia had called him.

He dragged her across the room toward the master bedroom.

She twisted her arm. "Stop! You have not upheld your part of the bargain."

He laughed. "Never bargain when you do not have the upper hand."

"We are not wed." She attempted to stop their progress with her free hand. "We must do this properly." She grabbed onto the door frame.

"We are." He yanked her free.

She cried out at the sharp pain in her shoulder.

He threw her ahead of him and then grasped her around the throat. "Don't make me hurt you."

Her heart pounded. Her knees quaked. Every nerve cried out. He had murdered before. Mammy. Perhaps more.

"Don't," she whispered, a desperate plea.

His cruel laugh echoed through the cold rooms.

⤞⤝

It took longer than Tom would have liked to get the documents that would allow Catherine to bring Aurelia and her children into Key West. Then he had to wait while Judge Graham spoke to the sheriff in the hall. Tom impatiently paced the judge's office.

At last the men entered the room, and the judge issued the search warrant.

The sheriff looked it over. "It seems in order. You realize DeMornay can retaliate if you're wrong."

"I don't believe we are." The judge stood. "Ready, Tom?"

"I was ready hours ago." He itched to finger the blade, small as it was, tucked in his belt. "I hope we're not too late."

The sheriff's eyebrows rose. "You think he's hidden all evidence?"

"I'm worried about Catherine. I should never have left her alone with him."

The sheriff looked confused, but the judge indicated Tom had an attachment to her.

Attachment? That didn't come close to the feelings bubbling inside him.

"If he hurts her . . ." Tom clenched his fists.

"Leave that to me, son," the sheriff said.

Judge Graham grabbed his top hat. "Come, let's go. I expect

the soiree will be ending soon. The missus won't be sorry to have missed it."

Tom preceded him to the door. "Did DeMornay give any reason for the party?"

"To welcome Miss Haynes home." The judge patted his coat until he located an envelope. "Here, read for yourself."

Tom opened the envelope and withdrew the ivory cardstock. It took little time to read. "'To welcome home the daughter of Lisette Lafreniere.'"

"So it says."

"You don't believe it either."

The judge shook his head. "I wish I could, but there hasn't been a party at Black Oak since Lisette left for her grand tour."

Tom absorbed that information while the judge opened the door. Tom went ahead, and the judge and sheriff followed. "How did Lisette's parents react?"

"They retreated into mourning. Perhaps the additional grant to her in their will was made as an enticement to bring her home."

"But it didn't."

"And her parents died not that long afterward, leaving Henri in control."

"With DeMornay. Is that when the plantation began to change?"

The judge glanced at the sheriff before answering. "It is."

Tom got into the carriage, and the judge followed.

"To Black Oak," the judge instructed the driver.

The horses nickered as if in protest. Tom couldn't blame them. That place made him uneasy too.

"Even with the sheriff along, you're taking a great risk," the judge remarked after they were on the main road. "DeMornay won't easily let Catherine go."

"I know. But I can't leave her there."

The judge turned to the sheriff. "We ought to bring reinforcements."

"I don't know a man here willing to set foot in Black Oak at this hour."

The blunt assessment made Tom cringe. "DeMornay wouldn't dare harm an officer of the law. But if we need more men, I could look for Captain O'Malley and the crew of the *James Patrick*. I'm not sure where they're moored, though."

"Can you spot them from shore in the dark?" the sheriff asked.

"If they're in the area and there's enough light."

"Very well. I know someone with a boat large enough to take you there and bring back a healthy contingent."

"But that could take too long." Tom feared what DeMornay might do to Catherine. "We need to arrive before the guests have left."

Then there would be witnesses. Then DeMornay couldn't touch her.

⌘

The master bedroom had always been locked. Tonight, the door stood wide open until DeMornay shut and locked it behind Catherine. He then pocketed the key and proceeded to pour yet another glass of spirits from a full decanter on the dressing table.

A massive canopied bed dominated the room. The gauzy bed curtains had been drawn to the sides and tied back with white ribbons. Pillows, bolsters, and a lush brocade counterpane covered the bed. A ponderous armoire and dressing table with mirror took up the bulk of the room, with twin chairs on either side of the bed. Their rich tapestry might have delighted

312

her on another occasion. Tonight, every item filled her with terror.

She summoned her courage in a last bold stand. "What do you mean by this? No gentleman would dare to treat a lady in such a manner." She even gave him the imperious gaze she'd seen acquaintances back home employ when an unwelcome gentleman paid a call.

It did not work.

He smirked. "You do not hold a title, and few would call me a gentleman." He grabbed her arms and forced a kiss on her. "Come, dearest. Surrender, and the world will be yours."

Had not Satan used a similar temptation on Jesus? The Lord had responded with Scripture that sent the devil fleeing. Yet she could not recall the precise verse.

Bold proclamation would have to do. "I surrender only to God."

He slapped her.

She stumbled and used the advantage to move toward the door.

He caught her by the wrist. "Not so fast. We have just begun."

"If you touch me now, I will not speak the vows."

"You will when you are with child."

Oh, the horror of that man. She cowered beneath his touch. Strength. She needed strength, but where could she find it?

The Lord is my strength and my shield; my heart trusted in him, and I am helped.

The fear dissipated a little.

He tightened his grip. "Don't you know that marriage is sealed when the intent to marry is made public and is then consummated? Vows only satisfy those who insist on the church's recognition."

She would not bear this insult against everything good and right. She planted a hand on his chest and looked him in the eye. "The Lord is my strength. He will shield me from all evil. He will help me."

Cool calm flowed into her with surprising strength. Though DeMornay cackled derisively, she saw a desperate man riddled with bitter covetousness. He might touch her body, but he would never have her soul.

"Stop!"

That voice did not come from either of them.

DeMornay spun around and then released her. Catherine fell backward a step and saw in the dressing room doorway a woman wild with purpose. Aurelia held a lantern high, a butcher knife in the other hand. Her eyes burned bright.

"What are you doing, Aurelia?" DeMornay attempted to circle closer.

The housekeeper lifted the blade. "Run, Miz Catherine."

"But he will harm you."

"Dere be nothin' this devil can do to me now. I'm goin' home to glory. You take my babes. Dey're waiting."

Catherine trembled. "The door is locked."

Neither combatant paid her the slightest attention. DeMornay thought her trapped. Aurelia sought death. But the door was only one avenue of escape. The window opposite the door was opened wide. She could easily crawl through it if DeMornay didn't stop her.

Aurelia inched toward the door. DeMornay must have figured that she was trying to unlock it for Catherine, but the housekeeper was too smart for that. She was giving Catherine an avenue to escape. All she had to do was run.

"Give me the knife," DeMornay said in that low, silky voice. "I promise you won't be harmed."

"You already hurt me every way a man can. You cain't have my Angel. You cain't sell my boys."

314

Catherine sucked in her breath. That's what DeMornay was doing. Selling slaves. Perhaps even smuggling them into Black Oak from Cuba.

"I would never sell them."

"Lies!" Aurelia spat at him. "All lies. If I gots to go to de fires of hell, I see my babes safe."

DeMornay lunged for Aurelia. This was Catherine's chance. She raced to the window, pulled up her skirts, and crawled through, landing on the veranda. Though she knew she shouldn't look back, one glance couldn't hurt. DeMornay had caught Aurelia's wrist, the one holding the knife. The housekeeper dropped the lantern and it exploded into flame, turning the rich carpets and bed into a blaze that surrounded the dueling pair.

"Aurelia," Catherine gasped.

For an instant, Aurelia's eyes met hers. The manic fire had dimmed, replaced by peace. She would give her life for her children. She trusted Catherine to save them. It was up to Catherine to ensure that.

After yanking her gaze from the expanding horror, Catherine ran around the veranda and down the steps. Her feet pounded across the empty yard. The servants were all supposed to be in their quarters, but a large man ran toward her.

She halted, fear squeezing her rib cage tighter than any stays. Would he stop her? Would he drag her back to the man who intended to lock her inside the plantation house for the rest of her life?

She steeled herself, hands fisted. She must fight, not for herself but for Aurelia's children.

The man ran past her, waving a hand in the air and calling out in a language she did not understand. He seemed not to see her at all, as if she was not there. Had the Lord veiled her from his sight? Shocked, she turned back just for a moment. Like Lot's wife, she froze.

The house was ablaze, flames leaping into the sky. No one could escape that inferno. That's what Aurelia had intended. She would make sure DeMornay never hurt anyone again. The enormity of her sacrifice weakened Catherine's knees. Would she have been so bold?

Forgive her, Lord, for she acted from love and desperation.

Catherine stumbled away from the house. Soon the rest of the servants would arrive and attempt to put out the blaze.

She could not dwell in the past. To make Aurelia's sacrifice matter, she must save her children. Where would Aurelia hide them? Her quarters? Too close to the other workers. The kitchen? Someone might be there. The sugarcane? Impossible to find. No, Aurelia would choose the first place she would expect Catherine to go. The pigeonnier.

Tom.

Catherine raced to the small wooden building. She pounded on the door. "Tom! Angel, Gibson, Hunt!"

What if Tom was still locked inside? She tugged on the door, banged on it again.

No answer.

Where were the children? She must find them, but that meant leaving Tom behind.

She felt a tug on her skirts and looked down. Angel.

She lifted the small girl in her arms and hugged her close. How would she explain that they must leave and their mama wouldn't be coming with them?

"He ain't there," Gibson said at her elbow.

"He's gone?" Her heart buoyed. "Where?"

"Don't know, but Mama said we's supposed to go with you."

"Yes." But her throat narrowed as three scared faces looked to her. "We must leave this place together. Stay close to me."

They hurried away. In the confusion and tumult of the fire, no one noticed one woman and three children. They walked past the cane fields and onto the road that paralleled the river. Where she would go next she couldn't say. Somehow, with no money, no carriage, and no help, she must bring three children to safety.

26

Tom didn't have to borrow a boat to search for Rourke. The captain had already arrived at the landing along with most of the crew. They gathered in force, lanterns in hand.

"I'm sure glad to see you." Tom forgot his subordinate position and clapped Rourke on the back.

Rourke looked surprised at first and then returned the gesture. "And I, you. We've been searching for you for days." He turned Tom toward the west. "Then tonight we saw the sky light up."

Tom's jaw dropped at the orange glow in the sky. "Fire."

"I'd say so," the sheriff said. "Better get the men together."

"From that direction, I'd say it's at Black Oak," Judge Graham added.

Tom's innards knotted. "Catherine."

"It could be the cane or one of the outbuildings," the judge suggested.

Tom recalled the lanterns placed next to the overgrown yard. Even if the grass had caught fire, it wouldn't make a blaze large enough to light the sky. The only thing that would . . . "It's the plantation house."

Rourke cut through the speculation. "My men will help fight the fire. You have a carriage. Would you bring Tom and myself and as many men as your rig can bear?"

"Of course," the judge said. "We can take four or five, including myself and the sheriff."

In the end, they squeezed eight into the carriage. Soon they were lumbering up the road as fast as the horses could manage. At this pace, all of Black Oak would burn to the ground before they arrived.

"I'll run," Tom offered. "Slow down and I'll hop off."

Rourke held his arm. "You'll do no such thing."

"But Catherine—"

"Is already beyond reach. If the house is on fire, she either got out already or has perished."

Though that offered no consolation, Tom knew Rourke was right. Flames licked above the treetops. No human could have survived such a blaze unless he or she had already left the building.

DeMornay. Tom clenched his fists. That deceiver could die. But what about the servants?

"Aurelia. The children," he gasped. "What if they're inside?"

"We must pray for their safety."

That wasn't enough. "I need to get there. I can run, and once I'm off the carriage it'll be a lighter load for the horses."

Tom edged toward the side, prepared to jump, but Rourke didn't release him.

"A dead man won't be able to help them," Rourke said.

Though Tom understood his caution, the image of Catherine surrounded by flames filled him with terror. He must get to her. He must ensure her safety. With a sharp yank, he pulled free and leapt off the carriage and onto the roadway. The impact sent him to his knees. The dirt was unforgiving. The stones bit into his hands, but nothing was broken.

The carriage slowed. Voices murmured. Rourke called out.

Tom scrambled to his feet and plunged forward into the shadows, at first stumbling and then running. The carriage resumed its course, slowly at first and then at a much more rapid pace. The crunch of wheels and clop of hooves quieted until he was alone.

Still, the dreadful glow of the night sky foretold a tragic end.

Tom struggled to catch his breath and had to slow.

Then out of the darkness, figures began to emerge, all huddled together.

"Who goes there?" Tom called out.

"Tom?" a faint voice asked.

Catherine. It was Catherine.

⌘

"They cannot have survived." Catherine clung to Tom, and he held her just as desperately.

"Who?"

"Aurelia and DeMornay. They were surrounded by fire, struggling for the knife." The image was burned in her mind. "I didn't want to leave, but . . ." Catherine drew a breath, hoping it would quiet the sobs that threatened. "She gave her life."

His hand, which had been rubbing her back in consolation, stilled. "For you."

"For her children. We must take them to freedom. Somewhere. I will go anywhere that guarantees that." The urgency pounded away selfish tears. "We must hurry before someone catches us and forces them to stay."

"No one will force any of you to stay." Tom broke the embrace, and the resulting distance between them made her shiver.

She pulled the children close. "I can't believe that. Only when I'm safely away from here will I rest."

Tom hesitated, and she realized he had no power to bring her anywhere. Captain O'Malley could, but he and his crewmen had raced to the plantation in the carriage.

"Forgive me for overhearing your conversation." Judge Graham stepped into the patch of moonlight on the road.

Tom started. "I didn't know you were here."

"I left the carriage when it stopped to lighten the load. A man of my age is not a great deal of help in fighting a fire." He turned to Catherine. "Mr. Worthington is correct. Papers were drawn this very night confirming your ownership of the plantation's, uh, property."

His glance toward the children left no doubt which "property" he meant.

"What if the transfer of ownership—" Even as she spoke, she realized it must have burned with the rest of the plantation house. "It's gone."

"If it was in the house."

"It was. I saw it."

"Then," the judge said, "you are majority owner of Black Oak. You might have to compensate your cousins for the loss of, um, property."

Catherine shuddered. The dream that had glistened before her all those years had become too tarnished to bear. This way of life relied on the oppression of others. She could not live with that. "Let them have the plantation."

"You are understandably overwrought. Even if the main house burns to the ground, the land has value. I urge you to at least offer it for sale."

Tom seconded the judge's recommendation.

"I cannot think on that." Her mind whirled toward the only thing that mattered. "All I want is to ensure these three children and their mother, if she is . . ." If Aurelia had died, she could not break that news to the children now. "They must be brought to freedom."

The judge nodded. "I understand."

"What of the other slaves?" Tom asked.

An answer popped into her mind. "Judge Graham, would you handle the sale of the plantation and use the proceeds to reunite the remaining slaves with their families? I suspect many have been brought here from elsewhere."

"That is a difficult challenge," the judge said slowly, "but a worthy one. I will do my best."

"Thank you," she breathed. "I trust you to handle everything. I must leave here as soon as possible and bring Angel, Gibson, and Hunter to freedom."

"We will." Tom rubbed the oldest boy's head. "We'll go to Key West. How would you like to be a deckhand, Gibson?"

The boy squared his shoulders. "I wanna be captain."

The men chuckled. Catherine blinked back tears, but it was useless. They came.

"Why you cry, Miz Cattrin?" little Angel asked.

Catherine couldn't answer while struggling to stop the sobs.

"Here comes the carriage," the judge announced.

Tom handed Catherine a handkerchief, and she wiped her eyes as the carriage pulled to a stop beside them.

"A total loss," Captain O'Malley said. "There wasn't anything we could do."

"Survivors?" Catherine whispered.

He shook his head. "Just the field workers. They were trying to put out the blaze, but a few buckets of water didn't make one bit of difference. I had them douse the kitchen and worker quarters so they have a place to live and something to eat for the time being, but arrangements will need to be made."

"I'll see to that," the judge offered. "I'll send for Henry Lafreniere in the morning." He nodded to Catherine. "If he agrees to your terms—and I suspect he will once he learns that he's not the legal owner and that a warrant was issued to search the house for evidence of trafficking slaves—I'll have the necessary paperwork ready for you to sign. We would like to have you as our guests tonight—you, the children, and Mr. Worthington. I'm sorry we can't house your entire crew, Captain."

"My ship is nearby. We have berths there."

Now that everything was falling into place, Catherine's strength ebbed. "Thank you for your kindness," she managed to whisper before the ground began to heave and the landscape to swirl.

"Sit her down."

"Bring her to the carriage."

She heard the voices but couldn't distinguish who said what. She swayed. Then strong arms lifted her. She nestled her head against his shoulder. Tom. She knew his touch, the scent of him, anywhere. He kissed her forehead, and she drew a deep breath.

He set her on a seat.

"Don't leave me," she pleaded.

"I'll be back once I get the children into the carriage."

She was willing to let him go for that long. "Return at once."

He laughed. "You can count on that. I don't plan to leave your side any longer than I need to." His voice sobered. "Ever."

The word washed over her as the cooler night air settled around them. Soon this would all be over. But Tom would remain. That was more than enough.

Cool sea breezes ruffled Catherine's hair two weeks later. As expected, cousin Henry had agreed to her terms at once. Their meeting in New Orleans was short and businesslike. Black Oak was no longer hers, and she didn't regret it. Days of sorrow and anguish had finally given way to expectation for the future. The sun shone. The breezes blew steadily, and the *James Patrick* made excellent time. How good it felt to let her hair flow free of any encumbrance.

Tom approached from the stern and met her at the forecastle.

"I'm never wearing a bonnet again."

"Never?" He joined her at the rail. "Not even to church?"

"Perhaps to church. You attend?"

"Every Sunday that I'm in port. Rourke taught me how important faith is, but I didn't really understand that until I met you."

Her heart swelled. "You're only saying that to win my affection."

"Did it work?"

She laughed. How good it felt. Here on the *James Patrick* she was surrounded by love.

The children had wept when she told them their mother had died. The boys soon wiped their eyes and feigned stony resolution, but Angel could not be consoled until Catherine repeated over and over that this is what her mother wanted, that she and her brothers make a new life with her in Key West.

"You will be free there," Catherine had told them, but they didn't understand what that meant. Aurelia had believed De-Mornay would soon sell the boys. Angel's fate—given what had happened to her mother—would have been far worse. It was all too much for her to think about.

Better to hold on to the future that Tom promised.

She leaned close to him. "You caught my attention the very

first day on the *Justinian*. That confident grin of yours was a challenge."

"Which you attempted to best, if I remember correctly."

"Naturally. You needed a little smoothing out around the edges."

"Isn't that like a woman," Tom said to Rourke, who had come on deck to peer at a passing island. "Always trying to change us."

"Successfully, if we are willing, and for the better." Rourke tapped a finger on his spyglass. "Take my advice. It'll go better for you if you submit to a little renovation."

Catherine laughed, but Tom looked chagrined.

She threaded an arm around his. "Don't fear. It will be practically painless."

"Practically?"

"Easier than raising three boisterous children."

He glanced at Gibson, who had taken his duty of ringing the watch very seriously, and the two younger ones, who followed on their oldest brother's heels. "I would look forward to raising them with you."

Catherine teasingly shook her finger at him. "Aren't you forgetting something?"

"The differences of culture?"

How witless could a man be? She huffed and moved away.

"What, then?"

She faced him, hands on her hips. "Don't act so dull-minded. You know exactly what I mean."

He leaned on the rail. "I suppose we would have to be married to raise children."

She gasped and spun away from the cad. "If that's what you consider a proposal—"

He caught her in a flash and stopped her protest with the sweetest kiss ever. The passion warmed her clear to her toes.

"Oh my," she gasped when his lips left hers.

"Is that a start?" His grin shone brighter than the tropical sun.

"A beginning."

"I have more persuasion where that came from." He leaned close.

This time she stopped him with a hand to his lips. "Aren't you being a bit forward? We aren't even courting."

He stepped back and bowed. "I have been courting you, my lady, from the moment I first saw you."

Normally she would have laughed at such silliness, but he wasn't jesting. When he rose from the bow, mirth didn't twinkle in his eyes. Neither were his lips curved with delight. This declaration was serious.

She drew in her breath. Was he . . . ?

"I haven't a ring to offer as a pledge, only my heart."

"You already gave up what was dearest to you for my sake—your father's ship. I still can't believe you didn't want to claim it."

He shook his head. "Not once I learned the purpose for which it had been used."

"Smuggling slaves," she breathed out.

"From Cuba. I could never sail such a ship."

"But what will become of the ship now that DeMornay is gone?" His charred body had been found alongside Aurelia's, still locked in mortal combat.

"Judge Graham promised to sell it and add the proceeds to your quest to reunite families that DeMornay had torn apart. At last Pa's ship can serve a noble purpose."

Tears rose in her eyes. "Thanks to the generosity of an honorable man." She squeezed his hand. "I wish to continue helping families." She glanced at the three children seated in a circle on the deck. "Not just Aurelia's children but any others God leads into our path."

"Our?" That grin resurfaced. "Then you will consider my suit?"

Though she wanted to cry yes at once, she could not resist a little fun. "No, I couldn't possibly."

His joy evaporated. "I'm sorry. I should never have presumed."

She let out a laugh before he tumbled into despair. "I'm not interested in a long courtship, Mr. Worthington. I am seeking a partnership of the highest sort."

Slowly, the grin returned. "Marriage? You will marry me?"

"If you ask properly. A woman does expect that much, even from a wrecker."

"Especially from a wrecker." He got down on one knee and looked up at her, his brown eyes twinkling. "My dearest Catherine, from the moment I first saw you, I knew you were the woman I wanted to spend my life loving. You are more beautiful than the most expensive jewel, more intelligent than most men, and so engaging that I cannot sleep at night without thinking of your laughter. Will you do me the honor of accepting my hand in marriage?"

She could no longer tease, not after such a declaration.

"I will. Yes, I will."

He leapt up and swept her into his arms. Then he gave her a kiss that made her forget everything that had happened and all that was going on around them. A sailor's whistle and laughter drew her back.

"Well done, Worthington," the men said.

Even Rourke was grinning.

Tom paid them no attention. He focused only on her. "From what you've told me of your mother, she would be pleased."

"She would. Love always came first to her. She would have adored you, Tom."

"And my father would have loved you." His grin was infectious. "Best of all, we love each other."

"That we do," she managed before he smothered the words with another kiss.

She let herself get lost in it.

A cry from above brought her back to the present. "Land ahoy!"

Tom ended the kiss, shot to the rail, and tugged open his spyglass. "Key West. Home."

Home. Her heart thrilled as she joined him, Angel at her side. At last she had found home.

Acknowledgments

First and foremost, all glory goes to my Lord and Savior, Jesus Christ, who is the Author of everything perfect and true. Thank You for letting me write these humble stories.

My deepest gratitude to editors Andrea Doering and Jessica English, who bring clarity to every story. You are the best! Thanks also to the wonderful marketing, publicity, and sales teams at Revell. Your work behind the scenes brings every book into the spotlight. Special thanks to Cheryl Van Andel and the whole team that creates such beautiful covers. I'm always thrilled to see your efforts.

Thanks too to my agent, Nalini Akolekar, who has been so supportive and encouraging every step of the way.

What would I do without my critique partners, Jenna Mindel and Kathleen Irene Paterka? Your keen eye and gift for story bless me richly. I'm so grateful that you are in my life.

And to you, dear readers, I owe the deepest gratitude. Thank you for joining me on this journey to Key West. I love to hear from you. You can contact me through my website, http://christine elizabethjohnson.com.

Christine Johnson is the author of several books for Steeple Hill and Love Inspired, in addition to her books with Revell. When not writing, she enjoys quilting and loves to hike, kayak, and explore God's majestic creation. These days, she and her husband, a Great Lakes ship pilot, split their time between northern Michigan and the Florida Keys.

Christine Johnson

WHERE ADVENTURE LEADS HOME

ChristineElizabethJohnson.com

Christine Johnson Author

ChristineJWrite

Also in the
KEYS OF PROMISE series . . .

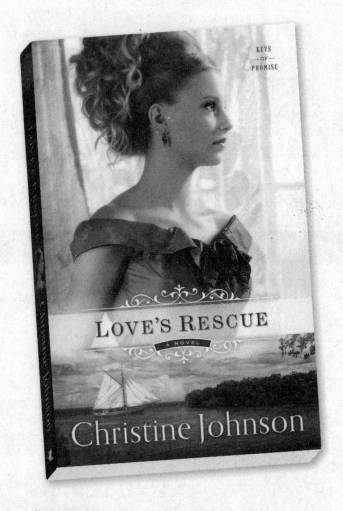

Can a girl enamored with the adventurous seas
ever be content with the tame life of a Southern belle?

Revell
a division of Baker Publishing Group
www.RevellBooks.com

Available wherever books and ebooks are sold.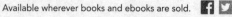

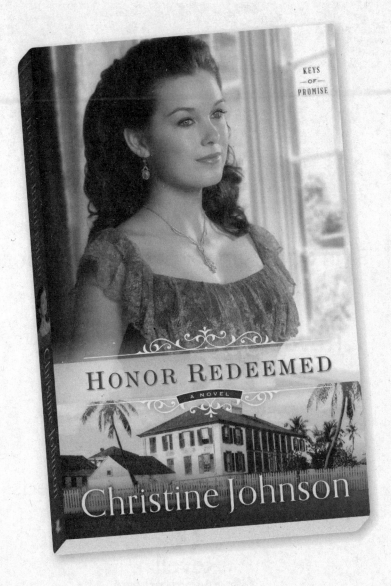

After the death of her parents, Prosperity Jones follows her love to
Key West—only to discover he's married someone else. Heartbroken
and destitute, how will she survive?